I no longer casually observe faces.

I can't help but see people in terms of spatial geometry, facial infrastructure. I ease myself under the skin, get a feel for the foundations. What is the underlying bone structure? How would I reconstruct his or her appearance if presented with their detached skull?

When your area of expertise is all around you — when it's at the very core of human interaction — it's impossible to switch off.

THEGIRL
ON THE PIER

PAUL TOMKINS

A NOVEL

For the missing.

ACKNOWLEDGEMENTS

With special thanks to Mark Lynch, Kate Ware and
Palomi Kotecha.

Further thanks to Neil Wheelhouse, Neil Burke, Mark
Allan, Jules Jackson, Carol Anderson, Chris Hadley,
Damien Parsonage, Chris Rowland, Claire Clifton,
Mairead Mooney, Eve White, Matthew Young, Daniel
Rhodes, everyone at Cornerstones, Roberto Rodriguez,
Araminta Hall, plus the fine folk at Matador.

Finally, an extra big thanks to my family, and anyone
I've so thoughtlessly forgotten.

Website: *www.paultomkins.com*
Email: *paul@paultomkins.com*

Matador
9 Priory Business Park
Kibworth Beauchamp
Leicestershire LE8 0RX, UK
Tel: (+44) 116 279 2299
Fax: (+44) 116 279 2277
Email: books@troubador.co.uk
Web: www.troubador.co.uk/matador

ISBN 978 1784621 049

British Library Cataloguing in Publication Data.
A catalogue record for this book is available from the British Library.

Printed and bound in the UK by TJ International, Padstow, Cornwall

Matador is an imprint of Troubador Publishing Ltd

MIX
Paper from
responsible sources
FSC
www.fsc.org   FSC® C013056

"*There is love of course.*
And there's life, its enemy."
Jean Anouilh

"*The job of the artist is always*
to deepen the mystery."
Francis Bacon

ONE

The sea surges across the shingle with the clack of a billion ricocheting billiard balls as *she* – this woman who transfixes me – floats past. I linger, looking through the crowd that throngs the promenade of Brighton beach; admiring her grace, her style, her natural beauty. I feel my pulse throb in my throat – its jugular thrum – and in my gullet sense my half-swallowed heart.

She turns, heads my way. I breathe deep as she passes, inhaling her scent: a mix of lotion, perfume, peppermint and seaside sweat. It stirs chemicals deep within my brain, strikes a primordial chord. She leans on the balustrade; I move to stand behind her, to one side, and pretend to look at a leaflet pulled from my pocket, acting the bemused tourist. Gulls – large, fierce – circle and call overhead. She turns. I take her in with forensic observation: arching eyebrows, naturally full lips, faintly olive skin, broad brown eyes that open wide between sweeping lashes. Stray hairs, escaped from pigtails, blow about her face, and she swats them away like flies. Graceful, but not ornamental.

Ninety-three: the year, the temperature. More than two

decades have now passed, yet in my mind it is still the present day. I close my eyes, and it's *happening*. I hear strains of music through the fuzzy earphones of her Walkman. I recognise the dark, brooding tune, but cannot place it.

I want to touch her – this total stranger. The urge is incredible. I am moments away from an arrestable offence. But I am not a threat to her safety; just a man who, for a split-second, has the wilfulness of a two-year-old child who doesn't want to take 'no' for an answer. Why *can't* I have her?

Just because. Just because.

The sea breeze blows a bead of sweat from her shoulder onto my face – a millimetre from my bottom lip, so I trail my tongue to taste the salt: a speck of saline heaven. Perhaps it is sea spray? No – it is her: her taste. I've not yet spoken to her, but I've already *tasted* her.

Checking her reflection in a compact, she doesn't engage the mirror for longer than is necessary; looking for a blemish, rather than admiring herself. She flicks something from her cheek, snaps down the lid. Done. It is at this point that I hear a cry, a strange guttural sob, and mistake it for the call of a seagull. I turn to see a boy standing alone, his cheeks ruddy beneath a blond bowl haircut. Bolt upright, almost statuesque, he wails with hands outstretched at the end of straight, quivering arms. I'm guessing he is six or seven years old, although I've never been good at determining children's ages. Passing tourists ignore his distress, unwilling to investigate a sadness that must have a simple remedy – kids cry, and sooner or later the parents intervene. Or maybe they are the other kind of passer-by, those who simply don't care. But the young woman is different. She sees that he is alone, and I can tell from her quickly altered expression that she senses a larger sorrow, an all-cutting pain; desolation, abandonment, the things that make us howl. With purpose she moves in, a saintly presence on the shingle. She hunkers down to meet him eye-to-eye; the denim of her jeans drawn taut across her buttocks, small ankle socks revealed as the turn-ups rise upon her shins.

I see her ask him a question. Her head tilts, an ear offered to the boy, but his reply is blurted out – too eager to have his words heard, too upset to do so with controlled breaths. Unable to speak clearly, he vomits staccato syllables. Again, a calming gesture. Again, reassurance. She wipes a tear from his eye, takes his hand. For a moment I think of offering assistance, but worry that I'll ruin her rescue mission, which she handles with an assuredness beyond her years.

She stands, leads the boy in the direction of the Palace Pier. I am about to move to keep up with the unfolding drama when a frantic mother appears on the scene, and clasps her son with suffocating force. In that second the panic recedes.

This is all it takes to confirm love at first sight. But what is that? Nothing more than lust, coupled with an overactive imagination? I can tell many things from the way this girl moves, the expressiveness of her mouth (I have already seen it turn up at the corners with miraculous geometry, as if elevated by abnormally-developed cheek muscles), the alertness darting from her eyes. It gives me a sense of her inner soul – or what I perceive to be her inner soul. In truth, everything I know about her, beyond the physical, and one single act of heart-warming kindness, is my imagination filling in the blanks. It is easy to experience such heady feelings for someone when instilling in them your every wished-for characteristic. She is merely a blank canvas.

The time: I need to be somewhere. And so I have to let her go — open my hands to set free the butterfly flapping against my palms, tickling my skin. But an indelible mark has been made on this, a day that will irrevocably change my life. Everything will forever lead back to this morning, when I took a walk along a seafront that would never let me leave.

TWO

I peeled a slither of Sellotape from the back of my hand; feeling it as keenly as flaying a layer of skin. I held the crinkled strip up to the light, staring at the arrangement of fine black hairs trapped like gnats on flypaper, and the mottled dust marks containing my DNA. I'd planned to repair a precious item, damaged five hours earlier in a violent marital struggle. Instead, I embalmed myself in transparent sticky tape.

Setting down the roll in temporary defeat, I returned my gaze to the mess of a lifeless face laid out on the bloodstained carpet. I studied the familiar features, slashed in rabid anger, scarred and disfigured, ripped and torn. Supine on the bedroom floor, pigtailed hair draped across her shoulders, she remained slumped where she fell in the early hours of the morning; one unmoving eye staring inquisitively back, asking *What did I do to deserve such unremitting brutality?* but unable to receive any kind of reply.

Uncomfortably cross-legged, I swore beneath my breath. The painting laid out in front of me – a portrait of a young woman, by an artist only at the fringes of fame – seemed determined to remain beyond repair. Having already spent ten minutes trying to stick it back together – stick *her* back together – I experienced only abiding failure. Utterly unable to avoid getting in a tangle with the Sellotape, I flicked and flicked as it clung to my fingers, and then, when I pulled it free, watched it curl worm-like up against itself. If I managed to prise a piece apart and straighten it out I found all tack lost. Eight or nine consecutive times I'd wasted a strip, and now the end of the roll had vanished; the scrape of a thumbnail unable to locate it as I twirled and twirled. Adrenaline burned my veins, my hands shaking. I'd only managed to stick together two pieces of matching canvas. A restorer would be appalled.

The portrait, of course, lay beyond repair. Painted only a decade earlier by Jacob Dyer, its worth – little more than a couple of thousand pounds in prime condition – vanished with this sudden and devastating alteration, reducing its price to less than that of its frame. But the elimination of its monetary value was not the issue.

A painting, worth so much more than a mere work of art.

* * *

The early hours of that morning came back via muddled memories, taking shape like slow-developing Polaroids. Every thirty seconds another shocking tableau gained resolution, pouring out from the mist.

Sprawled on the mattress, tangled in bedclothes, I heard the sound of vomiting drifting through the half-open en-suite bathroom door; repetitive jerks followed by rasping attempts to clear the throat and unblock the nose. I turned out of a knot of sheets, sat up. Evidence of violence surrounded me. Constellations of blood spattered the cream-white linen, culminating in a large circular pool on my wife's pillow. Clothes and ornaments lay tossed as if by frenzied vandals: drawers turned out, wardrobe doors hanging crooked on their hinges, and the apposite omen of a smashed mirror, in pieces on the dresser.

I could see my wife through the door to the bathroom; her back arched with the feline curve of a cat retching up the mother of all furballs. I felt unsure whether she vomited as a physical or an emotional response, or both – doubling-up on her as she lay floored, as she lay doubled-up. Slouched across the bathroom rug, arms embracing an open toilet bowl, it was over – so definitely over – but I wondered at what point she would feel strong enough to do anything about it. She forced bile from her nostrils. Slug-trails ran from nose to chin. Dried and darkened lines of blood covered her forehead and weaved a path down her nose and cheeks, bifurcating like forks of lightning. If she survived to get up, she was gone.

The true extent of Laura's recovery remained hard to gauge. But within two hours of waking she felt sufficiently revived to pack a few essentials into a bag and drive to her parents' house. She left without more than the briefest exchange of words. She confirmed she was leaving, and I accepted her decision. We understood it to be over; nothing before had ever been as clear-cut. I did not waste breath begging that she change her mind. I knew I would miss her, but she was doing the right thing. The *only* thing.

I sat beside the bedroom window and watched her depart, unconsciously performing my regular nervous habit of running the tip of a finger across the pronounced scar on the back of my right hand – a wound dating back a decade, to 1993, just over a year before we first met – feeling the bumps of damaged skin as she climbed into her car and drove away.

THREE

Rinsing hands stained scarlet, Jacob Dyer smiles. Some things refuse to be purged. His fingers squirm around a slab of pearl-white soap that turns a very faint pink, but no more. The palms still red. He grabs the towel hanging over the edge of the Belfast sink, squeezes it hard. Sanguine particles transfer to the white cotton fibres, but not enough to constitute cleanliness.

He crosses the room and enters his body into the composition of a window, almost self-consciously so.

"Everything you do is so purposeful," Black says, leaning naked against the wall.

"Beg your pardon?"

"Well, just look at you – standing there like that."

"Like what?"

"Like a living work of art, framed within the window." She crosses to the angular Marcel Breuer chair on which her clothes lie. "So considered. Most people would just slump against the window frame when looking out. With you, it's almost as though the looking out is secondary, an afterthought."

Jacob scans the Brighton streets below, choosing not to reply. He locates his glass of red wine, walks to the middle of the room. With his free hand he fiddles with a video camera on a tripod, arranged to film the session, but despite several prods, fails to halt the recording. The tape spools on, capturing him walking away from the lens.

Black gathers her clothes from the seat of the chair. She separates each garment from the mound they form with one hand, carefully reconstructing the pile in the arched cradle of her other arm. She returns her gaze to Jacob. "It's starting to sink in. It feels so final."

"You're leaving the country. That's fairly final."

He returns to the window, looking first at the sun's reflection on the sea before glancing down at the street below.

"Who are you expecting?" she asks. "Don't tell me I'm being replaced before I've even gone?"

"No, no. An old college friend. Haven't seen him in years. It was just a possibility, nothing confirmed. He said either today or tomorrow." He angles his head to see further along the street. "Incredibly nice guy, considering the breaks life has dealt him. I'd be far more bitter."

"You're bitter enough as it is," she says, laughing.

Still in a state of undress, Black stands with her big cushion of clothing. Clasping the disparate fabrics tight to her breast, she buries her chin in cotton and nylon and wool and lace, and with the constricted movement of her mouth noticeable in her enunciation, enquires, "Is my still being here a problem? Did you want me gone?"

"No, not at all. Anyway, if he was going to come today he'd have been here by now. I've never known him to be even a minute late in his life. He's a bit anal like that. I think it's safe to say it'll be tomorrow, if at all."

Black places the neatened pile of clothes back on the chair, short of one item: her knickers, thrown at Jacob hours earlier after a sarcastic remark. She begins to search the studio, crawling beneath a long low table, every inch covered in coloured tubs and cans of various sizes. She pulls away from the wall, one by one, the many blank or half-finished canvasses tipped like partially-fallen dominoes, to no avail; scuttles about the studio, dodging tubes of paint strewn across the floor; sifts under loose sheets of cartridge paper littered about the room, paying no attention to the pencil and charcoal sketches of herself depicted thereon. No sign of the garment by the broken easel, bent-up in the corner like a beaten heavyweight boxer. She wanders into the kitchen, widening her search. Whilst there she switches on the kettle, and drops a herbal teabag into a mug.

* * *

Still naked, Black wanders back into the studio, muttering "I don't believe this," half under her breath. Her gaze remains cast at the floor, until Jacob attracts her attention.

He turns to the door, holds out a hand in my direction.

Running uncharacteristically late, I have finally arrived. What I find remarkable is this: here *she* is again – the girl from the beach. Not only is she here, but she is *completely naked*.

"Black, I'd like you to meet Patrick."

She turns to the door, to where I am standing. And staring. I know it's rude, but I simply cannot avert my eyes; the particular nerve stems carrying the command severed by shock.

Black is similarly frozen. There is a momentary delay before she moves to cover her pubis with one hand and places the other forearm across her chest. However, in that brief suspension I have already taken a dozen mental snapshots. It is only when she moves to conceal her modesty that I realise it would in fact be polite to look away, and so begin to intensely study my shoes, scuffing them against the doormat; appearing to discover something profoundly existential in the word *Welcome*.

Despite moving behind an oriental screen to dress, she remains, in my mind's eye, at the exact spot I first saw her: some kind of apparition, caught in the mix of shafts from the four skylights – God positioning the sun until it becomes a follow-spot for the star on centre stage – so that when she finally turns to look at me an other-worldliness transforms the scene, and I am entitled to be dumbstruck.

At this stage it may be normal to undress, with one's eyes, the subject of the infatuation. But I have already seen her naked. Visually there is nothing left for the imagination; a form of perfection. So instead I move onto the next stage, and imagine physical contact. From across the room I feel the cambers of her flesh, the jutting peaks of bone softened by skin, the twists of hair uncoiled from their pigtails. My mind wills eager hands up and down her body, lingering at points of interest. My palms are warm, clammy, wet with sweat against her skin. I read goosebumps like Braille; stroke faint downy hair, momentarily pricked-up; with my fingertip encircle the birthmark on her thigh; stroke the tiny tubercles that populate her areolae. Only to an insane mind are these imperfections.

Normal people just don't enter your life in this way.

* * *

Jacob lives and works on the top floor of an old Victorian school, converted at the start of the decade into domestic dwellings. I have not seen him much since our college days, and this is my first visit to his current home. He shows me around with no obvious pride, acting more out of a sense of duty. Nothing, aside from his art, and getting drunk in the company of young men, appears to mean much to him. "Art, arse and alcohol," he has told me on many occasions, usually when intoxicated.

It's an impressive place. The ceiling has been removed, and the internal walls replaced with steel columns, resulting in a capacious loft apartment. An upper level – housing the living quarters – exists as a mezzanine, access to which is via a wrought-iron spiral staircase. So profuse is the sunlight permeating the broad windows that it's like being outside. I have entered a square lighthouse, with stunning views of the English Channel; only, an *inverted* lighthouse, illuminating the within, not the without. A single wall is constructed entirely of brick; great sheets of glass pan around the other three sides of the apartment. The effect is completed by mid-afternoon rays crashing down through expansive glass panels built into the high-arching roof. Such perfect light for his colours, he tells me, glass of wine in one hand, smouldering hand-rolled cigarette in the other. He then points out the array of daylight bulbs, rigged for night-time work. "For when the mood takes me," he adds through a puff of smoke.

Finally we come to a stop. "It's good to see you, Paddy," he says, fully aware that I hate the shortened version of my name. "What brings you back down here? You never explained."

"Do I need a reason?"

"Well, you're so rarely in Brighton these days," he says. "Unless you just never tell me?"

"No, you're right – I keep away. This time I had no choice. I needed to check something out for work."

"On a weekend?"

"It's a retail outlet."

Jacob doesn't even know what my job is these days, and doesn't think to enquire. "Have you been home?" he asks, prodding my arm in an accusatory manner, as if he already knows the answer.

"No."

"How long has it been? Is your aunt still alive?"

"Yeah, she is. Ten years. It's been ten years this summer. I still phone her – Kitty. Well, occasionally. But the cottage – I just can't bring myself to go back. It's too… well, I just prefer to move forward. You know how it is."

"Certainly do. Even so, you should go see her. But hey, that's up to you. It's your life. I have enough trouble making sense of my own." By this stage he has his back to me, walking away. "Cigars," he says, as he makes his way into the kitchen, adding, "Make yourself at home" once out of sight.

The studio, which dominates this level, smells, depending on where you stand, of oil paint, turpentine, damp rags, wet paper, leather and cigarette smoke. It is also a total mess. Chaos reigns; how a receding tsunami might scatter objects across a room. The floor at the centre of the studio is decked with newspaper, on top of which is lain clear plastic sheeting. This, in turn, is covered with Pollockesque trails and spatters of paint. Sable brushes – thick with desiccated clumps of yellow and orange and red – flower from glass jars on windowsills. Newspapers – yellowing by degrees from bottom to top – are stacked in one corner, reaching up to the height of the mezzanine. Jacob returns, cigar in hand, wine glass refilled, now sporting a battered pair of Ray-Bans, which he chooses to don whenever he's not painting. "I rarely read them, just have them delivered for the pictures," he says, seeing me taking in the collection of tabloids and broadsheets. "Although, occasionally a story will give me an idea." Beside these, a proliferation of items most people would label as junk, but for which he sees some kind of purpose, even if he is yet to decide precisely what that might be. For him, garbage is the start of a process, not the end.

Below the windows of three walls are smears and swabs and swatches of oil paint, haphazardly daubed in an effort to test the colour; no surface too precious – the studio a living, breathing part of the process, an active participant in the work.

Maybe *this* is art: an installation piece. The random nature of the marks could be transferred to a gallery with the brick and mortar intact.

I suggest this to my host. He stares blankly back.

In its entirety, the far wall is fly-posted to an inch-thick density with scraps of paper: vertical strata that an archaeologist could painstakingly strip away, expecting to discover centuries of activity, only to find that nothing had been adhered prior to 1991. It is a crazed, disparate montage of images: photographs, posters, leaflets, magazine and newspaper clippings, film stills, sketches, doodles, even 3D objects attached to masonry with six-inch nails, including a plaster of Paris mask Jacob cast from his own face, speared to the wall through its left eye socket.

Jacob and I are friends quite by accident – assigned adjacent rooms in the same student lodgings in the autumn of 1985 – and sometimes I'm very conscious of our different backgrounds and outlooks on life, even though we both spent our formative years in Brighton. While we studied the same art class, our temperaments could not be more contrasting. I am calculating, methodical, rational; he is spontaneous, off-the-cuff, radical. Although I am three inches over six-foot, and he just 5' 8", I feel somehow diminished beside him – as if my size is excessive, pointless. For some reason he took me under his wing at college, and in a way, perhaps I balance him out. As outlandish as he can at times be, he abhors bullshit. He knows I will tell it to him straight, even if he doesn't agree with what I'm saying.

Due to a dishevelled appearance – his unkempt hair is a knotted mess – Jacob looks much older than he actually is. He could pass for 45, and yet at 28 he's only a couple of years older than me. He has a beard that grows in clumps, a random proliferation of hair that only joins together at certain points of his face, and is at its thickest density beneath a sharp aquiline nose. Almost certainly an alcoholic – he refers to himself as a *wino* – he has recently taken to dabbling in various drugs, to further stoke his muse.

There can be little doubt he enjoys the contradictions to his personality, and wilfully embellishes them. If a stuffy art critic approaches him at a show then his response is to act ignorant, play the fool. If a viewer doesn't understand his art, he seeks to further confuse them. Undeniably homosexual, he claims the more ambiguous title of *bisexual*, even though I've never known him to show the slightest interest in women, beyond sometimes painting them. He hates giving people what they want, being the person they expect. He makes those in his company work hard, keeps them on their toes. Mostly appreciated by those who know him well, he is generally disliked on first impression, and often well beyond.

"When will they make bottles big enough to last beyond a handful of glasses?" he spits contemptuously, before shuffling off to locate and open another Beaujolais. His capacity for alcohol never ceases to amaze me, but it all seems to be part of a pure artistic temperament I just don't possess; what marks him out as a true artist, while I remain a mere technician.

Now alone, my eye is attracted to a cluster of photographs on the wall capturing extreme movement: G-force distorting a young pilot's face into an old man's gurn; a boxer taking a blow on the cheek – jaw-bending, nose-squashing, eye-popping, vein-bursting. War photography: bullets entering and exiting crania, faces exploding, amputees screaming, severed limbs curled on the ground like sleeping animals; a punctured dam of skin, blood flooding in pools. Beside these a selection of diagrams and illustrations relating to various diseases of the mouth. Further along, graphic photographs of operations and autopsies.

Black calls to me from the kitchen. "Would you like a cup of herbal tea? They're a special blend Jacob has imported from China."

I find herbal tea insipid. "Sure, that'd be lovely."

I lift one of the many sketches of Black scattered all over the floor: a drawing so rough it hasn't evolved to contain hair or fully formed features; just the coarse charcoal marks where each eye is positioned within the oval of her face, the tip of her nose and a stroke indicating the mouth. Beauty, reduced to a few lines within an ellipse. I could make a thousand – a *million* – marks on the page and not get anywhere as close to capturing her essence, but this is why I need time and effort to achieve a likeness, and he is the visionary.

I make my way back to the far end of the studio, to the collection of beaten-up leather car seats mounted onto wooden bases, and slump into one with its back to the collage. The disembodied engine of a Triumph motorbike – perspex sheet atop – has been reinvented as a coffee table. I take in my surroundings, awaiting Black to approach and hand me my drink: the moment we finally share the same small personal space.

Dressed in the clothes she had been wearing on the beach, Black brings through a tray of *Constant Comment* teas, the bloated bags left to float like dead sea mammals. She hands me mine, then sits down. I crave eye contact and yet as soon as it arrives I involuntarily look away. What am I scared of? I have grown increasingly confident around women with age and experience, but my attraction to her is such that I am fifteen again. I sip gingerly. The tea tastes of watery orange and sweet spices. Jacob briefly re-enters the studio, heading to the video camera, this time successfully switching it off. He leaves his tea – he still has a glass of wine in his hand – before wandering away to get changed. Black and I are left alone, and I am lost for words.

"Black?" I eventually ask. She looks at me, failing to realise that this one word is in itself a question, not simply an attempt to gain her attention. "An unusual name," I add.

"It's my surname. People began to call me it at sixth form college and it stuck from there."

"Like your eyes," I say. She smiles, half-heartedly, and I am not sure she understands what I am getting at. Has it come out as "I *like* your eyes"? I want to clarify that it was a comparison – that her eyes are fiercely black. But I don't push it.

"Um... that's a nice pendant," I note, looking at the silver locket which hangs around her neck, before realising that my gaze is dipping dangerously close to her cleavage. I avert my eyes, guiltily. She thanks me for the compliment, but the topic leads nowhere. Then, inspiration. "That was a nice thing you did earlier."

"What do you mean?"

"On the beach. With that young boy."

"You saw that?"

"Yes. I was on the beach too, nearby. I was very impressed. By the way you handled it."

"I hate seeing children suffer. It makes my insides quiver."

"Me too... I was going to help, but, well, you seemed to have it all under control."

She remains friendly, but slightly distracted. Fleeting eye contact comes and goes in waves. Just when I think I have lost her attention, and that she is off in another world of thought, she switches focus and our eyes meet with a sharp collision. I feel less unnerved when she is facing away; when she looks at me I feel the grip on what I am saying loosening, the thread of my thoughts starting to unravel.

It is only once Jacob returns, and acts as a conduit, that I relax a little. He provides the safety net, and I am buoyed by his ability to haul me into conversations, such as when he aims a few "Patrick likes such-and-such, don't you?" at me.

We sit discussing art. Black, it transpires, has just graduated from a degree course in photography. Some of the pictures on the wall behind us – a selection of medical students dissecting a cadaver – are hers. Finally I feel I have an 'in', a strong point of connection, a chance to tell her that I am also an artist.

"Anyway," she says, rising to her feet, "I'd best be going", before I have the opportunity to explain. My heart sinks. On her way to the door she grabs her canvas bag and yellow Walkman from the hat stand. "See you tonight," she shouts cheerily to Jacob. "Nice meeting you, Patrick," she adds.

"And you!" I reply, with a little too much enthusiasm.

"Tonight?" I ask Jacob, once the front door is closed.

"A little get-together. On the West Pier. Just a few of us."

"The West Pier? It's a wreck. It's not open to the public."

"Then we won't have any plebs ruining our fun. The invite stretches to you, of course."

I feel like a monarchist invited to the royal wedding.

FOUR

I'd never seen my wife like this, in almost a decade together. I didn't even recognise her: features distorted by rage, eyes distended with hatred and no little confusion. Her usual benign appearance – thin lips, narrow nose, small blue eyes, all of which framed and accentuated by a sharp mousy blonde bob – pinched inwards in rancour. Intoxicated – we'd both been drinking heavily – she looked like someone who wanted me dead.

At the heart of the altercation lay the painting of Black, which had hung in the spare bedroom for four or five years. Only in the previous few weeks had I found myself studying it again. Until then it had stopped telling me anything new; showing only the swabs of colour and the tracks of brush strokes. I had begun to view it as a series of textures, like a mountain range, with the many peaks and troughs of oil heaped in layers over one another; due to overfamiliarity, I saw only the medium, not the message. Then, suddenly, it spoke to me afresh. It found some new vivacity, alive once more. As a result, Black moved to the front of my mind. Nerves deadened and dulled by time were newly exposed, sliced open at the quick.

To my wife the woman in oils represented something altogether larger; Laura had it in her head that I was having an affair, even though the only person to cheat during our marriage was her. Maybe she anticipated revenge. Or perhaps, aware of her own lapse, she could not truly believe in someone else's fidelity. To be fair, she strayed during a period of separation, and her guilt was far greater than my anger. I fully forgave that momentary indiscretion, but her suspicion proved far more insidious. Something – and to this day I don't know what – tipped her over the edge. Full of confusion, she expelled vitriol in my direction.

"You bastard!" she screamed, pacing from our bedroom out onto the landing, throwing whatever she came across at whatever surface presented itself. I had to chase to look at her, face to face, before she turned away again, and launched the next object to hand. I ducked, and the mirror at the top of the stairs smashed as a clock impacted plumb centre.

"You cheating *shit*," she said, with the crazed glint in her eyes of someone whose mind was clearly well beyond making proper sense of anything. "You, *you*—" She circled the spare bedroom like a stir-crazy hamster mesmerised by the routine of her wheel "—bastard."

She didn't seem to hear a word I said. I went to take her upper arm, without aggression, to hold her still, but she wrenched it away with an exaggerated tug, leaving me cast in the role of brute. "Don't you touch me," she snarled, before picking up a vase and hurling it in my direction as I backed away. It sailed past my face, shattering against the far wall.

She stood facing Jacob's portrait of Black.

"Is it *her*?" she asked.

I hesitated, confused.

"It *is*! Oh good God, Patrick. You've *flaunted* it. All these years. You vile piece of shit."

"I've got no idea what you're on about," I said, furiously shaking my head.

Laura moved closer to the canvas. We had disagreed over the painting before, and, after defending my right for it to maintain pride of place in the living room, I eventually allowed her to move it to a less prominent position in the house. But now, to my wife, its significance seemed clear. This was not, as I told her, a random portrait from a flea market; it was evidence of my infidelity. Nothing I said could shake her from this conclusion.

Buzzing with a rage that seemed to stem from some electrical source – plugged into 20,000 volts – she took her door key and struck a deep blow between Black's eyes and, having pierced the canvas, dragged it down through her nose to the base of her chin; so visceral I expected an arc of blood to spout across the room. Before I could move – rooted to the spot, catatonic in disbelief – a second stab, this time at Black's shoulder blade, with the incision running at a forty-five degree angle, slicing through the opposite breast until flaps of material draped down, revealing the creamy blank reverse. She drew back the key again, her hand hovering over the painting, poised for a third incision. I had to act.

I grabbed her shoulders, span her round. No sooner had I released my grip than she flew at me; a rapidly uncoiling spring, expanding with exponential force. I sidestepped her wild lunge, but she glanced off my shoulder, into the painting. She would have head-butted Black's nose had her two-dimensional face not hung apart, exposing the backboard of the frame. Laura's body sprang back, strangely loose and pliant, uncontrolled arms flopping up then down and outwards in slow motion, head lolling back and to the side; her movements a mix of heavy rag doll and unbelted crash test dummy.

She came to a rest at my feet, flat on her back; a gash, about an inch in length, opening up on her forehead. This time the blood did gush, thick and red.

Guilt seized me, squeezing tight. Even though I was fairly certain none of this was my fault, I could perhaps have handled it better; not let things escalate to such an extreme. But I was also fairly inebriated, lost in a half-fog where nothing quite made sense. I lifted the dead-weight of her body back to our bed, and, in a rather pathetic token gesture, placed a plaster on the wound. And then, with her breathing steady and sure, I left her to sleep off the excesses and mania of a night to forget, but which, barring those vague moments of blackout, would remain forever in our minds.

FIVE

There is a head on my desk. With eyes firmly shut I run my hands over the skull: small, feminine, smooth between its fissures. I try to get a feel for the face: the curvature of the cheekbones, the jut of the jaw, the ellipses of the eye sockets; how these would have affected the tissues above and around. In time I will approach the skull more scientifically, with my charts, my high-precision ruler and my tissue-depth markers, but at first I want to work with impressions, instincts. My eyes may tell me most of what I need to know, and science inform my decisions, but the tips of my fingers will shape the reborn features. They need to become intimately acquainted with the contours. They need to learn through touch; learn like the blind. Upon this base I will build, in layers, the face of someone the world lost, or carelessly mislaid.

* * *

Absence has been a shadow cast by nothing – cast by the *missing thing* – since my childhood. For as long as I can remember I have been the one left behind, forever losing a grip on the relationships of my life. Sometimes abandoned – a pattern that began with my father when I was just six. Other times, such as in the case of a young woman who had such a major impact on my life, thwarted by circumstance; the intervention of a cruel twist of fate that to this day leaves me searching out a resolution. I carry a constant background concern, like the humming of a refrigerator that only comes to mind when you stop and listen. There's an underlying sense of panic, as I reel in the threads of those escaping, only to find an empty end to the cord. I cannot tie anything down.

The missing are my area of expertise. As such, it made sense to make them my career, albeit after failed attempts in other fields. Absence is my forte: there exist spaces where once stood people. It is my job, as a forensic artist and reconstructor of faces, to help fill those spaces, with that person, or with an answer. People slip from the radar of their loved ones, and a blip vanishes from the screen.

Faces of the dead stare down, from photographs and sketches lining the walls of my study, and from the eerie gazes of clay reconstructions lined along a shelf: an identity parade crying out for recognition. Then, in my desk drawer, a cluster of manila files, gruesome photographs escaping at the seams. On a daily basis I ask them *Who are you?* One day they will remember, and whisper their names.

There is another image of a missing person, the only one I knew personally, the only one who, as far as I know, isn't dead. It is in the form of an oil painting, shoddily stuck together with Sellotape, which hangs centrally within the room. In my top drawer I keep her file. But she is not *officially* missing. She resides in her own life, and is merely absent from mine.

* * *

Knowledge > grief. That is the key equation. People would much rather hear bad news than no news. They can *just about* handle the concept of a murdered son or daughter, parent or spouse, if they can eventually lay him or her to rest. The alternatives the mind throws up, in the lack of knowledge – in the dark of cluelessness – are often too disturbing to dwell upon. No one wants to think of their child lying in a ditch in a forest, cold and alone (not that the dead feel cold, or alone, but the thought still haunts the minds of the living). It's all just earth – bones in earth – but the difference could not be more pronounced. Closure means everything. Closure is the lid of a casket. Closure is a vicar's scattering of dirt. Closure is a gravedigger's shovel. It doesn't mean forgiving, or forgetting. And closure is such a trite word. It just means an answer. As long as someone remains missing, the story never ends.

I'm not religious, so I cannot pray for the missing. But crossing one's fingers seems too inconsequential.

* * *

I can't switch off, leave this work behind. I am always pondering the evidence, wherever I am. A torn item of a child's clothing strewn across roadside brambles: blown from the window of a passing car, or ripped from a frail and frightened young soul? A dew-dampened jumper at the centre of a park: a forgotten goalpost from a twilight game of football, or something more sinister? The discarded black thong: lost in a moment of drunken passion, or pulled down against its wearer's will? I pick it all up and bag it, just in case. Is it evidence, or irrelevance? I look for stories in everything. Stories where others see nothing. On the nameless (sometimes faceless, occasionally headless) corpses that remain free of identity there may be a series of physical clues.

Almost two decades on, and with Black's whereabouts unknown, I ponder every conceivable possibility, think of innumerable locations where she may reside. But the world is never bigger than when someone is cast adrift of your own personal sphere.

Plagued for decades by insomnia, I prefer to work at night, by candlelight. I place six to eight candles of varying sizes on a ledge above the table, along with a hurricane lamp. It casts organic light, alive in the room; animating the features as they take shape. It drops bristling shadows into recesses, flickers movement across pock-marked clay. It draws me into the subject. In these moments I am God, taking part of a real human and, for the first time since he or she took shape in the womb, forming features from scratch. How much more control can you have than literally shaping someone? Even a plastic surgeon doesn't delve all the way down to every last inch of exposed bone. But my aim is not to create a new look, or someone's idea of physical perfection. I need to find the faces of the dead, when alive; faces lost to decay, faces burnt away. Faces eaten by woodland creatures, devoured by insect life. Faces slipped away in the river's flow.

A person's features are largely determined by the shape of their skull, but there are many blanks in need of filling, where guesswork is inescapable. Noses, beyond the apex of the bridge, are mostly cartilage that rots. Eyes, each pair with their own distinctive gaze indicative of the life behind, can never be truly recreated. And hairstyles, eyebrows, beards and moustaches, all of which dramatically change an appearance, are often missing pieces of these kinds of puzzle; the colour and style of which can only be guessed at. Without evidence, there's no real way of knowing how to get a perfect likeness.

It's a slow process, with preparation paramount. I'm always eager to jump straight in, get my hands wet with clay; skip ahead to the point where it starts to pay off, when an identity takes shape. But everything constructed in layers relies on what lies beneath. I have to underpin the skin with the correct amount of simulated sinew and fat to turn a skull – hard bone – into a soft face. Ultimately it's about accuracy, not creativity. Then again, I don't possess the raw talent and imagination of someone like Jacob. I am competent at realistic portrayals and little else, and I've learned to accept that. I need a script to follow, rules to adhere to. Without these I flounder. I have skills, such as an obsessive attention to detail, and well-honed powers of observation, but little *flair*.

First I secure the various elements of the skull. Loose or dislodged teeth are glued in place. A forensic odontologist will assist if it's not an obvious case of slipping one or two teeth back into the matching cavities – it's usually obvious what goes where, like a nursery play-set. Next, the mandible is attached to the cranium. Slim foam spacers are placed in the temporomandibular – the hinge where jaw meets skull – to simulate absent cartilage. This is as far as I've got with the woman whose identity I am hoping to help discover. Found under piles of wood on Brighton's West Pier, no more than a bare skeleton: no flesh, no clothes, no jewellery. Just the wire from a bra curved beneath the bones, and a scrap of a label, on which the barely legible '32C'.

I never believed in psychic visions before I got into this line of work. But when you hold someone's disembodied head in your hands, its life vacated, it's hard not to experience some kind of connection with the person whose thoughts once resided within. With my eyes closed, and fingers clasped around what is now no more than an empty shell, an array of images filter through my mind. These are probably no more than the free associations of imagination. But occasionally I wonder if it's something more; something I don't understand, which will guide me in my work.

Can I see her face, smiling?

Next in the reconstruction process comes the numbered tissue-depth markers, cut to size and glued to designated points on the skull, plotting a course around the cranium: a kind of three-dimensional dot-to-dot, indicating the height to which the skin and tissue will on average rise, depending on the sex, race and build of the deceased. There are subtle differences between skulls of European, Asian and African descent, just as there are variations between male and female. The male forehead is usually more sloping, and has a projecting brow ridge area. The lower half of the face will be proportionally larger than in a female, due to a stronger jawbone. Teeth also tend to be larger in a man. In a female, the jaw is usually more obtuse, the chin more pointed.

There are also differences between these categories regarding the depth of the flesh. In a slender white woman such as this, the glabella – the smooth part of the forehead above and between the eyebrows – is half the average depth you'd find in someone obese. The mid-philtrum – the vertical groove on the upper lip, below the septum – is five millimetres on the work in progress, whereas even on a thin male of African origin it would be double that length. The skull of a black person will usually be recognisable by alveolar prognathism – a forward projection of the lower face – and the nasal openings will be wider than in a Caucasian. The faces of white people tend to be flatter, with zygomatic bones that slant back. It's not simply a question of skin colour, or delicate features, that differentiate between races and sexes; all the stage make-up in the world can't make a man of African origin convincingly resemble a white woman, or vice versa.

When there's nothing but the skull itself to work from it comes down to these kinds of distinctions to determine the race and sex, before reconstructing their identity. Make no mistake, beauty goes beyond the shallow depth of skin. In a number of ways it's possible to tell, with a fair degree of certainty, that the woman whose skull is propped upon my desk was good-looking. The gateway to the senses rot – nose, ears, eyes, lips, tongue – and in life these do so much to determine attractiveness. But what remains, in this case, is as close to perfect as I'll ever get to see. The bridge of the nose is delicate and petite, and the skull has a pleasing orbital shape to it. The jawbone, now secured back in place, presents a subtle curve that doesn't jar when viewed from any angle. Beauty is often about symmetry, and here the right side perfectly mirrors the left. The teeth, even now, are flawless. From the lack of wear and tear, and the half-emerged wisdom teeth, it's possible to say she was in her late teens or early twenties.

No one imagines themselves like this – a component, detached and placed on someone's desk as part of a working day. At one point in time this woman had her whole life ahead of her. She will not have stopped to consider this option, even had she sensed the worst. We have various concepts of our own death, and we have an understanding of what follows – not relating to an afterlife, but to the rituals of burial or cremation in front of a collection of mourners. It has a kind of comfort: that we will be missed, and that people will come to say goodbye. But *this* is unimaginable. No one thinks they will end up with their identity shrouded in mystery, reduced to an inanimate object onto which a stranger superglues plastic cylinders and overlays swabs of clay. Unless held captive, and given time to contemplate an unseemly end, none of this will have crossed her mind.

I no longer casually observe faces. I can't help but see people in terms of spatial geometry, facial infrastructure. I ease myself under the skin, get a feel for the foundations. What is the underlying bone structure? How would I reconstruct his or her appearance if presented with their detached skull? When your area of expertise is all around you – when it's at the very core of human interaction – it's impossible to switch off. It's not so much a case of taking work home with me, as it following. Is there something defining about a person's appearance – shallow scar, lazy eye, bulbous nose, distinctive mole – that would take no subcutaneous instruction, and leave me without a clue? Sometimes a conversation will come to an abrupt halt, or maybe even only skip a beat, and I feel caught out: that look from my companion – not fear exactly, but perhaps an acknowledgement of the threat of invasion, like a prey's wariness of its hunter – that leads me to think they've read my mind. I am looking too deeply. I am peering beneath the skin. I've gone too far.

It's like being caught undressing a woman with your eyes. Except I've been caught undressing a face.

SIX

"Holy *fucking shit!*"

The open-plan kitchen of Jacob's apartment, the door of an upright freezer ajar before me. Having mistaken it for the fridge

– hunting out something to snack on – I am confronted by a *human head.*

I jump back. And then — of course — draw the natural conclusion: it's *not real*, is it? It has to be a sculpture.

But no. Eyeball to eyeball, I can see that it is without doubt the severed head of a man of early pension years, icicles spiking from his prickly beard. I see a lost polar explorer – a Franklin, a Scott – exposed to the elements, peering through unblinking deep blue eyes glazed with a layer of ice. Those eyes, framed by powdered lashes, stare past me, at a fixed point on a blank horizon: at a world of white.

My appetite is suddenly suppressed. It is, without doubt, the most weird and unexpected thing I have ever encountered in my life.

Jacob brushes past. "Close that thing," he says, pushing the door shut before I have the chance. "*Fuck*, man. You could get me arrested."

"I could get *you* arrested? It's a fucking head. *In your freezer.* I was looking for something to eat."

"It's not what you think," he says, haughtily.

"No?" I say, still looking at the freezer, as if its door were still open.

"No."

"In what way? You mean it's not real?"

"No, it's real. But it's... complicated. It's *kinda* okay for me to have it."

"Ah, that clears it all up, then."

"It's a *cadaver*," he says, accentuating each syllable. "A friend smuggled it out of medical school for me. It's not like I went out and killed someone. All the same, it's not exactly something I should be advertising. At least, not until it's ready for what I want to use it for."

"I'd ask what that is, but truth be told, I'm not sure I want to know."

"Let's just say it'll be something a little more... *dramatic*. In a way, I'm doing him a favour. He'll live on, as art."

"I'm not sure *art* was what he donated his body to."

"Like he cares," he snorts.

"Ah – the failure of the dead to complain about their plight. They're just too blasé."

"Look, he was probably just a tramp. They're always tramps. Just some nobody, not missed by anybody. And this is the crucial bit – he's *dead*."

Another key difference between the two of us is that Jacob sees art as an excuse for *anything*; that art exempts him from normal societal boundaries and laws. Me – I care too much about such things.

At his behest I join Jacob at his easel, to inspect the painting of Black. I know how touchy he can be about his work, and purposely avoided studying it until invited. We stand within a rhombus of light at the heart of the room.

"So, this is your latest masterpiece?" I say, instantly regretting my choice of words. I perform a sharp intake of breath, perhaps willing them back into my mouth. They remain out there, hanging in the air, a verbal mist.

"Masterpiece?" he spits in hard syllables. "Who the fuck do you think I am? *Jeez*, man. Masterpieces are for artists who've been dead hundreds of years. I simply paint pictures, and, bizarrely, leave it up to others – often people who haven't a fucking clue – to decide whether or not they're any good. Half the time I don't even know myself."

"I walked straight into that. The wrong thing to say."

"Wait until I'm dead. Then you can talk about masterpieces."

Jacob respects my ability, but he knows I'm not a true creative force. That has been clear since college. Sometimes he includes me in his discussions on what it's like to be creative; at other times I'm blatantly excluded.

"It's always a great moment when you see a definitive progression," he tells me as we stand facing his painting, speaking in such a way that suggests I should feel enlightened. "Looking at an old piece and realising you've moved on to a whole new level. But at the same time, there's the eternal damnation of your mistakes, your poor works, being out there – you can't go and ask for them back, or instruct people to burn them. Monet destroyed his own work, y'know? Van Gogh – he destroyed his own work too. But they did so before the pieces were able to flee the nest. I'd like to track down and take a Stanley knife to some of mine."

"So... Black," I say, looking into her painted eyes. "She's very different from the life models you used to use."

"How so?" I can sense the mischief in Jacob's voice. He knows damn-well what I am getting at. The last time I saw his work it depicted men and women so overweight that their bodies had to invent new places to store fat.

"You know... she's just so ... *perfect.*"

"Oh, I'll tell her you think that."

"Well, compared to the models you were using before," I say, trying to play down my attraction to Black.

"The Double-baggers, you mean? Porkers? Fatties?"

"I'm guessing there was no accident behind the radical departure? There's a reason, right? You're commenting on the way beautiful people are treated differently to those less attractive?"

He turns, stands with his back to the easel, hands on hips. "To be honest, I haven't got a *fucking clue.* I paint what

I find interesting, but I'm sure it doesn't need me to suggest any meaning. Critics and audiences take their own meanings, make their own assumptions. I'm just holding up examples – a mirror, if you like. But a distorted mirror. Sort of like a fun-fair mirror. Y'know, presenting an altered reality. Reality, but one step removed. Maybe two."

"But it's about more than the surface, surely? Beauty being skin deep?"

"Is it? Is it really? Am I looking for the depth, the soul inside? I doubt it. If you think that, fair enough. I just want to try to examine the human body."

He tips more wine into his glass, to the very rim. He's on a roll. "It's *flesh*. Flesh and bone. And skin – loose or taut. That's my forte. I'd spent so long looking at the obese, the anorexic, the freakish. I wondered what it would be like try and capture something more flawless. *Perfect*, if you will insist on using that awful word. Does perfection have to be bland? Can perfection insult in ways other than being dull? Does beauty have to be some fucking god-awful, soulless airbrushed photo-realistic bullshit?—" I resist the temptation to interject that I like airbrushed art "—or could I represent it in a different manner, with different approaches? Could I be savage with it, and the beauty still shine through? Could I be tender with it, and not have it seem utterly sterile? That's what I've been doing with her all these months. Some have been successful. Others... well, the less said about those the better."

I am not sure what to make of the painting. At the risk of sounding dumb, and missing the point (and aware that even if I did find the point, Jacob would undoubtedly contradict me), I say, "It's beautiful."

And in its way, it is. But I mean *she's* beautiful. I want to express my feelings about the subject, not the art. It is Black who supplies the beauty, Black who takes the breath away. None of it is possible without her. She makes an otherwise blank canvas shine.

"Right, time for a piss," he says, and I am left alone with the painting. Black stands facing me, her arms crossed over her breasts, but with a hint of both areolae still visible. The painting is cropped just below the upper line of her pubic hair.

Despite not being a photo-realistic portrait it still bears an uncanny likeness to the subject – such large, piercing eyes. I move left and right, to see if they follow me and, sure enough, they do. The oil-stroke eyebrows are inverted Vs, the shape of a child's simplistic etchings of seagulls on the horizon: each with an upward sweep moving from the bridge of the nose out beyond the central point of iris and pupil, and then the sudden dramatic downturn, a short swish descending towards the ear; rendered with just two vivid arcing sweeps of the brush, up and then down, but still with enough femininity in each curve and delicacy in the weight of line to avoid looking odd. The lips are full, but not to bursting; nothing artificially inflated or altered. The nose is in no way petite or demure, but any other nose simply wouldn't work within the same setting. It fits her face.

Even the painting disarms me. Black, reduced to two dimensions and mounted onto an easel. But somehow a third dimension pushes out at me. For a moment I think I can sense a heat from the canvas, an aura enveloping the space I inhabit; clasping me, pulling me in. I want to touch her, even in this stillness, even in this flattened state.

SEVEN

Leaning against a promenade balustrade that despite the sun remains cool to the touch, I gaze across the water, staring at the narrow man-made structure jutting perilously out to sea, its brown-grey lattice sub-frame soaked to the knees; severed from the shore, having waded too far.

The pier comprises the concert hall – which in later years became a café – in the foreground, with its softly curved walls and arching roof lined with sweeping decorative flourishes; and the pavilion – which was first a theatre, then a restaurant – at the pier head, squarer in design, with oriental turrets and unlit lightbulbs arranged to spell 'WEST PIER'. Finally, the small rotundas: kiosks that once served the public their chocolate and cigarettes.

Throughout my childhood I would pass by, and each time it stared back, unmoved; ignored by everyone, it seemed, but me. In the evening, with the sun edging beyond the horizon, an unthinkable number of starlings would gather on its ornamental rooftops and railings. All at once they would blanket the sky in temporary darkness — a million tiny circles that merged, broke and reformed in various clusters, before banking east and out of sight.

My deep-seated fascination with the pier arose as an eight-year-old boy taken down to the shoreline by my aunt. I'd been aboard before, but by 1975, with it closed to the public, we were forced to keep our distance. This instantly rendered it exotic, mysterious; the sense of the unobtainable drew me in. It had become increasingly incapable of human occupation, decorated with signs warning against trespass; as welcoming as a nuclear power plant sounding its alarm. Despite the dangers, it possessed all the mystery and romance a daydreaming child could ever wish for. I imagined the buildings as suddenly deserted – at someone's order, halfway through lunch – and that in its final occupied moments everyone just stood up and walked quickly to shore. All paraphernalia remained preserved, kept as on that fateful day, frozen in time over the water. In my mind, china saucers housing cups of unfinished tea remained on the tables of the restaurant and café, topped to the brim with dust. A world of objects just waiting for the people who left them to return, when in fact they never would. The truth, of course, was far more prosaic. Imagination always has its rug pulled by reality.

I've wasted too much time, and have a list of things I need to do before this evening. I bid the pier farewell, aware that in a few hours we will finally be fully reacquainted.

* * *

The sun begins to dip towards the horizon, falling from a tie-dyed sky. Amber bleeds into red that fuses into purple that merges with the darkening azure. Clouds draw the colours into their plume.

Running late for the pier rendezvous after completing an errand, I stride through the narrow Lanes with their quaint, cramped shops that predate the antiques so many sell. I feel better for walking – the nerves smoothed throughout my body as I move. I'm still apprehensive, though – the tightness locked within my chest. If I stop my whole body will seize up. So I plough on, as if walking through invisible cement that I must not allow to dry around me. I'd just begun to relax in Black's company this afternoon, and now, with time to ponder how I am going to behave around her, I'm starting to unravel. I've barely eaten, and what I have consumed resists digestion.

I exit the Lanes, turn another corner, and as the pier heaves into view the usual cluster of starlings bursts from its buildings. For a moment they distract my mind from the need to impress. Before I realise I have crossed the coastal King's Road from the Metropole Hotel – where I have a room booked for the night – to Brighton's wide, promenading pavements, and then down one flight of steps, past a Mohican of moored sailing boats at rest on the shingle. Black approaches from the west as, from the east, I lope across unforgiving pebbles that distort my attempt to saunter. Our paths converge in the lengthening shadow of the pier. She smiles. I smile in return, then try to catch my breath.

My eye is caught by her scarf: a fluffy blue phalanx of feathers. It is an ostentatious gesture in an otherwise perfunctory outfit: snug-fitting denim jeans, thin black jacket carried under her arm, plain white blouse undone at the top three buttons, revealing a silver chain with an oval locket.

We are both late. Unsure if the others have already made their way onto the pier, we stand for several moments in silence, tied in an awkward knot of indecision. Perhaps we are each looking to the other to take the lead.

"What shall we do?" I eventually ask.

"They're already on there, right? I mean, they'd be here otherwise?"

I join Black in looking at the pier, thinking we see activity inside the pavilion. Squinting, we mistakenly identify sparks of orange sunlight glistening on metal as the glow of a torch, and birds flapping within the building as signs of our friends' movements. We take turns to call, and believe we hear muffled replies, which we will later decode as our own distorted echoes mixed with the sound of tourists further down the beach.

Black takes the initiative and wades into the water. The tide is fully out, with no swimming required to get to the point of access. I splosh in her wake. She locates a length of rope, tied to an iron railing this afternoon by one of Jacob's friends, and eases her taut frame into the air, hips shimmying, shoulders gyrating, as she ascends: a power-pack of efficiency. Her shoes clack against the trusses and girders as she uses them for leverage, pushing upwards. She displays surprising upper body strength. I am less agile, although I still manage to make it to the top, partly out of a determination to not look hopelessly weak. My innate clumsiness, however, has not deserted me, and my step is too heavy as I attempt to move beyond the railing. The floorboard beneath my feet snaps like a water biscuit, sending a section of railing, along with the rope, spiralling down. I fall gracelessly forward, landing in a heap at Black's feet.

My heart stops. I hold my breath, and listen to the wood supporting me, feeling for vibrations indicative of splintering within. But there are none; just a reassuring silence and stillness.

"Are you okay?" she asks, with the genuine compassion of someone who cannot bear to witness the suffering of others. I nod, feeling foolish.

She helps me up, and again I find myself trailing in her wake. She treads carefully on her way to the pavilion, and I follow behind.

We pause, take in our surroundings. Iron snakes coil decoratively around oil lamps. Flaking hand-painted signs for speedboat rides and bingo lie on the floor, covered with pigeon faeces and an array of broken artefacts. With each creak the balance between us and nature echoes. Wood, given by nature, felled, shaped and lain by man – then, in turn, degraded by the wind, the rain, the sea – is all that keeps us from a great descent, and the unreliable safety blanket of water below. None of it looks to have been designed to withstand the hostile environment to which it belongs. The only way that wood survives nature's ferocity is encased within its protective bark. Perhaps if it had been maintained, then the pier might have stood a chance. But no. Instead it has been left to rot, to the point where it is on the last of its many iron legs.

This time I take the lead. The sea, with its glistening reflections of the sun's final light, can be seen clearly through gaps in the floor as, with great care, we edge towards the pavilion. Tentatively, I bring my foot slowly down onto a crepitating board, testing it at first with a small amount of pressure, then a little more, and more still, until convinced it will bear my weight. With each step the process shortens, as our trust grows.

We take turns to call out for the others. Nothing.

"So, what now then?" I mutter.

"Inside," she says, confidently. "Jacob said his friends were going to tidy the place up. The rope was there, so they must be here somewhere, right? Probably hiding, pissing about. Dickheads."

* * *

The interior of the pavilion feels reassuringly secure. A thick, flat asphalt flooring covers the entire room; for once, the relief of not a single rotten board in sight. The remnants of a mirror maze lay piled up against the far wall: a clown's face, painted high above the door, still peering eerily beyond its film of grime. Our path in that direction is blocked by a mass grave of deckchairs, their skinny wooden arms and legs poking out beyond stripy material. To either side the view remains stunning: many of the windows that span both flanks are no longer glazed, but even the grubbiest panes offer sight of the sun setting over the sea.

We chance the staircase in the corner, fresh footprints cut into the dust suggesting Jacob's friends had recently trod them. At the top we find ourselves in a derelict dining room, a bent and broken sign for the Ocean Restaurant leaning forlornly against the far wall. Nearby, doors lie fallen from their hinges, flat on their backs beyond their frames. We are drawn to the light beyond them, out onto a coarse, bituminous balcony. Further steps would send us off the end of the pier.

Everything is in place for the party – all that's missing are the guests. Despite what Black suggested, no one jumps out to surprise us. As planned, someone has clearly been here at some point today: a small space tidied amid the detritus. To one side sit several cans of beer and plenty of snacks, plus an old portable cassette stereo.

"Some party," she says, standing with her hands on her hips. "I wasn't expecting the Ritz, but even so."

For a while we're both too taken aback by this unusual experience to speak. Eventually I break the silence. "So, who are these people that are supposed to be joining us?"

"No idea," she says, turning around. "I don't really know any of them, apart from Jez."

"Jez?"

"You don't know Jez?"

"No."

"Jacob's latest flame. Been a few months now. I think it was supposed to be mostly Jez's crowd here. Jacob was going to organise cabs to collect them all before meeting us."

"I see… So what's he like, this Jez?"

"Young, impressionable, although I've only met him the once. Drinks a lot, so in that sense they get along just fine. Of course, it's yet to take its toll in quite the way it has with Jacob."

"I look forward to meeting him," I say, with the strong sense that it won't be tonight.

EIGHT

Discovering the identity behind this particular skull feels unusually important, but for David Holford it's a life-long obsession. He was a young police constable assigned to protect the scene upon the discovery of her body, and then, decades later, headed up the region's newly-formed Cold Case Unit, which resurrected the investigation. Having retired early due to the onset of multiple sclerosis, he continues to work the case in his own time, with the department's blessing and its occasional assistance. Like the parent of a missing child, he regularly checks in with me for possible news, and offers ideas that might be of some assistance.

Our paths first crossed on a successfully solved homicide about fifteen years ago. All these years later he now has me reworking the forensic artistry on this woman, to see if I can come up with something that the original artist failed to capture with a sketch. Marina – named in keeping with her coastal discovery – remains David's one regret: his golden ulcer.

"Not for me", he has deadpanned on more than one occasion, with a self-pitying weariness, "the standard-issue carriage clock". Whenever he speaks, phlegm bubbles in his throat; the words filtered through a watery larynx. Eye contact is scarce. He may be talking to you, but contemplating something else at the same time; not ignoring you (at least so I like to think), but multi-tasking. Eye contact is reserved for the suspected, the *guilty*.

At the time of her discovery, David's superiors believed Marina likely to be a prostitute and drug user in her late teens or early twenties; the coroner's verdict suggested between the ages of fifteen and twenty-five. Needles were found at the scene, but not particularly close to the body. She fit no missing person's reports from the area, and nothing led back from the body toward an answer. David felt she might have been younger, and a runaway from London or further north, or possibly even mainland Europe. Dental work – so valuable in identifying a victim – didn't exist on almost flawless teeth: the lower set were slightly overcrowded, but that aside, they could have belonged to a film star. The cause of death was listed as a fracture to the front of the skull.

* * *

People to find. Needles lost in haystacks the size of the Isle of Wight. Tails to pin on donkeys, with eyes blindfolded. When the donkey isn't even in the room, the house, the city, the country.

Examples are everywhere.

The quiet and the still, set in relief from an upfront world: a field, a village backdrop. A hedgerow and a narrow country road. Nowhere specific, you feel. A young woman lies still on a mattress of long grass, central within the scene. To the north a church spire peers out above a cluster of oak. At its peak twirls a weathervane. Beside the woman lies a canvas bag, containing only scraps of paper and an empty bottle of pills. Her red dress, patterned with white polka dots, lies crumpled and creased upon her rigid frame. Cotton, it occasionally flutters in the breeze, rustling like a muted buzzsaw. Flies flit and jitterbug on her alabaster skin. Strands of hair are blown alive.

Who was she? This woman who overdosed when carrying no identification. I take photographs of her face, on which to overlay open, living eyes.

Between the bread-white sheets of hospital bedding: a frail teenage girl, puncture marks perforating her inner elbow; the insubstantial filling in a stale sandwich. Networks of tubes coil from her body, winding external veins and arteries. Beside the bed a space-age accordion rises and falls, rises and falls, its concertina folds breathing the dense rhythm of life.

Who is she? I am asked of a girl no one seems to know, a girl who will never awake. Again, I take photos, to add signs of life.

There are two kinds of missing person: there is the man or woman, boy or girl, who disappears, leaving behind frantic friends and family. Some are taken, others leave of their own volition. These are the lives without a body.

And then there is the body without its corresponding life: the unclaimed corpse in the morgue, matching no description on file, teeth correlating to no known dental records, fingerprints stored in no database, DNA unrevealing in the skein of its code (which, to itself, means *everything*; and yet to us, without a match, means nothing). The unmissed missing. You'd think someone, somewhere, would be concerned. There are few sadder fortunes than to be unwanted or unnoticed in death.

But being unwanted and unloved in life runs it close.

* * *

Six-years old, I took my seat on the train, clutching a shabby teddy bear to my lap: dear old Monty. Unconsciously I fingered the fabric of his bow tie, gripping it between index and middle digits, stroking rhythmically. It soothed in a way that would make more sense if I were the one being caressed. I felt excited, but also apprehensive: a strange woman sitting opposite in the carriage had me draw closer to my mother, seated beside me in her prim, pink two-piece suit, the skirt of which stopped just above her knees. As she spoke her breath oozed peppermint, which she used to take away the taste of tobacco. July, 1973. Mankind again voyaged those hundreds of thousand miles to the moon; we departed East Croydon, bound for Brighton.

Leaving her bag at my side, my mother told me to sit still as she went to find the on-board toilet. Her hand brushed my hair, with a kind of ruffling movement – neither fully mussing nor tidying; her hand lingering for a split second. I did as she said, and looked out through the grubby window – my fingerprints highlighted by a shaft of sunlight fragmenting through a lattice of trees. I traced a finger through the film of grime, drawing a picture: a smiling face. In just over an hour I'd be seeing my father, whom I had not visited for several months, and to whom I felt no great connection. With guilt, I wondered whether I indeed loved him, or instead simply *thought* I loved him. In truth, I did not really know him.

A shrill whistle sounded. It reverberated around the carriage and echoed in the distance somewhere outside as the train pulled away. My excitement – trapped in my chest and throat – ebbed down and out through some unnamed hole in my body as I saw my mother on the platform, her features set fast in a neutral expression. No wave, no smile. Nothing. Dead eyes.

I flung myself against the cold pane, pounded the glass with my tiny fists, and her head turned ever-so-slowly, mechanically, as the platform began to slip into my past, out of my life. As she shrunk her expression remained unmoved: her still, white-powdered face delicate and doll-like.

The train shuffled and bumped to the left as the track curved, and I did not get one last look at the platform.

I felt frantic, hollowed-out by abandonment. A baby cried in the next carriage, and I heard myself in its pain. Always insistent on being regarded as a 'big boy', I was reduced to a screaming infant. No knowledge, no understanding, just instinct.

I sat alone in the carriage, but for the middle-aged lady; the spectral mist of my mother's perfume a third presence. I answered her questions about my name, but could not explain why my mother had left the train. Eventually the woman suggested we open the handbag at my side. We found it empty, but for a silver St Christopher on a chain. This lady – whose name I did not even think to ask – would not leave my side until we met my father on the concourse at Brighton station, never to be seen again; but for that hour she became my family, my support system, as the train clunked and rattled its way south. The longest journey of my life – one giant train-ride for boykind. On that seat the distance to the south coast stretched 238,712 miles.

Amidst the terror and confusion I found comfort in the knowledge that my father waited at the other end of the line, and how he could make everything right – take me back to my mother, take me home. I may not have known whether or not I loved my father, but he was a grown up, a fixer of things broken. At least, that's what I thought.

Pale, gaunt and drawn, with perpetually greasy, greying hair and a moustache that never quite filled in, my father was neither a man's man nor a lady's man; he just bumbled through life, offending and impressing no one. Not that these failings occurred to me at the time.

The seaside should evoke happy childhood memories. Not for me. It transports me to the walk down to the beach with my father, hours after my mother abandoned me. Still teary, my hysteria passed with tiredness. Exhausted and dehydrated, I merely sobbed and spluttered. We wandered down the hill, my hand tiny in his; I can still sense it now, still feel those long thin fingers. From a vendor beside a Punch and Judy show he bought me an ice cream, but not even its sweetness could distract from my distress. Everything about that day is etched in a sensory bank that links to my mind's eye with searing precision. The overpowering lavender in the fug of the train compartment. The taste of vanilla in my dry mouth. The harsh shrieks of the gulls. And the smell of seaweed that squalled around us.

On the seafront he bought me a red balloon, which, like a beaten finalist, I carried as a worthless consolation prize. It bobbed at my side as we walked. And then it somehow slipped from my sticky-fingered grasp, its helium pulling it swiftly out of reach. I didn't even want the damned thing, and there it went, taunting as it jigged away on the breeze. Somehow my tear ducts found fresh moisture.

We ended up on the West Pier. My father led me straight past the giddy array of amusements lining the walkway inside the entrance. In no mood for entertainment I made no complaint. We moved into the Concert Hall Café, located a table. With great austerity he sat me down. I think he knew something like this might happen. He seemed so unsurprised. He'd brought me here to explain things, but at first we sat in silence. Tea and scones arrived, then my cola. I didn't feel hungry, but forced down my scone and sipped at my drink.

"She's ill", he said, as I chewed the cola-tasting straw. "Your mother. She's ill."

I remember thinking that there seemed nothing physically wrong with her, although some mornings she wouldn't get out of bed. "Don't worry though," he added. "She probably thought you were old enough to travel on your own. Y'know, a big boy now. You'll see her next week."

A day passed before we got the news: my mother had thrown herself under the next train to speed through East Croydon station.

I don't know why, but I tell those who don't know me – don't know my story – that my father was the one who abandoned me.

Actually, I tell a lie – I *do* know why. There is a normality to that scenario: fathers are known to do that kind of thing. There is no shame attached, unlike when a mother acts that way. *That* is personal. I mean, what could I have possibly done to drive her to leave me?

My father soon abandoned me, too. I was just eight-years-old when he died.

NINE

After two refusals I finally accept the call from a withheld number. My aunt's solicitor gets to break the bad news.

"I'm afraid it's terminal – she's dying."

News of my surrogate mother's cancer echoes on a patchy cellular signal, forty years after losing my true mother. But how shocked am I, at her age? Of course it upsets me, but it pales in comparison to the trauma of 1973.

An unusually warm weekend in a spring of murk, I sit on the grass overlooking the Art Deco lido at Saltdean, chlorine carrying on the breeze as I move to a more upright position upon hearing the news. Here to re-engage with my past – something I've found myself doing a lot lately – it's fitting that Kitty was already on my mind. I hear the man's words, but find myself lost in the sights of young people in the water, where once I stood. Back then, my aunt was the one at a distance, keeping an eye on the open-air pool from beyond its perimeter wall. Now it's me, looking not at someone I am expected to protect but at a vision of myself, in tight woollen trunks, all skin and bone in the shallow end, too scared to wade into deeper water.

"How long?" I ask, aware that the silence is mine to punctuate.

"Well, the doctors can never be sure. Months, if she's lucky. She'd like to see you, if that's possible?"

"Sure," I say, instantly flinching.

"She had a fall a while back – nothing *too* serious – and was moved to a nursing home. Maybe you could go and see her there?"

"Of course, not a problem," I say, relieved that I won't have to go to the cottage. "I'll visit her tomorrow."

These days I reside at a modest rented flat within earshot, if not sight, of the sea, not too far from the centre of Brighton; close enough to have visited my childhood home, and my elderly aunt, on many occasions, but I retain a strong aversion to that part of my past.

And yet explanations now seem vital. Over the years I've

wondered about my mother, and why she left me in the manner she did. But life got in the way; there was always an excuse to put off trying to find definitive answers. However, the last known connection to the person she was — beyond my own vague memories — lies in the balance, hovering over her own exit. I can't back out.

* * *

After a pause, as the echoing electronic chimes fade, the door opens to my aunt, although at first I see only her walking frame. As it's slowly revealed, her face bears the scars of time and illness. Shrunken and gaunt, she wears the clear yellow sheen of jaundice. Bags sag under eyes, webbed and veined with wrinkles. Puckered lines draw in around her lips. Ripples curve from eyelid to cheek, dimples forming further pathways. I am shocked at her pallor – death foreshadowing its arrival in sallow tones. Her hair, once thick and black-grey, hangs thin and bright white. Always so stoic in late middle-age, tears well in her eyes as I cross the threshold. It seems natural to meet in a hug, even though such contact never existed in my childhood. The weight of thirty years pushes down on us.

"I'm sorry I'm late," I say, looking around the tiny apartment. "I was held up with work, and I was going to leave it until tomorrow… but then I'd left things long enough."

"It's so good to see you, Patrick," she says, offering me a seat on the sofa. "I still think of you as a boy. Silly, really. Look at you! A grown man." Her voice sounds brittle and crackly, but the pace of her words remains unchanged from my childhood.

"I'm ever so sorry to hear your news. The cancer, I mean."

"At my age? Good heavens, I've got nothing to complain about. I've had a good innings."

"Are you receiving any treatment?"

"No, deary. I don't want any of that. What's the point? I can't go on forever."

"But—"

"No! No buts. I feel okay, most of the time. I don't want that dreadful poison they give you, hair falling out, all of that. I've maybe got a few months left. I prefer it this way. I have these lovely nurses who come to attend to me, so I'm okay for the time being. I expect they'll move me to a hospice or a hospital in due course, but for now I'm fine here."

"I'm sorry I never came to see you. It wasn't you. It was… *everything.*"

"There's no need to apologise. With what you went through, I'd have run away too. You had a rough start to life."

"I miss Mum," I say, tears now in my eyes.

"I do too. She was a good woman. She just… I don't know. She got lost along the way. Life wasn't kind to her, either."

"I want to know more about her, Kitty. I never knew her, not really. Not like you did."

"I'll tell you, deary, but not tonight. It's late and I'm tired. I get tired so quickly these days," she says, fishing around in a drawer. "Here, the keys to the cottage. Take them, Patrick. It's yours now."

"*Really?* I'm not sure I can?"

"Take them. *Please.* Sell the place if you have to. I've no one else to give it to. It'll go to you anyway, it's in my will."

"Are you telling me I have no choice?"

"Indeed I am, deary. Indeed I am."

"Thank you, Kitty."

"Your mother and I grew up in that house. She lived there for a while on her own, too. There are probably bits of her life still there, in amongst my old rubbish in the wardrobes. Oh, and under the bed. Take a look, see what you find."

TEN

A giant horse-chestnut tree stood a stone's throw from the lake that dominated the grounds to Kitty's cottage. Once a year, to my great excitement, it transformed into a toy dispenser: its autumnal branches filling with clusters of conkers – spiky green hand grenades – waiting to fall and explode. Those that landed intact I rolled with the sole of my shoe to break apart; careful not to damage the precious nut within. Even now, I can split the shell of any conker and my childhood will spill out. The richness of the reds and browns – swirling blends of carnelian, maroon and mahogany – remains a signature to that time in my life, when I studied each imperfect sphere as if a precious jewel or a miniature Jupiter.

Mid-October, 1975 – my first week at the cottage. Brilliant low late-afternoon sun stretched across the garden, its light more golden than at summer's peak, although a definite chill could be felt in the shade. I'd scattered the patchwork quilt of green, yellow, red and amber leaves, and the quarter-shells of blackened and withered horse chestnut segments, in the hunt for hidden gems. The insides of the fresh shells looked and smelled of apple; tentatively I tasted a piece, but it spiked bitterly on the tongue. I spat it out, wiped my mouth on my sleeve. The nuts – so plump and lustrous when first forced from their protective casing – puckered and hardened within days of placement on the windowsill, their skins tautened, and browned like old blood.

Then there was the broad broken oak, its bough split in two; sundered decades earlier, judging by the foliage growing over the tear, the wood darkened and weathered. No matter what nature had in mind, to me it was the perfect climbing frame.

Fortunately the cottage and its surrounding land provided this entertainment, as Kitty didn't have a lot of time for me. It can't have been easy for her, to have chosen a life without children and all the tiring responsibilities they bring, only to end up with little alternative but to adopt someone else's, whom she can't have loved like her own. I didn't find her cruel, but she wasn't the slightest bit maternal either, and in its own way that felt just as unhelpful. Nothing I did appeared to make her happy, but then she seemed to take so little pleasure from anything. In that way she resembled my mother; perhaps they shared a genetic depressiveness, or experienced the same childhood trauma; each wearing their weariness like a trench coat.

I still sought Kitty's approval, although without any great desperation. She had a way of saying "that's nice" that conveyed so little emotion; dismissive, meaning *Okay, I've heard you out, now leave me alone.* Like my mother, she had an absent air about her, her thoughts almost always elsewhere. She never laughed, and rarely smiled; showing no sign of being truly in the moment. Perhaps her distance suited me, as I didn't want to get too close either. In part I craved stability and reassurance, but I already knew only too well that with attachment comes an increased impact from any subsequent abandonment. So I spent much of my time alone, collecting conkers, skimming stones across the lake, clumsily climbing trees and drifting off into reveries that involved conquering the vast, verdant landscape.

* * *

Keys in hand, I leave the nursing home at dusk and drive the handful of miles to the cottage. Pulling into the short driveway – the grand horse chestnut visible on the left flank of the property – it strikes me how little has changed. All alterations lie within me. I can still taste that conker shell. I feel quite nauseous, fearing being dragged back to the person I'd once been, as if the *location*, and not my age, and the passage of time, define who I am. I have grown, changed, matured. But what if it all unravels and dissolves, like a salt crystal placed back into the sea?

The plan had been to head home after seeing Kitty, but having been given the keys to the cottage and the incentive of possible information about my mother, I found myself set upon a new course. As I step out of the car I've already concluded that I'll move in, possibly doing so as soon as the coming weekend. The lease on the tenancy to my studio flat is due for renewal, and, perhaps due to my restless spirit, I've always taken a flexible approach to where I live. I also work wherever that happens to be, which keeps things simple. In easing the key into the lock, I am already home.

The door swings open to an undisguised past. So much of the cottage survives from my childhood, almost preserved – like the houses of historical figures – as a museum. Kitty seemed to lose the urge to keep up to date when still relatively young; she simply gave up on following life's fashions. The nursing home doesn't have room for most of her furniture, but she is yet to get rid of it, so the majority remains where it always stood.

There exist concessions to the 21st century dotted about the place, but mostly where unavoidable: old appliances and furniture replaced with new after breaking or becoming obsolete, and the occasional relatively recent invention, like a microwave oven. The television set, however, was not even new when I left home, decades earlier. In the kitchen, the same linoleum floor and preponderate AGA sit with the table and chairs of my childhood, the legs of which still harbour bite marks from the mongrel Kitty took in during the 1970s. In the living room, the imposing grandfather clock, whose inexorable quarter-hourly chimes, and their particular notation, evoke long-lost images. Framed photos, either sepia or black and white, all faded and cracked, line the walls to every room; none apparently taken within the last fifty years, although there are some additions since last I was here. In between the array, a handful of empty spaces; dark delineations of pictures my aunt had taken to the home. On one wall hangs a stunning picture of the lake at sunset, photographed from the veranda: the silhouetted head and shoulders of a woman – probably my mother, judging by the curls – rising from the waterline as the surface shimmers with white streaks and flaring ripples.

I make my way upstairs. My old bedroom retains the same ancient furniture – bed, chest of drawers, wardrobe – although I removed all of my personal possessions the day I left home. I head to the window and look out over the lake; I could be fourteen or fifteen again, daydreaming. Aside from the further growth of trees and bushes, I experience the exact same view, framed in the exact same way.

And then, the spare room: *Genevieve's* room. Long gone – gone well before I ran away – I still sense her electric presence. Walking through the door an image jolts me; a vision of her, clear as day, sat on the bed with her back to the wall, scribbling in her diary. It flashes vividly in my mind, in a memory that also includes the posters on the wall, the records strewn across the floor, the clothes piled on the dresser: the objects of her story. And then it fades; I see the space only as it now is, stripped of her personality. The dreams and desires, flights of fantasy, borne of these walls. Where is Genevieve, a lifetime later?

Next, Kitty's bedroom: dim and musty, yellowing net curtains muting the twilight. As suggested I look under the bed, and in the wardrobes, but there is an overwhelming amount of *stuff*, tightly crammed into the limited space. How would I recognise my mother's possessions, even if I found them amid my aunt's lifetime of hoarding?

Sorting through it all won't be easy. It'll have to wait until another day.

ELEVEN

It got no better, in the days following our domestic apocalypse. Laura made an immediate exit, but most of her possessions remained. A curt text stated that her father, Mick, would be round to collect her belongings. She also made it clear that while she couldn't face returning to the property, I had a couple of weeks to find alternative accommodation before it would be put on the market. I tried phoning, to discuss her plans, but she refused to answer.

A day later, Mick duly arrived.

The knock on the door was met, deep in my core, with the kind of dread reserved for bailiffs or, worse still, underworld debt collectors who negotiate with the persuasion of baseball bats and knuckledusters.

No giant – I'd guess five feet nine – Mick was however the thickest-set man I'd ever known: a dense mass of stockiness, with the look, and accoutrements, of an East-End gangster. As a young man he'd spent time in the army, where he boxed to some distinction. And although he'd grown a little saggier over time – most notably in the loose skin beneath his chin – he'd also continued to bulk up and expand on a diet high in red meat. A veritable pit-bull of a man, beside whom I resembled an overgrown poodle.

"You know why I'm here", he said, standing right up against the door as I opened it. Minimal eye contact, words kept to the necessary.

We walked solemnly inside, heading straight through to the lounge. As he brushed past to lead the way our shoulders met in a brief moment of disturbing intimacy. I harboured fears that he was here to kill me. Or, more accurately, was *capable* of killing me, and was here. Ever since the very first meeting almost nine years earlier I'd felt thoroughly intimidated. His chunky fingers would envelope my relatively reedy digits whenever we shook hands. These handshakes were always painfully long and firm; Mick apparently unprepared to relinquish his grip until absolutely certain I knew of his strength, his innate capabilities, with every handshake a warning. Thankfully we were beyond such formalities now; otherwise I could see it lasting for days, with every inch of life squeezed out of a thoroughly crumpled set of fingers left to resemble broken twigs in a surgical glove.

I found equally unnerving his ability to say very little; to remain taciturn when it would be easier to speak, talking only in simple words when called upon – in my company, at least. In the company of others he could be positively loquacious. With me he was guarded, holding something back; I feared what the man thought but elected not to utter. Not the silent type, with nothing to say, but the strong and silent type, with lots to say, just never to me.

The relationship between father and daughter also disconcerted me, not least Laura's insistence on calling him 'Daddy'. Not 'Father', not 'Dad', not even an annoying but acceptable 'Pa', but this most juvenile of names. *Daddy*. It made my skin crawl each time I heard it. Likewise, Laura remained 'my little girl' to Mick, but it always felt to me in some distinctly unnatural way. After all, she clearly wasn't *anyone's* little girl – not any more. I certainly didn't want to harbour the sense of corrupting a minor.

But perhaps I already had. I had physically harmed his daughter, albeit unintentionally. I had broken her heart and helped ruin the life we were sharing, all in one highly regrettable evening. None of it is the kind of behaviour I'd expect any right-minded father to casually shrug off – and this particular father was far from right-minded. I could only conclude that Laura spared him the full details of her version of events, covering up the cut on her forehead with her hair. If she hadn't, I doubted I'd still be conscious.

Mick clutched a piece of paper: Laura's inventory, from which he listed items for me to locate. He also rummaged about without bothering to ask my permission – opening drawers, filing through papers, snooping in cupboards. The list existed for a reason, I wanted to point out, and yet felt powerless to object. I knew the man's thinking: his daughter owned half of the house and therefore he could do as he pleased, acting on her behalf. He took some unlisted electrical appliances – microwave, DVD player, toaster – perhaps just to make life awkward for me. But as long as he left all essential things untouched I decided to keep quiet.

The list generally lacked controversy. A good majority of the items were hers and hers alone: clothes, jewellery, toiletries, along with a couple of sentimental trinkets she didn't like to be without. There were just a few dual-owned possessions noted, and although not happy to lose them, in the circumstances I handed them over with an accepting shrug. Should a divorce ensue – and it felt unavoidable – then in time I would be losing a hell of a lot more.

Perhaps as punishment, perhaps as pre-planned vindictive spite, Mick set about tearing down streamers, unpinning decorations and dismantling the three-piece tree. The Anti-Claus, he packed up Christmas, to take away. Not that their household wasn't bedecked with gaudy tinsel and baubles; not that Laura in any way needed these things now. December 21st, and Christmas was officially cancelled.

Decorations detached and disassembled, Mick began to study Jacob's painting of Black, which was leaning against the living room wall, awaiting further repair. Here – on the surface, to someone like my father-in-law – stood a depiction of a nubile young woman, staring any onlooker in the eye in a state of undress. Where Mick might previously have accepted calling it art (whatever *that* was), I guessed he now thought it pornography; art being the excuse to hang an image of a naked woman on a wall. When he placed the painting beside the pile of confiscated goods I felt a rush of anger. *No way* would he be leaving the house with it. A link to both Jacob and Black; a link to more history and emotion than Mick could ever dream of. Somehow I had to broach the subject, and then possibly fight this colossal man. But he must have looked again, must have seen the light catch the lines of Sellotape holding the canvas together. He moved it away, back to where he found it.

Just as I thought things had passed off relatively peacefully, Mick emerged through the front door to collect the last remaining bag. He left it momentarily untouched as he approached. I felt my anal sphincter constrict, like an animal pulling itself into its shell. At the moment his club-like hand gripped around the neck of my t-shirt, drawing the material in across my chest – tight under my armpits, untucked from jeans – I feared projection into the adjacent kitchen, through a section of wall where there existed no door. Instead, he pushed me down onto a nearby chair.

For once he towered over me. His face drew in closer than ever before, as though he were about to kiss me. With warm, stale, coffee-tinged breath blowing against my skin, he simply whispered, in a tone far more sinister than any yelled threat, that should I not meet his daughter's deadline for vacating the house, he would kill me. About that I should make no mistake.

My legs still shook, some twenty minutes after Mick's departure. The shock hit me as soon as the front door closed tight (dead-locked, double-bolted), and I needed an immediate horizontal bearing. Somewhat surprisingly, I felt calm when facing the prospect of violence. My body told me I was ready: should things escalate beyond merely threatening and turn genuinely nasty, I had this notion that I would defend myself. However great the delusion, and however futile such attempts would have proved, my nervous system felt composed under pressure. It felt totally exhilarating. However, whatever primordial chemical reaction took place in my adrenal gland, in order to override my innate lack of courage, its effects almost instantly ebbed away.

The whole experience left me down and deflated; Laura's absence accentuated, the relationship's finality clearer than ever. Our marriage wasn't perfect, but Laura had been a companion, an ally. First it was her physical self, now the wider web of her influence, her touch, her taste. Next would be half of everything, split down the middle by an invading father-in-law with tape measure and chainsaw.

Without the DVD player I faced up to Saturday night TV, which I stared at over a microwave meal that, due to unforeseen circumstances, had to be cooked in the oven. As if being separated and friendless on a Saturday night wasn't bad enough, being forced to endure the mindless terrestrial programming – people laughing at their own stupidity – made it almost unbearable. The alternatives were a World War II documentary and a further investigation into the plight of Thalidomide victims, neither of which I felt mentally prepared for. I craved easy but engaging viewing, and found only the polar extremes.

When finally I dozed off in front of the glaring box, finding comfort and escape in sleep, the TV brought me back to reality with a start at two a.m., with the added truth that the broadcasting output only gets worse the later the hour. How I missed the test card of my childhood, the girl and her clown. I ascended the staircase, alone, and went to bed, alone.

* * *

Six months earlier we were set on a completely different course. Having safely navigated the first fifteen weeks of a pregnancy that didn't easily take hold, we made our way to Cambridge, treating ourselves to a celebratory weekend break. Laura wanted to revisit the city of her studies, and I was keen for a change of scenery.

With the half-hearted back-combed hair of someone who never quite mastered rebellion, a youthful Laura spent three years in the city studying maths, reading Sylvia Plath and listening to The Smiths and Lloyd Cole. Within a year of graduating she felt the calling of something more altruistic than banking – which, in truth, I could never imagine her doing – and started on the path to becoming a nurse.

For the journey she chose Abba's greatest hits for the stereo, *The Idiot's Guide to Pregnancy & Childbirth* as reading material, and with her hair, as had been the case for years, styled into a sharp, sensible bob. On the first evening we ate at a stark, stylish restaurant overlooking Parker's Piece: the square common, with its historic lamppost – the 'reality checkpoint' – plumb centre, separating the student world from that of mere mortals. From our table we could see children playing on this broad parkland; in our heads we projected futures onto our unborn baby, trying to imagine what he or she would be like at a similar age.

After leaving the restaurant we turned to stroll across the park. Suddenly Laura stopped by a grass verge, holding her midriff. She complained of severe cramps, which I put down to the meal disagreeing with her. But her face registered increasing agony, and it became clear through the crotch of her jeans that she was bleeding. Frantically I flipped open my mobile, phoning for an ambulance; emphasising the need to hurry, as if it's ever any other way.

I helped Laura lay flat on the grass, holding her hand; she squeezed back as if letting go would see her sucked out into the far reaches of space. I crouched, assuming the position I had expected to take in a birthing suite many months later; doing my best to reassure my wife as she endured excruciating pain. Cycles zipped past on the path, wheels passing within inches of our faces; no one stopping, or even slowing down. All the while our baby bled out in pools and clots.

Finally some passers-by came to our aid, not that any were

able to provide much help. But at least we were no longer alone.

The ambulance ride – all rattle and chaos – was both fast and slow, long and short. All I recall is swaying from side to side whilst trying to keep hold of Laura's hand as, with her face creased, she cried and groaned. It took an age, and yet we were at the hospital in no time. Then came the frantic rush along garish tungsten corridors, followed by the wait for a specific doctor who just happened to be nowhere to be found.

In some soulless, sterile room it was eventually confirmed as a miscarriage, with my wife suffering the indignity of an internal inspection to make sure nothing of the foetus remained; after which they supplied her with a strong sedative and a bed for the night. I sat in a chair at her bedside, trying, and failing, to get some sleep of my own. Eventually I lowered the rail and carefully climbed beside her, holding her tight as she slept on.

Looking back, I don't think we ever fully recovered. At first it brought us closer together, but after a while I couldn't bring myself to talk about it, and yet it remained all she wanted to discuss. With hindsight I can see how we drifted apart from that point on, unintentionally failing to meet each other's needs, locked in the silent, unacknowledged feedback loop of minor disappointments; although it still took a crazy night to bring things to a final conclusion.

TWELVE

It is growing colder – past ten o'clock – as Black and I watch the world from our isolated wooden tower, detached from human life, south of a country, raised above a sea. With no sign of the others we have agreed to wait it out. Jacob is notoriously unreliable, so neither of us feels particularly surprised. Besides, there's not a lot we can do given that I have destroyed the only practical route off the pier. The tide is now back in, and I cannot swim, while Black, somewhat understandably, says she will only leap into the sea in daylight. We have no choice but to sit tight.

"You see that?" she says, and I look, expecting a mini miracle: shooting star, oil tanker aflame, dolphins playfully soaring and dipping. But I see nothing.

"Down a bit. There. On the water."

"What is it?"

"A dead seagull. Look – its wings." And sure enough, wings become apparent, spreading temporarily as the carcass bobs on a breaking wave. Quite why it is such an unusual sight is hard to fathom. A sea bird, dead in the sea. But we both stare, transfixed. There is no other drama to observe, but all the same, it draws our attention on merit. There is something altogether larger occurring, something I can sense but not articulate. The lifeless creature makes its way to shore amid bubbles and spume, and is tossed back, time and time again, limp and pathetic, but undeterred. Can *will* remain after death? Is that what I am reaching for?

We look, but say no more.

The moon, obese and mottled, does something remarkable to Black's face: the kindest natural light, glazing her skin a faultless pale-blue porcelain. She sits with her knees close to her chest, drawing herself up into a ball. The body language is all internal, nothing expressed outward, toward me. Cigarette drawn quickly from its pack, she strikes a match, and her face explodes with colour. Her eyes have never looked so alive. She closes them upon an extended intake of smoke.

I inch closer, every few minutes. Unable to resist – like a petal whose emergence from the cluster is noticeable only through the eye of time-lapse photography – I am drawn towards the life-source in imperceptible movements. She does not appear aware of how close I have edged. I can feel the heat from her body on my arm. I almost expect static to draw its fine hairs towards her.

"Jesus, this is so fucking weird," she eventually says, flicking the smouldering butt over the edge of the pier. The fawn cylinder arcs in the air like a miniature distress flare against the night sky. We watch its pin prick of orange disappear out of sight, extinguishing silently in the sea.

We sit, Black and I, in our post-apocalyptic landscape: an assemblage of rusting poles, bent brackets and twisted ironwork, peppered with glass shards and erratic lines of splintered wood. Unable to think of anything to say, I study our surroundings. Moss grows wildly in a ruptured guttering above our heads. Decorative architectural features lie about us, ripped away or fallen exhausted to the ground. Everything – *everything* – is cursed with the pox of pigeon shit, which subtly fluoresces in the moonlight. Bird carcasses lie amid their own faeces.

Up close, the pier resembles a decomposing corpse: wrought iron braces and ties beneath a skin of wood exposed like a protruding ribcage, emaciated sinews barely able to contain the skeleton within; the regimental array of articulated bones: vertebrae and clavicles and sacrum, femurs and tibias and fibulas, phalanges and carpals and metacarpals. The structure rotting gracelessly away, displaying its innards, its splintered heart.

"I like your clothes," I note, forcing language into the silence. "They're nice," I add, somewhat redundantly.

"They're second-hand."

"They're still nice."

"I only buy second-hand. Well, mostly."

"Why?" I ask.

"Seems a waste to keep buying new stuff. And I guess it's wearing a form of history – stepping into the stories and lives of other people. I feel like someone else – at least at first – before the clothes have my own memories attached. I'd be lost without Oxfam and the Salvation Army."

I ask which photographers she most admires. I'm no expert, but from my schooling I know a few of the luminaries, such as Cartier-Bresson and Man Ray, and what they represent.

"Oh, lots. But I guess I'm most influenced by Diane Arbus. You know her stuff?"

Damn.

"Can't say that I do."

"I'm shocked. You really should."

"Yeah?"

"*Definitely.* I love the way she focused on these people, all kinds of outsiders. Y'know, transvestites, midgets, giants. And also normal people, but in unusual poses or situations. She had a style that was very revealing."

"She captured their souls?"

"Actually, I don't think a photograph can capture the soul,

because it's just one still, two-dimensional image. But she certainly captures *something* about the person. There's this one shot of a skinny boy in Central Park holding a toy hand grenade – at least I think it's a toy. His other hand is clenched in an identical fashion, as if it too should contain a grenade. Sunlight bathes him, through the trees. It's beautiful, almost tranquil. But it's his expression that makes it. So intense. He looks a sweet kid, but a *crazy* kid – like he's just necked a whole bag of sugar and six gallons of Coke."

"I think I know the photo you mean," I say, eagerly. However, I'm not sure that I do. There is certainly an image in my mind's eye, but probably because it's just been planted there.

"She once said 'What I'm trying to describe is that it's impossible to get out of your skin into somebody else's – that somebody else's tragedy is not the same as your own.' I've always loved that idea. The exterior tells us so much about someone, but you always remain on the outside, a voyeur. It's true, isn't it? Her suicide just adds to the poignancy of her work."

"True artists feel such extreme emotions," I say, sighing.

"She also said, 'I've never taken the picture I intended. They are always better or worse.' For me, that's the beauty of photography. You just never quite know what you're going to get. Sometimes it's a crushing disappointment, while at others there's magic in the play of the light, or in the movement, or the expression, and the elements conspire to produce something beyond your wildest imagination. It takes your breath away. It really does."

"I wish I shared your passion about what you do. About what *I* do, I mean."

"Maybe I'm just lucky." She says, shrugging her shoulders.

* * *

The bombshell is this: in just three days' time, Black is leaving to spend a year backpacking around Europe. I've only just had her enter my life, and already the exit looms. Why hadn't Jacob told me? I'd asked a few questions this afternoon, but he chose not to say anything. He didn't even mention that she'd finished modelling for him.

My chances of winning her affections – always slim – have all but evaporated. The need to do so sufficiently within a time frame of less than 72 hours renders them virtually redundant. With enough time, I *might* have stood a chance. But I'm not going to get her to change her mind about going away in less than half a week, nor do I see a way to make enough of an impact to have her hurry back to me upon her return.

"So why are you going?" I ask, absentmindedly spinning dregs of beer around the bottom of a can.

"I split up with my boyfriend, about a month ago. I needed to do something radical. And a year travelling around Europe with just a backpack seemed suitably drastic."

"What went wrong?"

"By the end, *everything*, really. But mainly it was because he was so controlling."

"And women aren't?"

"What's that supposed to mean? That I was?"

"No! Just that I've yet to meet a woman who didn't *also* want to be in control. Relationships are one big fight for the steering wheel. And if you do manage get a hold for a few minutes, she'll be back-seat driving."

"Men's egos can't handle not being in total control, dictating everything."

"Mine can."

She laughs. "Yeah, right!"

"Okay, look at it like this – I want my input to be valued. I mean, no one likes being *out of control*, do they? That sense of utter powerlessness. Okay, maybe there are a few people who like being entirely submissive in all aspects of a relationship – those who love being dominated. But I have no desire to be emasculated."

"So a woman having some semblance of control emasculates you?"

"No, no, you're getting me wrong. It's about balance. It's about being fifty-fifty."

"Nothing in life is ever fifty-fifty," she says. "There'll always be disparity."

"Well I can live with that. Fifty-five forty-five is okay. Even sixty-forty. I just can't live with being told what to do all the time, or having that sense that she's the one with all the power, the one who can make me crumble at a moment's notice. I can't handle eighty-twenty, ninety-ten."

I stop the thought there; let the next sentence fade to silence in my mind. I can feel that, for her, I would make an exception. I can see myself doing whatever she suggests. *Anything.* For the first time in my life I can envisage being a willing patsy.

In truth, we men stand no chance. We are not prepared for what the heart can do. We grow up with images of needy women awaiting rescue: the helpless princess falling for the heroic knight in shining armour. But we are the weak, the vulnerable. We are the ones known to fall in love more quickly, and to have the real trouble letting go. We are the little boys, lost and abandoned. Women are the ones who always find the strength from somewhere. Women pull through.

Black strikes up another cigarette, then re-ignites the conversation. "He also ran my confidence into the ground. Made me think no one else would want me, told me I was ugly. Told me I was worthless. Told me I was an embarrassment, that

I should never leave the house."

I look at her. Puzzlement must be clear in my face; I feel my eyebrows pinch and squeeze together. How can anyone who looks as good as Black, and who is a *normal human being* – one who doesn't eat her own flesh, drool, or defecate on street corners – be made to believe she is not what worthwhile men are looking for? Perhaps the problem with stunning beauty is the booming, metronomic clock that echoes inexorably at the back of the mind. I was attractive *yesterday*, but today it's all over. And while she has personality, character, intelligence, their worth has been undervalued by too many men for too long. Even by this tender age. Twenty-one still means a decade, maybe close to two, of being praised mostly for her superficial beauty. Perhaps taking her seriously as a person is the key? But what's the betting that the guy who gets to do just that also has to be tall, dark and handsome? Maybe I'm underestimating her.

"He was obviously unable to handle you," I say. "You weren't the simpering woman he clearly needs. That's all about him, not you." I think she hears me, but her reply seems to have been percolating since before I spoke.

"If I went out looking nice, he was paranoid. Anything sexy he'd say made me look fat. I ended up in baggy jumpers and saggy cardigans. More than a mere dab of make-up and he called me a tart. And God help me if I even *spoke* to another man. He'd have preferred me in an Islamic headscarf while out, but stockings and suspenders once home."

"That bad?" I say. However, already sparking in my mind is the bizarre vision of her in those stockings and suspenders, complete with accompanying burka.

"You deserve so much better. But then again, you're bright enough to know that."

She looks at me, and I think this comment has on some level

hit home. But she just continues talking about her ex, and I'm not so sure. "You really don't have to go to Europe to regain a sense of control," I offer, once she's finished.

"I know I don't *have* to. There are other ways, I know that. But it's a chance to have full independence, and a chance to take some interesting photos. I want to get away from taking pictures in a totally safe environment, an environment where nothing really surprises me or tests me. I want the pictures I take to really *mean* something, to have something at stake. A challenge. I won't know anyone, and don't speak any other languages beyond a few GCSE words. I plan to meet briefly with a friend in Prague at Christmas, but otherwise I'll be travelling alone."

"But is that independence? Won't you simply be more dependent on those who speak English? Those who…" I'm not quite sure where I'm going with this, or if I actually believe what I'm saying. I just want to form an argument to seed the idea of keeping her here. My words trail off.

"I don't agree. I will have to stand on my own two feet, rely upon my wits, far more than I do now."

"But can't you exert a level of control and independence *within* your life, not create a radical new life to fit the idea?"

"It's still *my* life. It's still me who's going to be overseas. I'm not changing my identity. Everything I experience will shape the person I am."

"I guess I'm just checking that you're being true to yourself, not doing something extreme for the sake of it. Not running away."

She laughs. "Well, I guess that's my business, not yours."

Not my business? If only she knew. I didn't ask for her to become my business – or go looking for it – but at this moment in time I feel like Black is the *only* business I have.

We fall silent, hugging our knees. Or rather, she is clasping hers, with such effortless grace, and I find myself mirroring her movements. My knees rest awkwardly around my chin, shins exposed above socks I regret choosing to wear. What does it say about a grown man to have cotton cartoon characters peering out from above his shoes? I see them as ironic, but a woman with the style of Black – with her thrift shop élan – would surely find them rather sad. I readjust my trousers, in the hope she doesn't notice. And while I'd of course like the opportunity, the prospect of her seeing my matching boxer shorts leaves me feeling uneasy.

Still, I'm nothing if not a dreamer.

After the extended period of silence, which, to my pleasant surprise, proves entirely comfortable – both of us temporarily stargazing – Black begins to quiz me with real gusto.

"So what do you do?"

"Do?"

"For a living."

"Well, at the moment, temporary work. In between careers."

"Careers?"

"Well, maybe *careers* is the wrong word. I dropped out of art college, when I realised it just wasn't for me. I felt too much of an also-ran amongst the bright young things – all those gifted Fine Artists like Jacob. I then managed to get into medical school. I'd always been fascinated by the human body, enjoyed life drawing and so on, and my mother was a nurse, so it all kinda fit. But turned out that wasn't right for me either and I just didn't have what it takes for all those years of study. Right now I'm temping in London, with an insurance company."

"I knew from a young age what I was going to do."

"Well, I knew what I was *interested* in. But I just wasn't

exceptional enough to be an artist or illustrator. Not creatively, at least. And in a very creative environment, I felt like an impostor."

"Why an impostor? I take it you'd earned your place there?"

"I had, I suppose. But maybe I was the one who scraped in by the skin of his teeth."

"Have you considered forensic art?" she asks.

"What do you mean?"

"Drawing people for the police, that kind of thing."

"No, not at all. What makes you say that?"

"A friend at uni was interested. Apparently there's no official course anywhere, but you can find specific workshops with existing artists. How much of your course did you do?"

"Which one?" I ask.

"Medical."

"A couple of years. Well, almost."

"So you must have a decent grasp of the basics?"

"I suppose so."

"And you must be able to draw reasonably well to have got onto a Fine Art degree?"

"Well, yes. Technically I'm fine. I just wasn't expressive enough."

"Well then. Why *not* give it a go?" This last point is put to me with an intonation that suggests I am already procrastinating, having not moved a muscle in the handful of seconds since she suggested the idea.

"I'll give it some thought."

"Is that all?"

"What do you mean?" I ask.

"Well, it sounds *ideal* – the perfect combination of your interests."

"It is. But I'm sure it's not as simple as all that."

I gaze up at the stars once again. Isn't that where you're supposed to find your future written? Its patterns make no more sense to me than Cantonese lettering on a glowing lantern.

Black moves through the doorless metal frame, out onto the sturdy balcony overlooking a broken wooden shed, beyond which nothing but the Channel. The best sea view in Brighton; only, not one you'd pay for.

I move to join her.

"Cigarette?" she enquires, holding the crumpled packet toward me, a solitary stick protruding.

"No thanks, I don't."

"Any reason?"

"No. I just don't. Tried once, as a kid, and that was it." But all of a sudden it seems like a good time to start; to just *do*.

She flicks back the lid of her silver Zippo. The noise it makes is a genuine *clink*. As the gas leaks before igniting, I take a deep breath; the smell is beautiful and comforting against the night air, as if the two ingredients, when mixed, form a perfect recipe. The tip of the cigarette gleams orange, and again the initial aroma of burning tobacco – mixed with menthol – is soothing.

"They're not coming, are they?" she says, confirming what I'm sure we've both long-since concluded. The shoreline is still fairly packed, but it must be around closing time. To the revellers at last orders we form two indiscernible shapes in the distance, whose earlier attempts at calling were drowned out by the waves and the traffic.

Black has a look – a double-take stare – where she fixes you with her eyes, relents momentarily, and then fixes you once again, only more intensively; checking to see if you are laughing with her, or at her.

"What's that?" she asks, breaking from one such stare to point at the chain around my neck.

"A St Christopher," I say, pulling the small silver medallion from under my t-shirt. "My mother gave it to me. Supposed to give you good luck on your travels."

"And has it?"

"I guess so. I'm still here, after all."

"So, tell me about your family."

"It won't lighten the mood, believe me."

"How so?"

"Parents divorced when I was a baby. Mother killed herself when I was six. Dad died when I was eight. No brothers or sisters. Brief time in foster care. Then went to live with my aunt, who never really wanted me. Not exactly your model childhood."

"*Seriously?*" she asks, eyebrows raised.

"Not exactly something to joke about, is it?"

"No, but... Wow. Such a tough run of events."

"Well, at least I didn't end up in borstal. Or worse."

"Why did she kill herself? – your mum. I mean, if you don't mind me asking?"

"I honestly don't know. She didn't leave a note. I didn't know her well enough, and no one really explained things to me. I took it very personally, though. Blamed myself."

"You poor thing."

Being *poor*, and being a *thing*, are not exactly labels I am seeking out. But together, in the way she says them, I feel validated. She puts her hand on my forearm, for just the briefest of moments. Even though she swiftly removes it I can still feel its heat.

The wind picks up, as a swift breeze gusts in off the water. Dust whips from the pier, pirouetting around us.

"*Ow!*" she moans.

"What is it?" I ask.

"Something in my eye," she says, rubbing furiously.

"Do you want me to have a look?"

"Don't worry, I'll do it." She tries to open the eye, then rubs it again. "Actually, if you wouldn't mind?" She turns her head to the moonlight, pulls down her eyelid. I draw closer, in a kind of false intimacy. She reveals to me a section of moist, private flesh. With my thumb and forefinger I help elevate the upper lid, as she darts her eyeball from side to side. Eventually a tiny foreign object, possibly a splinter of wood, swims into view. With the tip of my little finger I dab it, and it transfers itself onto my skin. There's the briefest pause as our eyes lock, and then in unison we both turn away. I flick the speck from my finger and we return to staring out to sea.

"What was your first broken heart?" she asks, turning back to face me.

"Genevieve. Genevieve Frazer. I was almost fifteen. She came to stay with me and my aunt in the summer of 1981. I'd known her before then, but a lot earlier, when we were both just kids. That summer was different. She was... *exotic*. There was something about her that just got to me on some deep level."

"How did she break your heart?"

I laugh, ruefully. "By never knowing that she even had possession of it. Actually, scrap that – she *must* have known. She knew how to play me. But maybe she didn't know how deep my feelings ran. Thinking about it, maybe she doesn't qualify after all."

"What makes you say that?"

"Well, don't you have to have been in a relationship with someone to be truly heartbroken?"

"I'm not sure," she says, slowly. "People can damage you in different ways. Ultimately, it's all down to the strength of what you feel."

"I mean, it's not like we didn't have *any* kind of relationship. I didn't merely watch her from a distance. We hung out together. I knew her. But if you've never been intimate with that person, then, well, obviously you've never shared a full connection. If you've never owned something, you cannot truly lose it."

"*Owned?*" she says.

"In the sense that they are *your* girlfriend or boyfriend. *Your* wife or husband. I don't mean you possess them like an object."

"Ah, okay. Let me ask you this – have you ever been more heartbroken than that first one with …?"

"Genevieve."

"*Genevieve.*"

"Probably not. I've obviously had proper relationships, but nothing felt quite as raw as it did that first time. I think I'd built this future for us in my head. I never properly thought it through, thinking back, but I *felt* it."

"Then she was your first heartbreak."

"You're probably right. So, what about you?"

"I had a few minor crushes, but I never really got all girly about pop stars or boys at school. Some of my friends would get so obsessed with someone, but I never really got that. I was always fairly tall at school, so boys in my year looked a bit odd to me, and they always seemed immature. And I didn't go for that whole 'older boys are so cool' thing – but they were less irritating than ones my age. Anyway, when I was sixteen there was this one older boy, Simon."

I laugh. "I bet he had a car."

"No… He had a motorbike."

I laugh again. "That's such a cliché!"

"I didn't like him *because* he had a motorbike. Well, a scooter, actually. A Vespa."

"When you said he was older, you mean he was a Mod from the sixties? Was he *in* his sixties?"

She kicks my foot.

"He was a *year* older. I thought he was interesting, at least at first. He was the guy that every girl in my class swooned over, but I soon realised that he was too self-absorbed, and my role was to fluff his ego. Still, somehow I let him get under my skin, and even though I didn't really like him that much, I was jealous when he gave other girls attention, and that made me think I was in love with him, which was stupid really, looking back. He dumped me because I wouldn't sleep with him. I soon got over him, but only after a week of feeling like my life was over."

We move on to discuss music. She tells me how much she loves the new Depeche Mode album, although I haven't even heard it. Still, I have at least heard of *them*, unlike her other suggestions. When asked the same question in reply I say The Beatles, because I don't think you can go wrong with them.

She then asks me about my favourite film, and again I feel uncomfortable that I'm not as hip or switched-on as her.

I pause to think. There are so many different *types* of film that I enjoy, but I've never really picked a personal favourite. My first thought is *Die Hard*, which I watch for escapist pleasure, but I'm pretty sure that this isn't a *Yipikaye motherfucker* moment. I quickly move on to consider the type of film *she'd* enjoy. Something arty and well-photographed. Something from the annals of film history. Something romantic, but not soppy or sentimental. In truth, there are not a lot of films in this category I feel able to discuss, given that I'm no movie buff. In the end I plump for *Rear Window*, although it's perhaps a little creepy, and not full of stunning cinematography. It is, however, one of the few bona fide classics I've seen multiple times.

"Oh, I *love* Rear Window!" she says, her eyes widening.

"Really?"

"Yeah! I wouldn't say it's one of my *very* favourite films, but it's still a classic. That set! It's amazing!"

"I know!" I say, nodding furiously. "I'd love to be able to walk around it. Imagine that? It's enormous!"

"How cool would that be? Who would you visit? I'd go and keep Miss Lonelyhearts company."

"The songwriter makes me laugh," I say, deciding against mentioning Miss Torso for fear of sounding shallow. "I love when he's drunk and knocks the pages off his piano and falls over."

"How pretty was Grace Kelly?" she says, nodding at her own suggestion. "What a stunning woman. So elegant!"

"Gorgeous…" I say, stopping myself from talking about the actress' tragic death. "I must watch it again some time."

"Actually, you remind me a bit of James Stewart."

"You're not the first person to tell me that," I say, dishonestly. Even so, it's clear that I'm more James Stewart than James Dean. But at least she didn't say James Cagney. "You really think so?" I ask.

"Yes. The shape of the face, I think. Nothing too specific, but there's something. Definitely."

"Interesting. Could be worse."

"He was a fine looking man. My favourite film is *Mirror*, by Andrei Tarkovsky. Have you seen it? It's the most beautiful film imaginable."

"Can't say that I have. What's it about?"

"It's not really a film that has a plot *as such*. Not a conventional one, anyway. The imagery is stunning, though. It's a collection of moods and feelings – very dreamlike. It's Russian, from the seventies."

"Sounds great," I say, thinking that it doesn't really seem like my cup of tea. But I can't help but feel that I would enjoy it in her company. I can't help but feel that I would enjoy *anything* in her company.

THIRTEEN

Laura did not die. But she may as well have done, given her altered status in my life. I suffered a bereavement, only without the accompanying sympathy a widower receives. Unless it's suicide, death is not rejection. You won't bump into a deceased partner with a new lover. You don't have to wonder what they are doing, or how happy they are doing it – because they are doing nothing. Your grief, with death, is acceptable, and indulged, and ritualised. Death doesn't divide up your friends, halve your property. Not that I ever wanted her dead – don't get me wrong. But it does provide a cleaner break. David and I sometimes discuss the issue, and while he never fully admits it, I sense he prefers that his wife was stolen away by death rather than another man.

For months after our split I pondered where the past *goes*, as it slips from our grasp. Where does love disappear to? Are there parallel universes in which the future we planned is enjoyed by other versions of ourselves? As I came to terms with our sudden separation, I asked myself if I still loved *her*, or if I loved the time we shared, and the future we were denied.

Laura became just the latest in a long line of absences. Our relationship, after we lost our way, was something I felt I could live without; my brain apparently incapable of understanding what it would miss until given no choice but to stare down that absence, feel its absolute hollowness. Every last drop of happiness infused during the relationship bled out as pain; the exact inverse of the good times revisiting in equal measure as hauntings, torments, nightmares. For a while our relationship was a phantom limb I could sometimes still feel, go to reach out with. Twitching, jittering; confused nerves sending corrupt signals.

We got on well, and, up until that night when it so violently combusted, never seriously argued. I always took that to be a positive sign – it meant we were somehow compatible. But a lack of conflict does not automatically make for the perfect union. Maybe we were just saving it all for that conclusive night.

The simple memories – the companionship – belatedly struck me as most important, as I came to terms with life as a single man. In a swimming pool, somewhere warm, holding onto my shoulders, piggybacking through the water. Reading in the garden: paperbacks and newspapers on a summer's Sunday morning. Coffee and hot chocolate in a quaint café, sheltering from a storm. Laughing – laughing, at anything. And smiling.

Laura's heart, in terms of its capacity for love, was the opposite of the Grinch's; in her case, two sizes too large. She felt, physically, the pain of others, and helped to soothe it. She possessed the same affinity with animals; hating suffering of any kind. Laura not only wanted a cat, she simply had to have the three-legged tabby at the shelter, abandoned by its owner and then overlooked time and again by visitors. And so Maisy came home with us, her stump swinging gyroscopically as she walked, her balance somehow unaffected.

Arguably the greatest gift ever bestowed into my hands, Laura's compassion could not dampen my restless spirit, which nagged and gnawed at me like a febrile disease. Even though it may have been beyond me, I wanted to *create something*: a lasting work of art, something perfect, a statement to endure. I wanted to leave a legacy; and yet I did not know the form it should take, or if I actually possessed the necessary talent to even attempt it. All the same, that restlessness overpowered my better judgements.

Over and over – even now – I ask myself if life with Laura, rather than my fantasies about Black, represented the truer form of love? Or is it all, no matter whether formed from years of intimacy or concocted from imagined hopes and dreams, confined to our head?

Is love, no matter how it happens, *all in our mind?*

It seems we simply feel what our brains tell us to feel. The message can be right or wrong, real or imagined, genuine or no more than a trick, but ultimately it's all the same: just chemicals and electricity, creating thoughts and emotions.

Is our relationship *out there* – wherever 'there' is – floating into distant space? Or is it all still *here*, locked inside the dense networks of grey matter?

Around this time I took to carrying a journal everywhere. On the inside cover I wrote: *Believe what you see, as later it will be refuted*. I wanted to write my life story, for what it was worth, but never managed to finish it. Even now, various freehand drafts are piled up in my study, on loose sheets and bound in notebooks; different versions of events, scribbled down, annotated, crossed out, rewritten. On my trusted Smith Corona I typed up diary entries, but nothing was ever completed.

In those months I discovered that a cherished memory can transform into one of pain if there's a change in the relationship with those involved. The past, therefore, is never set in stone; what we subsequently learn will colour what we knew and experienced at the time. Good memories turn bad, with a sense of loss or betrayal, and yet bad memories rarely turn good. The best we can hope is to recall the comfort provided by loved ones in times of crisis, and by those pertinent, reassuring songs that somehow keep us going.

FOURTEEN

Where the cottage has changed since my childhood is in growing old, wearing down; fading, flaking, crumbling, mouldering. The lustre has long-since disappeared from the patterned paper, which has grown dull in patches and soiled in others. The paintwork is chipped and peeling, the white gloss turned yellow. The house itself seems structurally sound, but the cosmetics are in grave need of attention. I need to rip this place apart.

It is spitting with fine rain as I lift the last of the boxes from the back of the car, carrying it through to the living room to put with the others. My life's accumulations seem pretty scant, when laid out across the floor. I've faced several crossroads over the years, where moving on involved paring down belongings to the essential, plus those few luxury or sentimental items which enrich my existence. Stacked together, it doesn't amount to much.

I score a key through the tape fastening the boxes, peel back the flaps. I lift objects mummified in newspaper and bubble-wrap and place them on all available surfaces. Three sculpted busts are of vital importance to me – reconstructed faces from several years ago: a woman discovered behind Brighton train station, a homeless man found sheltering on the seafront, and a woman washed up in the Adur. I want to know their stories.

But nothing matches the emotional pull of the painting of Black. When I've decided which room I'll use as my study I will hang it with pride of place. Even now, every time I look at her face I feel that she is staring back – staring only at me.

* * *

Despite having fully settled back into the cottage, the childhood feeling of isolation is never far away. The last thing I needed at the age of eight was another new school – my third in three years – but Kitty lived in a different catchment area to my father and the foster family with whom I briefly lived, so there was no choice. That first day at St Edmunds, after the autumn half-term, was like stepping into a cage of prepubescent hate. Word soon got around about my status as an orphan, and my reluctance to make eye contact had me pegged as a 'weirdo', even at such a tender age. A lack of sportiness meant that I was an obvious target for bullies, with some declaring me a 'poofter', on little evidence other than I was quiet, thoughtful and uncoordinated.

One moment stands out, as clear today as it was then. Pushed to breaking point one lunchtime, I punch one of my tormentors in the mouth, feeling thrilled as his split lip leaks rich blood. I imagine grabbing his hair and smashing his face into the concrete. However, in a swift response, I find myself on the wrong end of a beating – inasmuch as you can get a 'beating' at that age. (I've since worked on the corpses of those for whom the term is far more appropriate.) As I grapple and grasp at my opponent the onlookers shout 'Errr, *queer!*' For my troubles I am dragged by a teacher to be caned and demeaned by the hateful headmistress, to add insult and injury to insult and injury.

While it didn't stop the playground taunts, no one dared touch me again, knowing that even if they beat me to a pulp I was not afraid to inflict some damage in reply. Even so, friends hardly announced themselves in their droves. If you opted to hang around in my presence you would be inviting bullies to find you guilty by association. As such, I spent evenings and weekends with my face pressed up against my bedroom window, looking over the lake in the back garden, or, in better weather, out in the sprawling cottage grounds, inventing games, discovering potential hideouts, alone but for nature.

Both my prison and my liberty, then as now.

The cottage had been in my mother's family for several generations. By the outbreak of war just she and Kitty survived. They lost their mother to cancer in 1935, and their father, who boasted a proud record of never having taken a sick day from the accountancy firm at which he'd worked his whole life, dropped dead of a heart attack late in 1937.

My grandparents, long lost to me before I even entered this life.

Is tragedy *genetic?*

I'd never really appreciated it – not that a son necessarily would – but my mother was once a beautiful woman. Perhaps she hadn't aged as well as she might. My memories are, after all, of someone who was fifty, but the photos secreted around the cottage reveal a striking woman almost unrecognisable to me: loose mousy-blonde ringlets that suited her youth – reminiscent of Carole Lombard – and, looking at her fresh face in one black and white picture, a hint of a late-teen/early-twenties Judy Garland about the fall of her features and the fullness of her lips.

I never even existed when she was truly alive.

* * *

A week has brushed by since I saw Kitty. Sorting, unpacking, searching: removing my world from bags and boxes, finding it all a new home, overtook my days. Walls were shorn of paper, and white emulsion applied, as I pared back the past. Anything of my aunt's, bar obvious junk and large furniture, I shunted upstairs, to further fill her bedroom, which now resembles a shrine.

I can't continue to put off seeing her. It's time to return to Hove.

Visiting my aunt assuages some guilt, but in its way it's also rather soul–destroying: the unnerving proximity to old age and illness, to imminent death, both with her and within the nursing home itself, which reeks of incontinence and bleach. I can't help but think that we should have had these conversations long before now.

I arrive late-afternoon, on a day of evaporating cloud. We

hug once more, but this time it feels forced. She makes some tea – in a teapot, which strikes me as quaint – and asks if I will carry it through on a tray with some biscuits. We exchange pleasantries, and I ask after her health. "Mustn't grumble," she notes, out of habit. There are periods of silence as we eat and drink.

"So," she says, setting down her empty cup on its saucer and peering over her glasses. "How are you settling into the cottage?"

"Fine. It's nice to be back. Weird, but nice."

"I don't suppose you'd be good enough to take me over there?" she asks. "There are a couple of things I couldn't find when they rushed me in here."

"Funny you should say that. I wanted to ask you about what stuff might be my mother's? I could use your help."

"Then let's go."

"You mean now?"

"At my stage of life there's always less chance of tomorrow."

Kitty is still able to walk with the aid of her frame, although she's noticeably slower, even within just a week. I help her into my car, fasten her seat belt.

"How did you end up with the cottage?" I ask, as we pass along the shoreline. "Didn't Mum live there before you?"

"She did. It was towards the end of the war. I'd started teaching up in Glasgow after university. Then the time came when I wanted to move home. Around that time your mother started getting ill and had to stop nursing to spend some time in, well, I suppose they called them *institutions* back then – although you must understand that it wasn't one of those awful places, with straightjackets and all that. She got better, over time, but she never wanted to live back at the cottage. Any time she came back to visit it made her feel ill. So she moved to Croydon, and I took the cottage."

I let her talk. By the time she finishes we are on the winding country lane that leads to the cottage. The giant horse chestnut heaves into view. Once parked I grab the walking frame from the boot, then help Kitty out of the car. Her eyes, big behind oval lenses, light up at the sight of her home of nine decades.

"I have to warn you, I've made a few alterations," I note. "Nothing major, mind."

"That's fine. It's your house now, deary."

"I've not thrown anything of yours away, though."

"After today, unless there's something you want, just chuck the lot of it. Set fire to it for all I care, or give it to the Sally Army."

We enter the house, and she takes in the changes. But she passes no judgement; she knows her time is short, and that, in the grand scheme of things, cosmetics mean nothing. She heads first to the back room, which is now my study. The ornaments that once lined its broad shelf have been replaced with reconstructed skulls, and this clearly takes her by surprise.

"Your stuff – it's up here," I tell her, leading her to the stairs. "All your things are in your bedroom," I add, helping her up each step, one at a time. On the landing we face Genevieve's room.

"Do you remember Genevieve?" I ask.

"Of course I do," she says with a scowl. "My memory's going, but it's not *that* bad. She was a real handful, that girl. Trouble."

"Her mother – Alice. Did she ever give up hope?"

"No, I don't believe so. Drove her to an early grave."

"And she never heard anything?"

"No, nothing. Mind you, I don't think any of us were surprised. She'd done it before, and she'd do it again, we all knew that. We hoped that she might grow out of it, but no, it wasn't to be. God-knows what happened to the girl in London. We all feared the worst."

"She had her dark side all right. But she could be nice, too."

"She drove me batty. And what she did to her poor mother – it's unforgivable, really. Teenagers never think, do they? So selfish."

With a delicate touch Kitty strokes the walls of the landing, where I've yet to start redecorating; her arthritic hand trailed gently over the tired wallpaper. I follow her into her bedroom. "This is all rubbish," she says, referring to everything on view. "The good stuff is in the wardrobes and under the bed. Along with more junk."

"I did start to have a look, but I didn't know what was yours and what might have been Mum's. I didn't want to sort through it without you."

She stands beside the bed and begins to slowly lower herself, but then, with a few inches to go, trusts the give of the mattress and flops down onto her backside. The springs twang, but she remains upright, wobbling. "Bring me that stuff," she says once steadied, gesturing towards the first wardrobe.

I open the mahogany doors to boxes, carrier bags, hard-backed photographs, folders, loose papers and all manner of bric-a-brac, whose airtight cramming holds them in place. One by one I attempt to pass them across to my aunt without the rest spilling onto the floor.

It takes over an hour to sort through her possessions, and, knowing that time and energy are on the wane, she doesn't spend long on decisions. She looks at each item, then quickly places it either to the right or to the left, onto the patchwork quilt. Discard, keep, discard, discard, discard, discard, keep, and so on, with the discard pile growing higher as she tires. Some boxes and envelopes are opened then dismissed, the contents warranting no further inspection. "All this," she says, looking to her right, "can go in the bin."

The sorting complete, I make room on the bed beside her – casting the discarded pile to the floor with the rest of what she considers disposable – as she collates a handful of objects to show me. With hands shaking she presents photographs of their childhood: two skinny sisters in gingham dresses on the front porch; slightly younger sisters, paddling in the lake; a fair bit older and seated around the dining table, Kitty now in her teens and wearing glasses, my mother's full, relaxed smile a shock.

"I'm glad I saw these again," she says, handing them to me. "But you should have them now." I consider protesting – how can you give away such precious mementos? – but it's not like Kitty will have much more time to appreciate them.

"You can't take any of it with you," she says, looking around the room. At first I think she's giving me an instruction, but adds, "You leave it all behind," and I understand.

She hands me an old ciné film, encased in a yellow Kodak envelope. "I've no idea what's on it," she says. "It was your mother's. I've no idea what ever happened to the projector."

"What can I do with it?"

"Can't you send it somewhere?" she asks.

"Probably," I say. "I guess these days there are places you can send most things."

"Ah, these are what I was after," she says, tucking some scraps of paper into the pocket of her cardigan. It seems invasive to ask what they contain, and she doesn't offer an explanation. She simply moves on to the next item in the pile. I recognise it instantly: it is Monty, my childhood teddy bear. "This is yours, I believe," she says, holding him out to me like a midwife passing a newborn. One touch of his bow tie puts me back on that train, rattling away from my mother's existence. He seemed so much bigger, then. Now, my hand stretches right around his waist. I slip him into my bag.

"Ah, these," Kitty says, handing over a clutch of letters grouped together with an elastic band. "You might want to read them. They're from your mother's younger days."

I quickly scan a page pulled from the first envelope, reading it with the sense that my mother was somehow cheating on my father, decades before they even met. I feel a sense of betrayal, that she knew love in her youth. Unwilling to confront the final paragraphs, I fold the paper and slip it back into the envelope. Maybe once the shock has worn off I'll be able to read them, from start to finish.

"You're your mother's son," Kitty states, matter-of-factly.

"Pardon?"

She hands me a photo. "I see her, in you. I notice it more, now you're all grown up." She then tuts, softly. "You're almost her age. You know, when she…"

I hadn't really thought about it before. But yes, it's now less than a handful of years until I'm fifty. How did I ever make it this far?

Kitty is clearly tiring as we descend the stairs. Her whole weight – which admittedly isn't much – is pressed into me as I hold her upright. After the final step I release her into the curved embrace of her walking frame. I go to open the front door, but she wants to see out the back. Slowly we shuffle through the patio doors, out onto the veranda.

"It's such a lovely view, isn't it?" she says, looking across the shimmering lake, to the tree with its broken bough, and beyond, to the woods in the distance, before turning her head to take in the entire panorama. "I shall miss it," she sighs. I drink in the same crepuscular views: dappled golden light on the long grass, angular shadows falling across a field of rape, the drifts of smoke from a distant bonfire, a handful of low pink clouds in sky. I take a deep breath: there's a strong scent of rosemary and rapeseed in the air.

"What was she like, when you were children here?" I ask.

Kitty pauses. "Quiet and shy, with outsiders at least. But she was also a little mischievous. Keen sense of humour."

"She wasn't as serious, back then?"

"Good heavens no! That came much later. It's funny, I remember a lot of my childhood better than I remember this morning. I can still see your mother running around the lake, she must have been ten or eleven, round and round, as if she was competing at White City. She loved to run. So full of beans."

"Were you happy living here?"

"We were. Life was simple, at least until our mother died. She – your mother I mean – would have been thirteen. It affected her badly – it did us both. She had got over it, somewhat, by the time she left school. But I think it was part of what undermined her, when times got tougher."

"It's silly," I state, clearing my throat, "but I still think I should have done something, back then. I was just six, but I can't recall being six without knowing what I know now, as if I was equipped to intervene, when obviously I wasn't. I just wish I'd known *some* of it at the time – enough to say something that might stop her."

"We live and learn, Patrick. In that order."

FIFTEEN

The clay smells foetid, but it's an aroma I've not only become accustomed to but actually grown to like, due to its associations with creativity and achievement. I use a rare organic compound, as opposed to the more heavily oil-based variety popular with my peers, because its humus is all part of the cycle of life. A wealth of dead plant and animal matter has dissolved into the clay over millennia. The ground then gives up this substance which, in turn, helps create an identity for someone deceased, who will themselves, when that identity is discovered, return, boxed up, to the soil. There is something about organic clay that gives more of a connection to the process than the Plasticine used by others, or the computer modelling that, I fear, may soon make such skills obsolete.

As with any portrait, the eyes hold the key. But how can I get them right without anything to refer to?

Given that those made for dolls and taxidermy have unnaturally large irises and too little of the white space that surrounds them, it's essential for maximum realism to use synthetic eyeballs from a medical retailer. I plump for brown eyes, on account of it being the most prevalent colour amongst the population. If definite proof of hair colour exists — say blonde or auburn — then I might opt for a shade of blue or green, but with no such evidence I stick to the laws of probability. I tear off two golf-ball sized slabs of clay and force them into the hollows. I then sink the glass eyes into these soft sockets, at just the right angle, careful not to push too far. Aligning them within the recess is a delicate balancing act: a ruler bridging the bony arcs of upper cheekbone and eyebrow ridge should lightly intersect with the tip of the cornea. Once in place, I pad the circumferences with more clay, to further secure them.

The phone rings. Expecting it to be David, and unwilling to be distracted, I turn up the music on my stereo. Even now, in this age of digital music, I persevere with vinyl on a turntable, sticking mostly to records from the '70s and '80s.

All thirty-two numbered tissue-depth markers are in place, the glue dry. I slice a strip of clay roughly ten centimetres by three in length, tapering to between four and six millimetres in depth, and run it down from one peg to another. Next I take a strip of similar length and place it horizontally, from left to right, as the underpinning to eyebrows. I step back: the skull appears to be wearing an inverted cross on its forehead. From here I work outwards to the cheeks, then down through the lower jaw, until the clay joins in a mask encompassing the majority of the markers. At the end of this stage, for which, it must be said, creative talent is not necessary, the sides of the face and the forehead are covered, but the central area – nose, mouth and what surrounds the eyes – remains untouched, the bare skull showing through. All underpinning, along with some flesh, has been applied, but what follows is the artistic side of the process. What follows is the *appearance*.

With a Boley gauge I measure the front six teeth, the size of which largely determines the width of the mouth. My aim is to give her an open smile. I usually only go down this route when there's something like a snaggletooth or an unusual arrangement – or even absence – of teeth, because broken, missing or crooked teeth can often be the one distinctive feature of which we can be certain. However, teeth like *these* demand to be displayed. If you have teeth like these you are not ashamed to show them. It complicates my task, given that the facial infrastructure alters, as the muscles pull and stretch the corners of the mouth: the cheeks plump, and push the eyes into more of a squint. But it has to be done. I lay two strips of clay and curve them into lips, pinching away the excess thickness of the upper, fattening the lower. I'll return to it later, to smooth it all out, but I first want to establish a rough idea.

How the lids arc over the synthetic eyeballs is another process where a millimetre here or there, either in terms of thickness or shape, can radically alter the look. I carefully lay the first thin fronds of clay. What starts as the widest possible stare – unnaturally bulging eyes – recedes into a natural expression once the lids are in place and smoothed down. A tiny pea of clay is pushed into the inner corner of each eye, to replicate caruncles. The canthi – the inner and outer corners of the eye – are fractionally lower on the inner edge, either side of the nose. As such, the eyes need to appear fractionally tilted.

According to studies comparing rebuilt faces with existing photographs of the deceased, the nose tends to be the most accurate feature in reconstructions. And crucial for this accuracy is the nasal spine – the base, in between the nostrils – which can often be missing or damaged. In this case I'm fortunate. A nose dictates so much of a person's attractiveness, as the facial centrepiece. It's not so much the size, but how it suits its surroundings; its proportion to the rest of the features. Judging by the nasal spine – which here is small and upward in projection – and the slender protrusion of the nasal bone (the bridge), this young woman most likely had a neat, diminutive nose. A narrow nasal aperture adds to the theory of delicacy.

I take a measurement of the nasal spine, and multiply it by three to get the full length. This can then be joined to the projection of the nasal bone, with a dab of extra clay for some kind of neat bobble or furrow at the tip. I fill in and encircle the cheeks, to get a nice round look, and, with fresh pieces of clay, create small, delicate ears that I add to the skull once fully shaped.

She is evolving, returning to life. A physiognomy is apparent, an existence harked back to. She is far from finished, but to someone, somewhere, she might already be alive.

SIXTEEN

Time: then and now. My six-year-old self, dressed awkwardly in new black trousers and a heavily starched white shirt with grubby cuffs, standing at the edge of the lake, which dominates the grounds to Kitty's cottage. The water is so still, so lifeless; a mirror reflecting the sky, the tree line. I grab a stone, pull back my arm with the grace of a sportsman – a cricketer at the third-man boundary – and in a swift forward sweep release it with a flick of the wrist and a follow-through of the hand that splays the fingers; something occurring instinctively, to produce the best leverage. No one taught me, I just know.

It skims across the surface of time, dipping below, skipping above. The mirror cracks, and then gradually reforms.

One heartbeat later I am thrust into middle-age so fast it knots my stomach, and the existence of the stone, like my childhood, my youth, my potential, is nothing but a ripple on the water. The memory of that day four decades ago – the day of my mother's funeral – is eerily fresh. Beside the lake I drift back to those moments when, having been kept away from the service itself, I snuck out from the solemnity of the wake to play by the water's edge.

Daydreaming, and with the total detachment of an aerial perspective, I see my younger self pull from his trouser pocket the St Christopher left to him by his mother, and launch it across the inky water, using the same technique as with the stone; hard and low, although it only skips once, the chain dragging it down. Nothing more dramatic than a flurry of bubbles marks its descent somewhere out towards the centre.

* * *

Yet another of those childhood days that would stay with me forever: just eight years old, and positively racking them up. I came home from school and, as usual, let myself in. I had a key, even at that age: my father could not be relied upon to be awake or to hear the doorbell.

At first I failed to sense a problem, but even the mundane details of those few minutes have stayed with me, such as how the low spring sunlight streamed through the coloured glass panels on the door and painted the radiator with Art Deco rays; the football pools coupon lying on the mat; and the exceptionally strong smell of coffee that in itself suggested very little, other than my father had just brewed a cup. Little did I know that, several hours earlier, I'd become an orphan.

If never apparently right at death's door, my father shuffled furtively near its porch. I took his genetic inheritance of being slim, but at no point have I ever been as scrawny – possibly because, unlike him, I didn't smoke or drink more calories than I ate. He had a greyness that permeated his entire existence, from his sallow complexion to the dull suits he wore at the council's waste management services. That was, until he lost his job two months earlier.

A good man at heart – gentle, with no anger or malice – but also undeniably weak. He wanted me in his life, but seemed ill-prepared for the burden of full-time cohabitation. When a week here and there became a full-time obligation, it took its toll. And with the loss of his job went the last little sparks of life.

I made my way into the living room, half expecting to see him stretched out on the sofa. With no sign there, I went into the kitchen. The lingering smell of coffee suddenly made sense: the percolator was on, a cup of oily black liquid resting beneath its spout. Something felt wrong, but it wasn't yet clear just *how* wrong it could possibly be. That would change once I made my way upstairs.

I found my father semi-naked on his bed, full ashtray beside him. He looked asleep, but even paler than normal, apart from a slight reddish-purple colouring to his skin where it met the mattress. Dampness radiated across the bedding, and there was a smell of urine in the air, rising above the coffee. His jaw looked unusually – *unnaturally* – slack, his eyes firmly closed. Despite all this, it never occurred to me that he had died. I didn't understand alcoholism or depression, but by then I knew enough of my father's odd behaviour to think that, not for the first time, he'd simply fallen asleep and pissed himself. But the more I watched him, the longer I went without detecting a breath. Perhaps flickers in my vision – those swift blinks – concealed the movement of his chest? It was only when I touched him, to try and wake him, that I recoiled at the coldness of his flesh.

I didn't cry; at least not right away. I simply stared at him. Even though I think I *understood* he was dead, I kept expecting him to move; the man I knew would always shift sooner or later, would always awake from the drunken stupor, the near-coma.

I sat on the end of the bed, and eventually, after thinking about his hand in mine when he met me from the train twenty-one months earlier, I began to cry. He never did hold my hand like that again, and I never again felt as close to him as I did that day. I must have been in a state of shock, as, despite some tears, it didn't fully sink in. Indeed, it felt slightly surreal, as if I were a mere spectator, watching myself from a distance. I covered my father's body with the bedclothes, closed tight the bedroom door and went downstairs to watch *Crackerjack*.

I consciously held off from dialling 999, even though I knew it was the thing to do. Facing radical change once again, only this time I would have even less of a clue where it would take me. I'd recently seen *Oliver!* on TV, and believed that being an orphan meant an awful existence. Aside from my aunt Kitty, I had run out of family – at least those I knew about. Delaying the inevitable – and I think I knew that it was inevitable – gave me the chance to stay at the place I had come to call home, before strange people came in and decided my fate. I felt helpless and confused, and at times terrified, but also like I'd been initiated into an adult world where parental control presented no issue, a world where I could be my own boss, at least until the harsh realities of how to cook a meal or find money to spend on food came calling. For the time being I got by on snacks from the fridge and the larder.

I fell asleep on the sofa after *It's A Knockout*, waking to the test card hours later. I went up and grabbed some bedding, along with the increasingly careworn Monty from my room, and returned to the sofa. I left the TV on, but turned down the volume to mute the drone. The little girl and her clown kept me company throughout the night.

It would be a long weekend in the house with my father's body.

Looking back, my father's funeral proved a rather pathetic affair. Given that I hadn't been allowed to attend my mother's cremation – just the wake – it would be my first. I therefore had nothing with which to compare it. Only years later, with the aid of hindsight, did I realise that more than a handful of people should be present for the laying to rest of a man of his age. After all, he wasn't some pensioner who'd outlived all his friends; he simply hadn't accrued any. An only child, he lacked the siblings to boost the tally with their own partners and children, while his own parents were both long-since deceased. Kitty, two neighbours and a couple of council colleagues paid their respects. That was it. Five adults and one child.

My father had not drawn up a will, nor discussed any plans for where he wished to be buried. As such, he ended up in the graveyard of the 12th century church in the village nearest to where Kitty lived. After the service we filed slowly and silently back to her cottage, and that was it: both parents in the ground.

* * *

The cries of scruffy children rose to the third floor window beside which, in a shabby armchair, I habitually sat. Only a couple of months into life with a foster family, it felt like an eternity, interred in that block of flats. Eventually Kitty took me in, but not until I'd endured a spell as an outcast in a brutal housing estate.

I listened to the step-divers play, launching themselves as far as possible, before one of their number marked in chalk the length of the jump. Beyond the step-divers a dozen-or-so boys kicked and chased a sagging sack of plastic — a football, once — swarming over the concrete wasteland, from one end to the other, where pushbikes with buckled wheels, crumpled sweaters and bent-up traffic cones substituted as goalposts. Each kid fought for the right to be next to lay leather to its embarrassed shape as they spilled across a boundless pitch. No touchlines, no bylines. Casually they circled the burnt-out Cortina chassis as if it were just another opponent. They strayed to beneath my window, in amongst the step-divers, with straggle-haired waif assuming possession of the ball from straggle-haired waif, skinny girl landing between them on white chalk line.

I looked on from above, omniscient but excluded.

Perhaps those five-and-a-half months, alone and cooped up, intensified my love for the cottage; by the time I arrived there, I had come to appreciate just how oppressive life could be. I had never lived in splendour with either of my parents, but each home proved comfortable enough, and, even though I never really thought about it, relatively spacious. Then came the stint at Tyrer Court. Although a nice enough couple, Mary and Alan did not welcome me into the lap of luxury. He worked as a long-distance lorry driver, which took him away a lot, and her time was spent as a housewife. They'd fostered before, but only ever girls, and I'm not quite sure Mary knew how to relate to me. To be honest, I don't remember an awful lot about *them*; what sticks in my mind is confinement and boredom. My future at that point remained uncertain; Kitty had been approached about my adoption, but she had only very recently undergone the first of two hip replacement surgeries. She had yet to indicate whether or not she'd ever be physically capable of taking me in, although perhaps her psychology also held her back.

I had no friends with whom to enjoy the summer holidays. One boy from school looked a potential candidate, but he went away for the entire duration. I'd tried to fit in with the kids of the estate, but lacked the sportiness and sufficient rough-and-tumble. The widely-known fact that I lived in a bedroom with pink walls adorned with flying unicorns did not help with this early form of street credibility. The gentle girls welcomed me to play, but while I appreciated the offer, I only saw that as adding to my problems with the boys. Other girls – those who hung out with the tough lads – would push me, spit at me, safe as part of a gang. Perhaps I could have toughed it out, but my resistance waned, and isolation, while tormenting, just about trumped bullying and abuse. Thankfully Kitty eventually rescued me from this purgatory.

My stay at the cottage remained blissfully free of complication, until the arrival of Genevieve Frazer.

SEVENTEEN

Did Black have a precursor? Indeed she did. I first met Genevieve when I was eleven and she thirteen, and then again a year later. At the time girls remained an irritant, an alien life-form to be distrusted and fought with. Plain and slightly plump, and although not exactly a tomboy, she had a willingness to at least sometimes join in with my games. This of course endeared her to me, and we got on well, despite our different interests. The first girl to ever feel like a proper friend, I was grateful to have someone to hang around with, irrespective of her gender. I sensed that she cared for me; at that stage she seemed genuinely concerned with my well-being.

Genevieve's mother, Alice, knew Kitty from their schooldays. Originally from Sussex, Alice now lived in Derbyshire, and had taken to sending her daughter to the cottage for the summer. A widow, Alice worked irregular hours, and childcare had long been an issue. The south coast, and the cottage, struck her as the ideal retreat for her daughter in the holidays. However, at fifteen Genevieve felt old enough to stay at home in an empty house on the evenings and nights her mother worked, exerting her authority in several heated arguments in order to do so. Genevieve betrayed that trust by running away to London with her boyfriend, only returning after six weeks in the capital, as the relationship ended in violence. A year later there arose the chance of seaside work in Sussex while she contemplated a return to school for A-Levels – something she had the intelligence to do, if she applied herself. Her fractious relationship with her mother had once again reached breaking point, so time apart was considered wise by all concerned. Genevieve was granted some of the autonomy she craved, within the relatively secure setting of Kitty's cottage.

But something happened that summer in 1981, when I was fourteen and she sixteen. In the two years since I'd last seen her she had transformed into something new. She now hung on the verge of womanhood. Hitherto uninterested in the contents of a girl's blouse, something about the development of breasts on Genevieve's once shapeless body struck me as a kind of alchemy: flesh turned into miraculous curves whose form represented a type of perfection. From the widespread fascination with them that surrounded me, I knew that they would one day appeal on levels I didn't yet understand; I knew how I was *supposed* to feel about them. But when I did – when the penny dropped – it just hit me so quickly: moving from an abstract concept to a stern reality in one moment as she stepped from the car, her contours clearly visible within a tight red t-shirt. The *shock* – so exaggerated due to their existence on someone with whom I didn't associate them – floored me. *Desire* arrived that day: an androgynous girl, with tomboyish ways, reborn in alluring adult form; as changed as butterfly from caterpillar. Where I'd never been anything other than superficially attracted to either girls or women, Genevieve, who occupied a glorious middle ground, captivated me.

She seemed different in so many ways. As well as the development of those curves, her face had altered shape. She'd lost some puppy fat, but more than that: the angles had refined. Make-up – a new addition – only accentuated the metamorphosis, and I reacted to the redness of her lips, contrasting with her powdered pale skin, with a similar gut-level yearning to that evoked from her new-found shapeliness. Had her mouth grown and her teeth straightened? Had her cheekbones swollen, accentuating her eyes? And the hair: deeply dark, with startling bright red streaks.

Her clothes that summer were mostly black or white, with the occasional addition of a red garment — neck or head scarf, belt, shoes, t-shirt — that would pulse against the monochrome materials. She looked like a pop star: part New Romantic, part Goth, part glamorous siren; still an alien life-form, but now one I wanted to intimately know.

Two years earlier she had been a devotee of the *Grease* soundtrack, with its overriding sense of innocence and poppiness. Her new taste in music, which I'd hear from my room over the coming months, was jarring: The Cure, Bauhaus, Leonard Cohen, Siouxsie & The Banshees, Killing Joke and the like, with their bleak and foreboding tones. Duran Duran, in the top five with *Girls on Film* (which also happened to be on her playlist), proved about as left-field as I got. What I heard from beyond her door summed up the new Genevieve: strong, independent, brooding, with moments of beauty undercut by an undercurrent of darkness, and a certain detachment.

That first day, as she stepped from the car, my nerveless insouciance disappeared; rendering me awkward in an instant. Her openness vanished, replaced with a closed-off coolness; the new outer casing not merely cosmetic, but, it seemed, an impenetrable veneer. That first day I did not know whether I felt love, lust or loathing.

EIGHTEEN

Almost midnight. The stillness of the day has given way to movement in the air. The wind grows and dies in erratic bursts. Zephyrs swirl around our bones, darting like invisible starlings, as, below, the resonance of waves amplifies and the pier trembles and shakes. Woodwork creaks and bows, ironwork rattles and chimes, and a bird flaps its wings in frantic flight. In the darkness these sounds add fleeting menace to what has been one of the strangest days of my life.

Black pulls from her pocket a small lump of brown resin wrapped tightly in cling-film. "I take it you haven't smoked this either?"

"Pot? No, not really my bag," I say.

"So you won't be wanting any now?"

"Well…"

All of a sudden, it seems like the most natural and essential thing in the world. Even if she is going on only the shortest of trips, I want to travel with her. I want something to bring us closer, onto a shared level, and this could be it. But like a departing ship, I have to get on now or never if I am to experience the same ride. "Go on, then," I say, hoping to fix onto her wavelength.

She smiles to herself, nodding as she stares down at the kit stretched across her lap; a gesture that implies she isn't sure I'm cut out for even the lightest of narcotics. She constructs the joint with the care and precision – and steadiness of hand – of an expert model maker. She begins by heating the clump of brown resin, picking off tiny scabs as they soften and placing them in a line along the length of an open Rizla paper.

"You didn't tell me about your family?" I say.

"No, I didn't. I guess my childhood wasn't ideal either. I don't have a father — at least not one that I know of. I was *illegitimate*, as they say. Mum was pressurised to give me up, but she kept me. It was a struggle, though."

"I bet."

She looks up from her work. "We clashed a lot, in my teens. But I'm grateful now, looking back. I didn't appreciate the sacrifices she was making."

"You don't, at that age."

I watch as she trails her tongue along the side of a cigarette, from butt to tip – the tiniest hint of saliva deposited – before peeling back the damp white strip to reveal a cylinder of tightly compacted tobacco. "True," she finally says, studiously laying the tobacco over the cigarette paper, evenly spreading its tangled fibres as she pulls apart the weave.

"You've done that before," I note, as she licks the adhesive strip and seals the joint. With the excess paper at the fat end twirled into a tight tip, she takes the thin end between her lips and strikes down on the lighter. The tiny burst of gas is audible, and the surfeit of paper briefly burns bright white-orange. It flares again upon her first drag, and she exhales like someone expelling her last breath. She smiles broadly and passes me the baton.

I manage to inhale without coughing, although just a single intake of smoke is enough to set my vision gently spinning. Within seconds I feel light of head and body, but it's not an unpleasant kind of giddiness. Black takes longer, more intensive drags, to my quick, tentative tokes.

"What's your deepest, darkest secret?" she asks, staring me hard in the eyes; a gaze of interrogation.

"I don't have any secrets."

She snorts. "*Everyone* has a secret."

"Maybe my secret is that I don't have a secret," I note, smugly.

"Or that you *do*, and you bury it in a secret about not having a secret," she says, passing the joint.

"Maybe… Although if that *was* my secret, it's no longer a secret. And then that would mean I have no secrets."

We both pause, then laugh. The joint has burnt down to a hot remnant of roach, which she discards with a casual flick.

"So what's yours?" I ask.

"My secret?"

"Yeah. Seeing as you brought it up."

"You've seen me naked," she says. "That's a kind of secret. I don't share that with many people."

"Although Jacob was lucky enough," I note.

"He paid me," she says.

"So that's the secret to seeing a woman naked?"

"You seemed to manage it for free."

I take a swig of beer, to wash away the taste of smoke. "How did that come about? Working with Jacob?"

"I was down on the seafront, near the boat sheds, looking at some stall selling quirky jewellery. He came up and introduced himself, and asked if I'd be interested in modelling for him."

"Didn't that seem a bit sleazy?" I try to imagine doing the same thing. I'm pretty sure I wouldn't get away with it.

"I knew who he was. I'd been to a small exhibition of his work, and his art just got to me. I felt honoured. Really honoured."

"So you don't normally do that kind of thing?"

"Undressing for strangers for money? No, not normally."

"So, any *proper* secrets?" I ask, with a gentle nudge of the elbow.

"Aside from being half-crazy?" she says, with no clear hint of irony.

"We're *all* half-crazy. Half-crazy all the time, or totally crazy half the time. Come on, you can do better than that."

"Says he who has no secrets."

"Says she who asked the question in the first place."

"Okay," she says, "I'll tell you, if you promise you won't share it?"

"That's the golden rule of secrets. They go no further."

"In theory."

"With me, in practice, too."

"Okay, in that case I'll tell you," she says, settling herself with a deep breath. "I recently helped to, um… steal a body."

She clearly expects me to be shocked. I'm not. "Would it happen to be a bearded old man?"

"How did you know?"

"I met him, in a manner of speaking. Or what's left of him. In Jacob's freezer."

"Oh my god," she says, shaking her head. "He promised he wouldn't tell anyone until he was ready to exhibit."

"Promises, eh? Actually, it was my fault. I was nosing around. I stumbled across him, in all his frozen glory. And in fairness, Jacob never mentioned your name in connection with it."

"I'll get someone into *big* trouble if this comes to light."

"I don't plan to tell anyone. That said, is there much of a trade in bodysnatching these days?"

"They're worth a lot of money, for medical purposes. Not quite worth their weight in gold, but not far off. Although this one had already been worked on, with his organs removed."

"At least you didn't get involved in grave digging. I mean… you *didn't*, did you?"

"Don't be silly."

"Just teasing. Sorry."

"Look," she says, fiddling with her lighter. "I'm not proud of it. But art has to be about taking risks."

"Did Jacob tell you what he's going to do with it?"

"Some kind of elaborate sculpture. On a big scale, although to be honest he was a little vague. I knew someone at medical school and helped set up the… well, *theft* I suppose. I regret getting involved… and yet at the same time I don't. It could end up being *meaningful*. But that's not the end of it."

"No?"

"No. I've told him that if anything happens to me he can have mine, too."

"Your what?"

"My body. My head."

I am stunned into silence. I understand the words, but on some level it just won't compute.

"Your *head?*" I eventually say, my voice an octave higher. "If you die?"

"Yes. Why not? I'd rather that than just rot in a box, or burn away. What's the point of that?"

"I don't know what to say. I mean, you're *serious*, aren't you?"

"About art? Yes, I am. Deadly serious – no pun intended."

"Well, it's your life, I suppose. Even when it's at an end."

"Indeed it is," she says, and then she laughs, out of the blue. "But life's great, isn't it? So precious, so fragile. If you don't appreciate it, why even bother continuing to exist?"

"My heart just keeps beating on my behalf."

"But you have fun, right? You experiment? You *live?*"

"I do, but you make life sound so much more vital. It can be like that, but it can also be filling time, in between those things. Waiting."

"Wait too long and it's gone."

We both fall quiet, and I wonder if all this time I've been living, or simply waiting.

"So…" Black says, smiling as she breaks the silence. "How would you feel about posing for me?"

"Posing?"

"Yes. Here. Now."

"You're kidding?"

"No, I'm serious."

"Um… I really don't know. I feel very self-conscious in front of a camera." She just stares at me. And it's not long before I relent. "Oh, okay. I suppose."

"Naked," she states, matter-of-factly.

"What?" I splutter, choking as beer catches in my throat and shoots up into my nose.

"Naked. Nude. No clothes. You really need me to explain, Patrick?"

"Full frontal? Surely not full frontal?"

"Why not? Should we be afraid of the penis?"

This comment seems to work on two levels, and I'm unsure as to which she means: should society be scared of the exposed male member, which it does so much to cover up, or should we – she and I – be afraid of *my* penis.

"You mean right now?" I ask, fidgeting nervously.

"Yes, right now."

"Here?"

"Where else? It's not like we can go anywhere. It's a great location."

"But why naked?"

She tuts. "Do you need an art history lesson?"

"Of course not."

"Well then."

"I really don't know. I'm not—"

"Look, you've seen me naked. So I think you should. Actually, I think it would be rude of you not to. *Very* rude." She's now smiling.

Phrased like that, and with enough alcohol and cannabis in my bloodstream to sufficiently lower my inhibitions, I cannot refuse. And there is no denying that I feel distinctly honoured. Uneasy, but honoured. In some way it feels like a form of immortalisation. But where do I fit with her admiration of Diane Arbus, and her pursuit of freaks?

Fortunately I don't look too bad naked. In a strange way, and contrary to how most people feel about their bodies, I perhaps look better than when dressed; finding clothes that properly fit is the main problem. There is nothing special about my body, but equally, there is nothing desperately wrong with it. It's elongated, but also fairly toned and sinewy, and free of anything unsightly. As long as it's not being asked to perform anything particularly athletic at the time, it's okay.

"So, whereabouts are we going to do this?" I ask, looking around.

There is an area behind us in which she sees possibilities. An old octagonal kiosk at the south-west section of the pier head – one of the few relatively sound structures – offers the chance of 360° views. She explains how, depending from which direction she shoots, the backdrop could be the kiosk, or purely sea, or the two main buildings on the West Pier, or the Palace Pier, or the shoreline, with each giving a different perspective. The eight sides to the kiosk are fairly identical, with the exception of the door panel, so, she suggests, it could appear that the world is rotating around me. She briefly shrugs her shoulders, intimating that it might not work, but her general demeanour is one of inspiration calling. I follow her to the far edge of the pier. Part of the kiosk's signage remains intact, but all of its windows are smashed to varying degrees. Its roof has fallen in on itself, and other junk fills its inner space.

"Don't you think this lends itself to nudity?" she says, reaching in her bag, "The total unexpectedness of it. And also the contrast – I can already see it in my head – between smooth skin and the darkness, the decay, the coarse materials. And then there's the sea, too, which adds all kinds of symbolism."

I nod, unsure of what to say. I love seeing her like this, fired with enthusiasm. I feel excited at being the cause of this new-found animation; ignoring the likelihood that it is just a response to her own ideas, and I am no more than an object to shoot. She removes from a padded camera case – itself wrapped in a waterproof bag – what looks like an antiquated museum piece; the kind of camera Kitty used to have. "With *that?*" I ask.

"This is a *Leica*. Anyway, quit stalling."

"*Totally* naked?"

"Totally."

I start to undress with my back to Black – which is somewhat pointless, seeing as I will be turning around. She begins to hum the music that accompanies stripteases, but stops when I threaten to change my mind. My cartoon boxers are scrunched down in one movement within my jeans, so that I am at least spared that particular embarrassment. The tight neck of my t-shirt then snags against my chin and ears, as I wrestle with my own clothing like a child, before my head finally extrudes.

The whole experience is at once unnerving and invigorating. I have spent the evening harbouring crazy fantasies about being naked in her presence, but this is not quite what I had in mind. And even though I am the only one undressing, and that it is not for us to be intimate, there is something very arousing about being wanted in this particular way. If it's not exactly how I fantasised, it is still more than I could have ever realistically expected.

Fully undressed, I turn around, and she smiles. It's not a leer, nor a look of joy or amazement, but it is, all the same, a *smile*. Is she merely approving of my compliance, my courage, or is there more to it? And then, almost instantaneously, I am under closer scrutiny. Leaning against whatever stable surface she can find – walls to the pavilion, a bench designed into the curve of the perimeter rail, a small turret-like shelter – she works with slow shutter speeds to eke out what little light there is, rather than opting for the unforgiving glare of a flash; something for which I'm extremely grateful. She asks me to stand perfectly still, so that the world beyond me moves as the camera lets in light.

The viewfinder's unusual positioning on the Leica means that the body of the camera does not obscure her face, and she does not close her other eye, as so many people do. I imagine that she is touching me as the lens is directed over my body, and even more so as she moves toward me; I sense my skin prickle as I come under greater examination. My heart is beating ten to the dozen. Standing only feet away, she pauses to take off her jacket, and the curves of her breasts become clear, and her smooth, taut belly as her blouse rides up. I start to wonder if she too is planning to get naked – to come closer still, to touch me. I think back to the moment earlier in the day, in the studio, and how she looked.

"That's enough," I say. But she is standing over my clothes; before I can reach them she grabs my boxer shorts, and starts to dangle them over the water.

"Give them back," I plead. I smile outwardly at her playfulness, but inside I'm angry at my vulnerability. "*Please*, Black," I beg, my weakness now showing.

"Spoilsport," she says, handing them over with a sly smile.

NINETEEN

Like a name that cannot ease itself from the tip of the tongue, the appearance of this reconstruction is eluding me. It's been a week since I've attempted any adjustments. For days, half-finished features – modelled and remodelled time and time again – leered and taunted from the wonky armature. Feeling beaten, I lay a sheet over her, to obscure her power. But I can't keep putting it off.

I don't know why, but I just can't get it right, get *her* right. Already she has taken three times as many working hours as normal, and I'm unsure whether I'm getting closer to, or further from, actually finishing.

When it comes to art, simplicity in the work of others is what I envy. I have forever been dogged by a compulsion to add, and add again; to embellish, to overcomplicate. In this line of work it's not too much of a failing, and I do eventually come to a stop, when I force myself away. But right now I cannot get close to a sense of completion.

Why am I being so precious about this one in particular? No matter how hard I try, the features I lay down just don't match the appearance alive in my mind's eye. Maybe what I've created is how she looked; but somehow I expected – *wanted?* – her to appear different when the clay came to rest. More than any other head I've worked on, this feels personal.

Perhaps there's someone in particular that I want this face to resemble. I just can't tell anymore, can't double-guess my own motives. Have I thought it could be *Black?*

Yes.

But not in any logical manner. While there are a number of similarities, this woman died a decade before I even met Black, so in no feasible way can this be her skull. But perhaps my urge is to *make it* her. Maybe, with this orb of bone, I have a chance to recreate the one who got away. The building blocks are all here, and if I can eschew science in order to take a little creative licence with, perhaps, a hint of black magic and a dash of necromancy, I can summon her spirit. Silly, I know, but at this late hour, with the low lighting and the soft music, my mind plays tricks.

While both involve capturing reality – or certain interpretations of reality – when it comes to our art, what I do is very different to how Black worked, back in the pre-digital age. Mine is considered, laborious, as an image builds over days, sometimes weeks, layer upon layer. But her art dealt in fractions – *thousandths* – of a second. It doesn't mean that no preparation went into a photograph; foresight and planning necessary to picking the location, where the defining moment might occur, and then composing and recomposing the shot. A photographer would work at the prints – choosing what to crop out, and how to get the right contrast in the developing process, after dozens, even hundreds, of negatives are exposed. Then there were the technical considerations, such as what lens to attach, which film stock to use. But it mostly came down to that one split second, when the index finger depressed the shutter release.

She tried to stop time, whereas all these years later, I try to restart it.

Perhaps it's this woman's story – or what little is known of it – that confuses me. I knew none of the specific details of the case at the time I met Black, but many years earlier – when still just a kid – I was vaguely aware of the discovery of female remains on the West Pier. Estimated to have been dead for around a year, the police found only a skeleton and scraps of underwear beneath some upturned wooden kiosk panels. Eventually she made her way to me.

* * *

David hasn't been looking too well of late. Although the severity of the symptoms fluctuates, multiple sclerosis has a tightening grip on his central nervous system. Most of the time he requires a walking stick, although occasionally he'll get about unaided. Although only in his late fifties, he appears much older: patchy grey beard, peppery flecks of red poking through; bags beneath the eyes, puffy sacs packed with *experience*; the eyes themselves, dim and glaucous behind large, thick-rimmed bifocals, constantly darting back and forth; liver spots spreading across his temples, stopping at the point where his hairline would have been before it began to recede; skin loosening around his neck and across his forehead. Perhaps he was a real *bastard* in his day, when the need arose. It was, after all, an age of brutal interrogations. But he now carries himself like a harmless granddad, complete with knitted pullover covered in food stains and cat hair. Sometimes he breathes heavily, but words rattle out of him like ack-ack fire. He talks at me. Not for the first time he riffs on the toolkit of the killer, having seen something on my desk: "Ah, duct tape. No matter the M.O., there's *always* duct tape. You should need a licence for that stuff." And then he falls silent, and inhales through pursed lips, as if taking an extended drag on his favourite cigarette.

"Don't you ever just want to let go?" I ask, as he looks out at the lake.

"Let go? What of?"

"Marina. And all the ghosts."

He laughs. "As if I could. You see this?" He rolls up his sleeve, revealing the green-blue tattoo of a crudely-inked anchor. "It's just like this. It's not quite as vivid as it was, but it stays there. It might as well be a picture of this girl."

* * *

Despite my initial uneasiness, I now feel fully at home at the cottage, making the most of the large back room, with its broad windows and French doors, as my study. Even though I sculpt mostly at night, there are times when I need as much natural light as possible, for my work, but also to keep a steady mood. It's strange being finally able to treat the property as my own. I keep expecting to have to ask permission to make an alteration, such as when taking down and burning the old net curtains.

I find myself working on Marina from noon onwards, as soon as I get up. Most days David turns up unannounced – but not unexpected – after lunch. He is forever at a loose end, lost since the death of his wife. Retirement suits some men and kills others; this special project saves him from the latter fate. He hobbles about behind me, unaware that I find it intensely irritating. Sometimes he'll stand looking over my shoulder, and I feel my hackles bristle, but he usually moves away before I need to ask. He rarely stays longer than an hour. I think he needs the act of setting off to a destination, to loosen his limbs. Whatever he asks about the case and my progress could easily be done by phone in a matter of minutes, but this way, when including the slow walk, it can be stretched out over a couple of hours.

With tenderness and spittle I smooth bumps of clay like a mother pressing down a toddler's hair. I depress divots around the temples, scoop excess material from beside the nostrils. The clay dries into the furrows of my fingerprints, and in return their swirls embed into the model. With every press of thumb and forefinger my identity sinks itself into the work, an enduring craftsman's mark.

Alternating between a scalpel and slim wooden spatula I refine the clay, whittling away a thin strip in order to adjust her eyelids. I can only trust that this gaze is met by someone who knows, in a heartbeat, that they have seen it before. I apply a fraction more clay to the nose and chin, smooth it down. I plump the lips, tweak the ears. Is it her yet? When will I know to stop?

"Still no closer to an identification of the tramp?" David asks, referring to the clay bust on the high shelf, which he stands inspecting. As a question it's almost ridiculous. Successes in this line of work are few and far between; across the entire industry, half of all reconstructions go unrecognised. Of course, that just means any eventual identification provides that much more of a reward. It's often as if the only race you ever win is at the Olympics; in between, you finish nowhere.

The homeless man in question was found five years ago, sheltering (somewhat unsuccessfully) in the boat sheds on the seafront. He was a mess: torn clothes, wicker hair and a face of leather, part of which had slipped from the skull like a melted waxwork. From the very first moment I felt fascinated. Like Marina, his teeth were in remarkably good condition; as if he'd only fallen on hard times relatively recently. Unlike Marina there *was* dental work, with three fillings, but thus far it's proven to be of no help: you need some kind of solid lead in order to find records with which to make a comparison. No older than forty, and possibly a bit younger, hypothermia had stolen him away one winter's night, several weeks before his discovery. The cold weather slowed the rate of decomposition. Like an unannounced character arriving in the middle of a novel, only to then disappear, he possesses no known back-story and no future plot-line. The same is true of Marina.

"How can no-one miss this girl?" David says, angling his head at the bust on my table. "I can't be the only person who really cares, can I, Patrick? Not that I'm saying that you don't. But you know what I mean."

"She's so beautiful," he adds, having finally moved in closer to inspect her. Despite not being quite finished, an essence is finally present. I feel a slight chill – a sprig of hair springing up on the back of my neck – as I try to view her as if for the first time. It's almost there.

"This is her," he says, forcefully. "I just know it. Seriously. This is finally how she looked. Jesus, Patrick, *this is how she looked!*"

TWENTY

It shouldn't be *this* funny. It helps that we are more than a little drunk and slightly stoned; after all, playing with the carcasses of dead birds is not your average Saturday night activity.

We find ourselves competing in a game that, as far as I can imagine, has never been played anywhere else in the world. It begins with one of many desiccated pigeon carcasses found in the giant hall, which Black shuffles out onto the balcony with a plank of wood like a hockey player easing the puck across the ice. She then draws back the wood and whacks the bird out to sea. Silliness, passing the time, but before long it has evolved into a competition, for which rules are hastily devised.

We choose only the dry, crisp carcasses – not wanting to touch, even with an arm's length of wood, the recently expired ones, still plump with foetid meat and littered with maggots and god-knows what else. And anyway, the flatter ones are more aerodynamic. We line up side-by-side, adopting golfing stances. On her call we swing and send our dead birds as far out to sea as possible. I win the first round, but only by default; neither of us makes a clean contact, but at least mine goes in the right direction. Having seen her first effort plummet into the roof of the wooden hut and break up on impact, her second soars almost gracefully – albeit with the simple linear trajectory of a frisbee, sailing way beyond my faltering bird, far out towards the offing, and even managing to skim across the surface to gain extra yardage. We find it strangely hysterical.

My next effort proves my best yet, flying with a satisfying sureness of purpose; an easy victory. "Luck, pure luck," she claims, nudging another pigeon into position. Once mine is in place she attempts to sabotage my swing, but I spot the interference and playfully push her away. She nudges me back, before we settle into our stances. On our next attempts my bird seems the favourite until it arcs back around and crashes into the pier.

"That one's a homing pigeon," I say, and feel the reward of a belly laugh booming out beside me. Before long she is doubled-up on the floor, and I too feel the elastic-snap of stomach cramps. I collapse beside her, and it signals the end of the game.

In every sense I feel like a winner.

Having lost count of the cans of beer I've consumed, in addition to that one joint, I cannot claim that my faculties are unimpaired. But this night has felt like no other. It's nearly three a.m. and although Black, now lying down, is visibly wilting, I still feel fairly alert. Her head rests upon my jacket, which is stretched across my thighs, just above my knees. She speaks with her eyes closed. Every time I think she has fallen asleep she proves me wrong. From telling me little at the start of the evening she has progressed to baring her soul, while in return, I start to feel philosophical.

"What were you like as a child?" I ask, contemplating

whether or not to stroke her hair. I decide against it, for now, and listen to her talk.

"A bit overweight. Very shy, and awkward… Very sensitive. The plight of other people really upset me. I think I had an excess of empathy. There was a disabled girl at school – she could walk, but with crutches – who the others used to tease, and I just wanted to hug her. I also used to go and put flowers on the grave of a girl who was a similar age to me, who was also a Suzanne. It was a really old grave. Those around it were well kept, and still had visitors. She was forgotten." She pauses, sighs. "I really don't know what happened to that little girl."

"How she died?"

"No – I mean *me*. I don't know what happened to the person I was, where she went."

"It's so weird how we change," I say, laying my body back, so that I am now fully reclined on the balcony, staring up at the night sky. "As a kid I used to know the order of all the planets, from the sun to the edge of the solar system. Now I just know us and Mars. I've forgotten the order of the others."

She mumbles something, showing just enough interest for me to continue.

"My life is so insular, so *Earthly* these days. I used to notice the stars, when I was young. Now, if I happen to see them at night, it's like, shit, when did the stars get turned back on? And the planets – I guess they're there, amongst the specks of light. But when do you ever get the chance to think about stuff like that? The future, the Space Race, men on the moon – it's all the past. It's like the Big Bang. The universe has been constantly expanding ever since – until the point when it will stop expanding and start contracting. It just seems as if our appreciation, our outlook on the universe, is already drawing in."

"I can't get my head around how insignificant we are," she says, in a gentle, pleasant drone. "We're nothing."

I look across at the Palace Pier, now silent and dark. "I spent so much of my childhood on that pier, in the arcade. I'd go there with a few two-p pieces – maybe even ten-p pieces too, if I was lucky. I'd put them in those coin-drop machines, where you watch them slide down the chute, and onto a ledge, and a buffer comes forward and pushes them down onto the lower level – kinda like a coin waterfall, I guess. You know the ones I mean?"

"Uh-huh," she murmurs.

"The coin would fall just right onto the lower level, yet when the final pusher came forward and forced my coin into the others it failed to tip this huge cluster over the edge – what seemed like a small fortune just hung there, suspended. Yet the thrill if some *did* fall was huge. I might spend as much as a pound, just to hear the sound of falling coins. I'd get back maybe fifty pence, yet leave feeling like a winner.

She nods, and I continue. "I remember when they got their first Space Invaders machine. I'd go and stand nearby to watch over the shoulders of older kids as they played . They were like these Zen masters or something; at one with the machine, their fingers a blur of movement. I'd only dare have a go myself when no one else was around to watch. I wasn't very good. Most of the time I just lurked, lost in a semi-circle of silent onlookers. I think I spent hours at a time, just watching these tiny little sprites go from side to side."

"I liked Pac-Man," she says, then laughs, softly.

I laugh too, mirroring hers in tone and duration, although in truth I never really cared for that game. I find myself staring out at the tiny lights of a tanker on the horizon, a leviathan passing in the night. "There was this one time – I must have been about twelve – when I went on the waltzer at the end of the pier. I don't know why, as I *hate* fairground rides, always have. As it gained speed this attendant guy started spinning my carriage. It was horrible, and I was screaming for him to stop, but he just kept on spinning, spinning, spinning, and I'd catch sight of his face with each rotation, and see him laughing at me – laughing harder the more upset I got. I left the ride in tears. I was at that age where I was trying to learn not to cry but hadn't quite mastered it, and it kinda just blurted out. He found it hysterical. I got off and puked over the side of the pier. The *bastard*."

I look at Black, laid across my thighs, as she mutters something indiscernible in reply. And then, for a moment, she falls silent. She brings her hand to her mouth, to stifle a yawn. Slightly chapped and cracking, she holds a finger up to those dry lips, tracing a line across the skin. As she parts them a tiny bubble of saliva expands and explodes.

She is perfect.

And that perfection is a double-edged sword. It pulls me in, and then says *Who the fuck do you think you're kidding?*

But this is the story of my life. Like a heat-seeking missile I am drawn, with unerring precision, to the explosive outcome.

You do not casually walk away from a woman like Black, be it of your own volition, or at her – or police – insistence. Even now, just hours into our acquaintance, I fully understand that. Men possessed of greater virtues, better looks, superior intelligence and more unshakeable self-belief could not get out intact. There is something almost hypnotic: the light that universally draws the moths, time and time again, no matter how durable the species; the mistake they *always* make, no matter how they evolve.

Everything in my life, be it advertising, television, music, books or the movies, has told me that a woman like Black represents happiness, excitement, fulfilment, completion. Winning her affection – having her say she feels the same way about me – could be the prize that finally confirms my true worth; the elusive, all-pervasive thumbs-up that nothing can overrule, not even my propensity for self-doubt. Being with a woman this alluring, this breathtaking, will plug the pockmarks of my self-esteem. It will elevate me to some new dizzying height. Dazed and in a constant trance of ecstasy, I will thank my lucky stars every morning upon waking beside her. She, and she alone, can solve my problems. She is my happily ever after.

That is, until I run an alternative, non-Hollywood scenario through my mind, playing the advocate of my own devil. What if it is too crippling, too paranoia-inducing, to be with a woman whom others – Adonises, alpha males, millionaires – will not be slow to pursue? Even if Black declared her love for me, could I ever allow myself to *believe* her? Even my fantasy is not permitted the chance to run smoothly. I'm already scared of losing her, before I have even come remotely close to winning her.

I know all of this – and yet I cannot correct myself. Maybe I am less heat-seeking missile and more Kamikaze pilot, experiencing moments of consciousness as the plane throttles towards its target, the outcome avertable by one movement of the joystick but my mind unwilling to force that evasive action.

Black can validate me; and in a weird way, *only* Black. Now that I have met her, I have set in stone the mandate that excludes all others. Maybe she is the most elusive and unobtainable woman I've ever had the fortune – or misfortune – to meet, and spend genuine, intimate time with. You never get to meet the film star, the pop icon, so she remains unreal; but if you had the chance to spend several hours alone with her you'd conceivably stand *some* kind of chance. You'd exist on her radar.

I exist on Black's radar.

TWENTY-ONE

Cluttered, chaotic, but full of welcoming light during the morning hours, Genevieve's room lured me over the threshold. I knew I shouldn't be there, but when left alone at the cottage I felt unable to resist trespassing. The sweet minty aroma of patchouli only added a further pull. Only here for the summer, she had brought, and accumulated, so much stuff. I wanted to know her; who'd she'd become but she wasn't telling.

Her *room* would.

I'd always enjoyed art, and earned good marks at school, but Genevieve was the first person I'd met with an inspiring talent. For a while it was all she cared about, and, somewhat inaccurately, the only thing she felt any good at. Having turned 16, she began considering abandoning her education for her new passion: music. Neither Kitty nor Alice were aware, but I'd overheard her talking on the phone about how she wanted to be in a band. The new wave of art-school groups popping up at the time were an influence, although she was still too young for college, and no longer saw the need to follow that route. I could already see that she wouldn't look out of place in a band like The Human League; she had the look, the attitude, and that seemed to be what counted.

The walls to her room were lined with a dozen posters,

including reproductions of artworks that were far darker and harder to grasp than the likes of Magritte and Dali (who were about as obtuse as anything I'd hitherto studied). One print – of a painting by Francis Bacon, whose work I'd never previously encountered – hung above her bed. Entitled '*Triptych May-June, 1973*', its three separate panels depict a seated man in some kind of small dark cubicle, his face and body seriously distorted, as a sinister black shadow bleeds across the central canvas. Genevieve must understand stuff like this, I concluded. It just left me uneasy and unnerved. It made her all the more untouchable.

I walked carefully, on tiptoes, over the littered carpet. Fanning out across the floor by the record player in the corner were a collection of long play records, with *Songs of Leonard Cohen* at the top of the pile, its vinyl snug on the turntable; another artist whose work felt beyond me. So dark, so foreboding, although from my room, with her door closed, I could never clearly hear the words; just menacing melodies and a bruisingly deep voice that caused the cheap speakers to rattle and the floorboards vibrate.

Having imbibed such weighty works, it perhaps came as no surprise that Genevieve had clear artistic talent; learning from the best. I'd rifle through her scrap books and cartridge pads, poring over expressive illustrations and doodles, etchings and sketches. She had a lightness of touch and a freedom with her strokes that left me both inspired and dejected; admiring the art, but with my own talent put firmly in the shade. However, it infuriated me – the sheer waste – that she had no great desire to do anything with it. In her future she saw only the supposed freedom of life in a band. She lived in the clouds.

I continued to root around. On her bedside table I found a book about old black-and-white films, the kind in which I saw no appeal. It didn't seem to fit with the rest of her taste, although it did go against the grain of contemporary mainstream culture. My obsession with Indiana Jones, and the *Star Wars* movies, with their vivid colour and bombastic action, contrasted starkly with *Casablanca, It's a Wonderful Life, Brief Encounter* and Hitchcock's classics.

Her underwear, some of which lay loose on the dresser top, was almost exclusively black. That in itself seemed incredible – it had never occurred to me that such items could be anything other than white, or the off-grey and beige of Kitty's strapping undergarments pegged like lifeless torture victims on the washing line. I opened the top drawer, to find more lingerie. I couldn't help but take a set, even though I had no idea what to do with it. They had not only touched Genevieve's flesh, they had done so in the most intimate of places. It felt as close as I could realistically get.

I had gained access to her inner sanctum. But her possessions, and the obfuscated meanings behind them, left it feeling more like an exclusion. A short corridor, but a world away. How could I ever understand this girl? How could I ever be *suitable?*

* * *

A sultry Saturday night of freedom: Kitty away in London ahead of the royal wedding, staying with Alice in a hotel for the week, the pair planning to line the Mall as Charles and Diana passed by. Genevieve, charged with looking after me, did not show the slightest bit of interest in the task. Of course, I didn't exactly need babysitting, and cared even less for the embarrassing notion that she might believe I required it. At nine p.m. I told her I planned to head to the cinema with school friends, to see a showing of *Raiders of the Lost Ark* that wouldn't finish until almost midnight. I'd already seen the film twice. I said goodbye to Genevieve – interrupting her hair-drying, from which she barely batted an eyelid – and made my way to the Cinescene on North Street. I met with Tony and Steve in the foyer, but once the film started I began to feel tired and feverish, and before long, a little nauseous. I just wanted to get home and lie down. I whispered my excuses, and snuck out.

The last throes of twilight faded as I walked home from the bus stop; yet the night remained blissfully warm. None of the cottage lights were on when I got back. I let myself in, and walked upstairs in the dark, to my room at the back of the house. I shut the door behind me, collapsed onto the bed. I'm not sure if I'd actually fallen asleep, or just hovered on the edge, but my ears pricked at sounds outside.

A boy – no, I'd say a *man* (in the way that, contrary to now, boys in their late teens seemed like fully-formed adults) – stood upright in the lake, at a depth just above his waist. Standing on the bank: Genevieve, dressed only in skimpy black underwear. My heart began to pound, my mouth filling with saliva; aroused to instant alertness, as if inhaling smelling salts. Her skin lit by an irradiant moon, I couldn't avert my gaze.

The man began to splash water in her direction, and Genevieve began to shriek and yelp as she took evasive action. She displayed a certain lack of grace in the way she ran in panic, accentuated by her near-nakedness; I was used to seeing her fully composed and in control. She seemed a different person to the one I knew; having fun, and, for once, clearly not the boss of the situation.

The man – she shrieked the name *Darren!* – then crawled out of the lake and began to chase her around the perimeter; she slipped, squealed, and he dragged her toward the water, with an alligator's predatory ease and efficiency. Her yelps grew more frequent, like a child being tickled, and when her body hit the water she yelled at the top of her lungs, before both sank below the surface. They emerged in each other's arms, her legs wrapped around his waist. She was facing the house, but unaware of my presence. In one quick movement with his right hand Darren unhooked her bra – to me, a kind of magic trick – and she was totally naked. She began to ride up and down, and I felt this incredible excitement matched by a sense of disgust and anger – betrayal, even – and my nausea returned. Dizzy, I turned away from the window and vomited into my hands, holding them close to my mouth so that the sound didn't give me away. I made for the bathroom to wash away the sick.

As much as part of me wanted to, I couldn't bring myself to look outside again; I just lay on my bed, hearing the splashes and moans, even with the sheets pulled tightly over my head. Tears filled my eyes as I willed my mind to switch off, to bring silence, and the blessed relief of sleep.

TWENTY-TWO

There is one other important woman in the story of my life, the link between Genevieve and Black in a chain of fascination.

A glorious summer Saturday in 1985, in the right place at the right time. She fell, and then I fell. We were strangers, sat next to one another on the curved concrete balustrade of a Trafalgar Square fountain, seared by the sun; each unaware of the other, and the fact that we were about to become acquainted. It all hinged on one small gesture. Without thinking I casually threw my crust to the pigeons. They reacted with such fast, fluid belligerence; their movements as a mass apparently so chaotic, yet they never once collided. They did, however, dart and swirl about the girl beside me, and in panic she leant back and that was how she fell.

My fall was less literal, but it began with hers.

I jumped up, swivelled round and leant over to help her out, as Japanese tourists viewed the impromptu street theatre. As I eased her up – she took my hand with no hesitation – my eyes were inescapably drawn to her delicate white underwear, which popped vividly against the lightly tanned skin beneath a clinging cream dress. I'd seen prettier girls, but she had a certain *something*. Quickly I pulled from my bag a cotton tracksuit top, handed it to her. Once she'd wiped her eyes she realised her dress was no longer particularly concealing, and quickly wrapped the top around her midriff. And then, with a clear French accent, she thanked me, warmly.

"I hope you don't think I just tried to drown you?" I said, trying to sound nonchalant; pleased that the words came out as the right sounds, in the right order.

"Of course not!" she said, with the broadest smile. "Unless you are owning the birds?"

"The swans belong to the Queen. I own the pigeons."

"I'm Isabelle," she said, laughing, offering a straight arm.

"Patrick," I replied, brimming with excitement as I shook her hand; careful to attain the right level of pressure for feminine fingers. I'd just turned 18, and this was the first time I'd introduced myself to an alluring stranger; doing so in the heart of London, to a French woman, felt so grown up. She was 20, and perhaps more accustomed to such behaviour; I was, by contrast, a mere novice. She was the first *woman* I fell for, and in a way it reminded me of the awe I felt for Genevieve.

We sat on the plinth in the shadow of a black lion and talked, then went for a stroll, stopping at a couple of pubs with outside seating. In the evening she invited me back to her half-deserted halls of residence in Battersea, and we barely left her bed for the next three days. It was established right at the start that I was due to attend art college in Glasgow in just six weeks, and she was a few weeks away from returning to France, with her year in London almost up. There was a strict time limit, and we both knew the tryst could not last beyond August. That gave it an added frisson; we both wanted each other, but equally, we were keen to get on with our lives in other areas.

For once, I didn't even dream of more. I lived in the moment, and enjoyed every precious minute of it.

TWENTY-THREE

I can't recall the last time I sat and quietly watched the sun rise. Indeed, have I *ever* actually done so? Experiencing it from the vantage point of this pier makes it all the more vibrant. It's such a primal part of human existence, but our awe of that burning giant – bringing light on its journey across the heavens – is no more; we simply don't deify what we feel we understand. A phosphorescent halo at the horizon forewarns of its impending arrival: an envoy running ahead to herald the new day. Before long the sun itself is inching over the horizon. And as the world before my eyes is painted in luminescent oranges and blues – and with Black dozing softly against my shoulder – to have never previously experienced this seems like a kind of gross negligence. The moment feels truly transcendental, almost spiritual. This is my mystical morning. This is my new life.

I've tried my damnedest to stay awake, to not miss a moment of this night as it turns into day. Black had earlier promised to do the same, only to succumb to light sleep on a couple of occasions. Awake again, and upon seeing what I see, she angles her body to a more upright position, to take it all in. But she does not pull away from me. Against the odds, the most beautiful woman I have ever met is still huddled up to my side, gripping my upper arm for support, as my jacket shrouds our shoulders. But with this bliss comes the daylight that will make our exit inevitable. It is the most perfect moment of my life, but no sooner am I aware of this fact than I realise that its end is imminent.

Spinning blue lights flicker in the distance on the shoreline, bright cyan stark against the morning haze. The lack of a siren lends an eerie quality to the scene; another visual distraction disconnected from our island existence. What appear to be an ambulance and two police cars speed into view, then disappear behind a row of houses. We look more closely, trying to work out the exact location. It's impossible to tell for sure, but the lights are reflecting on properties close to Jacob's studio. His unreliability is legendary, but suddenly we're considering an alternative explanation for his absence.

"You don't think…?" she asks.

I *do* think. At least I *think* I think. I keep the moment on hold, choosing not to say anything as I try to convince myself otherwise. In truth, my mind is a jumble. I'm obviously concerned about my friend – if something has indeed happened to him – but also about how such a turn of events would affect my relationship with Black. A connection could be broken. Then again, perhaps a tragedy would unite us?

"Look – they've gone," she says, cheerily. "False alarm."

However, it's not long before she says it's light enough to safely leap into the sea, and what reason can I possibly offer to have her stay *here* instead?

* * *

I believe it to be my earliest memory – but it can be hard to put a definite chronology to such distant, fractured recollections. Perhaps I have sensory impressions that predate it, but no actual events spring to mind.

It belongs to the cottage, at a time when I lived in Croydon with my mother. Our own house appeared so suburban, so urban-planned. By contrast, Kitty's property sprawled, almost unconfined, across the landscape. And the lake – well, that fascinated me. A great big expanse of water – *in the back garden*. Another world.

Early afternoon, high summer: it must have been Kitty's 50th birthday, because I remember bunting, colour and cake. I guess I was three or four years old. The kitchen heaved with the presence of strangers. I kept wandering outside, to find some space and freedom. All of this would perhaps have been lost like a million other nascent memories, had it not proven such a uniquely strange day. Unlike my father, my mother wasn't an alcoholic, but she did drink to excess in social settings. If running outside offered my escape from a large group of people, then drink provided hers. And on this occasion she had passed all sensible limits. She'd already got into an argument with someone, and I saw her ushered out into the front garden, to be calmed down.

My desire to explore took me out the back, to the edge of the lake. I could see tadpoles just beneath the surface of the water, and poked at them with a twig. And then, from nowhere, a sense of overwhelming panic as I found myself submerged; I don't recall the slip at the water's edge, just the moment when I understood that trouble *had me*. I have no idea how long it lasted, but even now, in my mind's eye, time remains slowed. As I flailed, I felt a clutch of fingers grab my shirt and haul me out.

To my great shame I can't recall the name or the appearance of the man. Perhaps I was told at the time, but his identity faded long before I realised just how important it was to remember. It certainly wasn't someone I knew – and yet I literally owe him my life. Another minute, maybe less with such tiny lungs, and I'd have drowned. He'd seen me from the kitchen window, and raced to my rescue. Sodden, I made straight for my mother, whose reaction, as she came running around the side of the cottage, was one of total hysteria; stumbling, crying, mumbling. The growing crowd of people parted for us to embrace, but once in her arms she violently shook me. She screamed, I shrieked; both of us increasing in volume as she had to be pulled away.

Weeks passed before I saw her again. I was shipped off to my father's. As it had in the lake, time slowed; it seemed an eternity, and I carried the guilt of being bad, the guilt of having forced her away. My fault; always my fault.

* * *

The hush of the wash, as waves broke gently beneath the pier, had been the only accompaniment in the final hours of darkness. Every so often a more voluminous wave would crash with a surprising crescendo of noise. Mostly, though, it soothed: the calm, rhythmic sounds of sea meeting shore.

But now, as we stand side by side and stare down thirty feet into the water, it doesn't seem quite so benevolent. The beach is deserted, apart from a woman walking a collie in one direction, and a jogger vanishing towards the horizon in the other. I cannot let Black see my fear. Fortunately the water is not dangerously deep, but that provides a different problem: I've no idea how sufficiently it will break our fall.

"What do you reckon?" I offer.

"Looks okay to me," she says, bright and bubbly. She stands near the edge, clutching her waterproofed camera.

She goes first: plummeting into the water, swallowed whole by a breaking wave, and in an instant coughed out several metres closer to shore. Visible for a second, then gone; just a collision on the surface of lambent ripples and spume. An arm, a foot. A patch of clothing. Another wave, and lost again. Then, even closer to shore, she is upright, dancing, kicking her feet through the shallow water. It provokes in me a slight sense of panic: that familiar fear of abandonment. She is safely down, and I am still nervous atop this rickety platform: a high-board diver who cannot swim. I remain stationary, recalling the shallow depth of the lake all those years ago, and my utter helplessness in it. I feel Black's eyes on me, sense the time I'm taking. My mouth is dry, my stomach churning.

But fear begets bravery. I launch: a split second of flight, then total immersion. I feel myself dragged under – unable to gain control – but soon I am floating on an inbound wave, shoved into shallower water, and through ears filled with brine

I hear Black's whoops of delight as I crash safely ashore.

At several stages over the past nine-or-so hours I've thought *the current moment* to be the pinnacle, when it comes to feeling alive. But *this* – this will take some beating, as the sound of her cheers and the beat of my heart resonate in bubbling eardrums, and as, through stinging eyes, I take in the final stages of sunrise. Every fibre of my being is atingle. My legs are shaking, but I feel an exhilaration that circuits every inch of my skin.

I take her outstretched hand, and she leads me from the sea.

TWENTY-FOUR

This is how she looked! However, David's words don't equate to an identification. The woman's appearance finally feels right – I share his optimism on that – but decades after she died, will anyone recognise her? All those hours spent alone in her company, mostly at night, staring deep and hard; all the time aware that this is *someone*. Rather than simply see her case resolved, I want to *know* her, in life. Of course, professional pride and ego mean that I want identification to be swift, and for people to get goosebumps upon witnessing the likeness; to commend me on my amazing work, my unique talent. For the sake of everyone concerned I want a solution, so that a killer comes to justice and that good men – particularly David – can remove a weight from their shoulders.

But above all else, I want a story to go with the face. I

feel a kind of love for Marina, one based on proximity and imagination. Maybe it's almost Frankensteinian, in that I want to bring her back to life. Ludicrous, I know, but on some level I want to experience her *as she was*. Maybe some old ciné film would suffice: enough to sense her movements, as well as her likeness. But on a deeper level I crave more. It's the story of my life: desiring the impossible woman. And none – not even Black – could ever be more impossible than Marina.

* * *

She first came to me, Marina, wrapped tightly in manilla, one memorable morning at the end of 2002.

The day began with the phone sounding, shrill and insistent, as I lay submerged in a deep winter's sleep. For a foggy-headed second, with the quilt drawn over my ears, I did not recognise its signature bleeps, the staccato notes entering into my dream as a dance track on a distant radio. Eventually I fumbled and located the handset, as Laura, with ears plugged, slept on.

"Have you heard the news?" David asked breathlessly. "Get yourself down to the pier", he said, his words swift and tremulous. "As quick as you can, Patrick. Hurry, lad." I could tell he was already there: the familiar rush of the dispersing tide, the wind howling into the mouthpiece, the echo of a gull. His signal failed before I had time to argue.

Half a mile from the West Pier, David's news became all too apparent. Despite the fine rain and sea-spray blustering about me on the promenade, the landmark on the horizon looked clearly altered as it moved into view. My heart sank: the structure – a symbol of unfathomable endurance – had suffered a near-fatal prolapse. The central section had dropped away, the walkway declining at a 45° angle in both directions to form a 'V', its base lost in the shallows. Rows of supports beneath the Concert Hall had bowed and snapped, causing the southern half of the building to teeter just above the waterline; an optical illusion suggesting it was sliding slowly into the sea. The pavilion, at the pier head, now stood even more isolated. The country's most exposed Grade One listed building, earmarked for special concern – nil by mouth, priest on standby – simply crumbled; dismantling itself, washing away its central section – its heart? its soul? – in the manner it had for so long threatened, as waves and wind lashed and ripped. Enormous planks of wood turned into juddering gliders that could hold their poise in the gale for no more than a split second before crashing into whipped-up waves. Smaller timbers splintered and dove into the water, bobbing haphazardly to shore. Tubular iron struts snapped and submerged in violent descents, lost from view until they washed up on the shingle.

I couldn't yet pick out David amongst a hundred-or-more onlookers, in front of what could have been a stricken whale in shallow water; the crowd unsure of how best to intervene, before concluding that nothing could be done. Manpower stood no chance against such weighty catastrophe.

All the while, a crime scene – and a love scene – washed itself away.

Hours later, David and I sat nursing drinks in a gloriously warm pub overlooking the sea, as the storm raged on. "Have a look at this," he said, removing a manilla folder from his holdall.

"What is it?"

"An old case," he said, placing the folder on the table, and giving it a tender pat. "Go on, look."

"What's it about?"

"Marina. The girl found on the old pier."

I placed my hand on the folder, and kept it there.

"What's the problem?" he asked.

"Nothing, no… no problem," I said as I finally lifted the thick file. Crime scene photographs – large, and rich with colour and clarity – spilled out over the table, along with notes, drawings and typed statements.

"What am I looking for?" I asked, moving my pint glass to make more room.

"Something."

"Can you be more specific?"

"No. Because I don't know myself."

I looked at the images, perused the notes.

"Anything jump out at you?" he asked, wiping a thick white cloud of Guinness from his stubble with the back of his hand.

"Just that it's the pier. And that the remains are skeletal. I'm not sure what you want me to say?"

"Take a look at this," he said, pulling a sheet of cartridge paper from the bottom of the file.

"It's good," I noted, as he held up a sketch of a young woman. "But obviously I don't know how true to life it is, just from looking at it like this."

"Thought not. Ah well."

"But it looks like it was drawn by a competent artist. I've seen worse."

"You think? I want to reopen the case, but I've been told it must wait. Too many others on the go already. One day I'll get onto it, if they let me. One day, before I retire."

"You've got a while left yet, haven't you?"

"Maybe," he mumbled, behind his pint glass, before falling silent.

The photographs also provided evidence of my own dramatic

encounter with the pier. Both Black and I had of course alighted safely – ours was not a crime scene – but something monumental had taken place that night, too. And while the elements had wreaked further havoc in the decades between the capture of these images and our time aboard, it remained recognisably *ours*.

Over the following years, in pubs across Brighton and in visits to my house, David provided snippets of the investigation, until I gained the full picture. The body had been located inside the south-western kiosk, against which I had been photographed all those years later; her bones discovered beneath piles of detritus. Although the debris supplied a degree of protection from the weather and the sea, it proved no place for the preservation of evidence. An entomologist had shown that, due to specific insect activity, she had died the previous summer, which at least provided something to go on. Nesting pigeons had defecated and died all over the scene, and the discovery occurred a long time before the ultra-fine forensic detection now commonplace.

At the time of the pier's violent collapse, Marina's skull remained stored as evidence, not even afforded the dignity of an unmarked grave. For years, despite bringing the case to my attention and poring over it on numerous occasions, David never asked for a fresh attempt at capturing the girl's likeness. That finally came earlier this year, as he sought out one last desperate attempt at jogging a memory.

And now that I have finished that work – now that Marina is complete – he wants to box her up and take her away, so that she can be filmed and photographed by the media. He wants to show the world.

But after all this time together, I suddenly don't want to let her go.

TWENTY-FIVE

The time I'd been craving: alone, in Genevieve's company. Of course, she needed a favour; nothing with her ever came without a catch – something I'd become acutely aware of as the summer unfolded.

The previous night she'd lost a silver heart-shaped earring gifted by Darren, and wanted me to accompany her back to the scene: a secluded area beyond some woodland, to which he had recently introduced her; and as such, I guessed how the jewellery went missing. An hour or so before dusk, she had me follow her.

As we walked, the surroundings became increasingly rural. The pavement wore away into nothing more than an unkempt gravel path, which itself faded into a dirt track beaten out by feet and bike tyres, sandwiched between wild grass, leading us down to a shady wood. The chimes of an ice cream van, pulling away on a country lane beyond the trees, carried on windless air; the signature tune of an off-key *Three Blind Mice* diminishing with every corner turned.

We cut through an area densely populated with trees. The sun pierced the tangle of branches in thin straight beams, casting a spotlight on swarms of gnats, bobbing and weaving like crazed atoms, and the expansive spider webs crafted between oaks and ash. "Not far now," she said, as I rubbed at my itching eyes. "Just a little bit beyond this churchyard. But first, follow me. There's something I want to show you."

Blackcurrant bushes, left to reach out unfettered, grew wildly over the path to a graveyard. She led me through the lines of granite and marble, over to one shabby grave, where she stopped and knelt.

"Who's this?" I asked, before even thinking to look at the inscription. For some reason I just defaulted to Genevieve, almost becoming dumb in her presence. She knew stuff, and I didn't.

"Doris Florence Lindley," she said, as if the name should mean something. "She's just ten years old," she added, the present tense used in a matter-of-fact way. "She died on the Lusitania."

"The Lusitania? What's that?"

"A ship that sunk in 1915. I've visited her a few times this summer. But no one else does. Not any more. It breaks my heart." She wiped gravel and moss from the tombstone, and I got to see a side of her I'd not previously encountered; at least not since she'd been reborn as a self-possessed, aloof creature.

"It makes you wonder," she said, sitting down beside Doris' plot, as I remained standing.

"What?"

"If anyone will visit *our* graves. I think we just assume that people will. But they won't, not always. There comes a time when it stops. Has to. We all get forgotten."

I didn't know what to say; transported beyond my comfort zone. I thought I knew what she meant, but felt unable to articulate it for fear of sounding stupid. Cross-legged, chewing on a blade of long grass, Genevieve's eyes swelled, red and moist. Perhaps I'd been invited back into her world, after a couple of years' absence, but I didn't feel assured enough to relax. Finally I sat down, doing my best to look at ease.

"Come on," she said, "let's go."

The old Victorian arch of a disused railway line led through to a small, naturally enclosed meadow: the secluded area to which Darren had introduced her. Their beer cans from the night before lay to one side, along with a smattering of cigarette butts. "It's got to be here somewhere," she said, looking either side of a blanket-sized area of grass flattened the night before. I got down on my hands and knees beside her, and combed the ground. Eventually I located the earring. Her relief made me smile, although it merely helped her to appease her boyfriend. I wanted to be part of this world; I wanted to be Darren, older and able to attract Genevieve. Instead I was just a lackey who'd crawl through long grass on hands and knees.

She sat and lit a cigarette, pulled from a fresh pack. I sat close by, and this time she didn't pop straight up. Discarding the cellophane wrapper, she silently held the packet out to me, the lid tipped back; presenting me with my chance to be like Darren. She'd never seen me smoke – because, of course, I never had – but she didn't take that for granted. To take a drag without looking like a total novice was a trick I obviously couldn't conjure. I coughed and hacked as soon as the smoke connected with the top of my lungs, which sought to rapidly expel the foreign substance. Genevieve laughed, and my cheeks further reddened. "First timer?" she said, grinning as she stated the obvious. "Aw, bless you."

I choked, unable to reply.

Even with the ignominy of failing to smoke with even the mildest hint of success, let alone sophistication – not to mention several further examples of my naivety – the day still felt magical; perfect weather, and an adventure to new places, both geographically and emotionally. I seemed to relax a bit more as the hours passed, but never enough to let down my guard.

On the stroll home she took my hand in hers. Looking back, I'm sure she meant little by it; with hindsight, just a casual gesture, maybe even harking back to our childhood friendship. Despite her aloofness, she could be a very tactile person, and with no one else around, perhaps it had simply come my turn. But at the time I felt utterly *electrified*. I'd harboured fantasies about her all summer, but this one meeting of palm in palm felt better than anything I'd yet to imagine. Returning to my bedroom, my head span faster than a seaside waltzer.

* * *

It was just after five a.m. when Genevieve woke me, whispering my name over and over – so that it drifted into my dream – as she gave me a gentle prod on the shoulder. Dawn breaking, light eked in fragments through the gaps in my curtains. I could see her quite clearly, once my eyes adjusted.

I sat up, acutely aware of my nakedness beneath sheets which, in the heat, I had almost turned out of. As planned, she had left the cottage a week earlier – the middle of August – to return to Derbyshire, and I hadn't expected to see her again that year. With Kitty in hospital having recently undergone another hip replacement operation – she was due out the next morning – I had the house to myself.

"Patrick, I need your help," Genevieve said. "Do you know where Kitty keeps her money?"

"Eh?"

"Money. I need some, and Kitty must have a stash somewhere. It's kinda urgent."

"Are you in trouble?" I asked, awake but disoriented.

"No. Well… not as such. Obviously I *might* be, by tomorrow. But by then, y'know, I'm sure I won't care and it really won't matter."

"What do you need it for?"

"I can't really tell you right now – or rather, I shouldn't. But I'll tell you if you tell me where she keeps it."

"I don't know."

"You don't know if you'll help me?"

"No, I don't know where she keeps it. And I don't know if you taking it would be a good idea, even if I did."

"Stop being so fucking moral. It's *important*." She leaned in closer. "Will you help me to look? *Please?*"

"I just don't think it's a good idea. And I might get the blame."

And then she kissed me; out of the blue, like a violent attack. Her lips felt thick and warm against mine, her tongue sliding slowly and unobtrusively into my mouth. I instinctively closed my eyes, but it ended almost as quickly as it began; I barely had a chance to worry about what to do in return before she eased out of the clinch. It wasn't just the kiss that left me flustered, but the way she put her hand on the back of my neck, and drew me in. By the time she let go my mind had emptied. Her tongue, and those fingers – I could feel the painted nails stroking neck hair and impressing on skin – sent a spark through my frontal and temporal lobes to short-circuit my speech, and it rendered me this mute boy, disarmed and, momentarily at least, mentally incapacitated. I knew what had just taken place, in terms of the physical event, yet beyond that I felt dumbfounded. Too confused to smile, too baffled to be elated, my body betrayed its teenage reaction. I scrunched the sheet up around my waist, but it only served to draw her attention.

"I'll make it worth your while," she said, placing her hand on my thigh. She smiled, and at once I felt both weak and strong. My speech returned. "Let me get dressed," I said, looking towards the door, "and I'll see what I can do."

It's not something I ever saw myself agreeing to: being voluntarily struck around the head by a beautiful girl, to blacken my eyes and bruise my face, in an attempt to defraud a loved one. Paths open up in life, and down them we amble; and while we can later evolve and refine the kind of people we are, we cannot change the things we have done in previous stages of our existence. They stay with us, evoking pride if we feel them to be abiding achievements, or shame if we drift from the person of that moment in time. Of course, this incident inhabited some grey middle ground: not the decision of the person I *was*, but made under the influence of the person *I wanted to be with*. I knew it contradicted many of my better instincts, but went along with it all the same.

They were without doubt the most conflicting minutes of my life. Pain – not received through masochistic desires but from a concept of future pleasure. Unease – for the betrayal of the trust of an aunt who had been given little choice but to take care of me (which, in many ways, made it worse than had she been a voluntarily adoptive parent who gladly opted in to the whole situation). Pride – at my bravery and Genevieve's gratefulness. Humiliation – at the weakness I felt. Excitement, too. But in the pit of my stomach the adrenaline mixed uneasily with the gut-based skewer of shame. I could get into trouble on so many levels, and yet the rewards distorted my thinking.

The downstairs back room, overlooking the lake. Genevieve sat me in a wooden chair dragged from the kitchen, tying my hands behind its stiff back. We hadn't properly discussed how we'd approach the task; I assumed that I'd have some control over the damage caused to my own body, perhaps even administer it myself, but she forcefully took charge. I was to experience *real* suffering, as part of a faked robbery.

The pain of the first blow paled as successive strikes spiked nerves already smarting, the sting digging deeper and deeper each time. But after a while, certain areas seemed to numb – although I also found myself entering a zone of pain control through intense concentration. When agony permeated the mental barrier I tried to hold on to the notion of the reward, just minutes away. She had to stop soon. Failure to stick to her side of the bargain would leave her vulnerable to an exposé in retaliation; as much as I craved her, I wouldn't allow myself to be *completely* duped. And then it occurred to me that she could choose to leave me permanently silenced: comatose, brain dead, deceased. For the risks involved it would make little sense. Still, I was at her mercy. More blows rained down.

"Enough!" I finally implored, my head dizzy, my left eye closing. "Leave me conscious!" As I spoke, through lips cracked and swollen, I could taste the sharp iron tang of blood as it slipped onto my tongue and down my throat. She relented, stopping to smile broadly at me. I saw it as a kind of thanks, a sign of appreciation, but perhaps she was merely admiring her handiwork.

She undid my fly, and, as promised, my reward followed. My swift climax was like an injection of morphine, quickly followed by the stabs of guilt that, minutes later, slipped away with the heaviness of my eyelids.

It was hours later when I awoke, uncomfortable in the chair, my face throbbing as the sun arrowed into swollen, watery eyes. Genevieve had gone, and I had no choice but to wait overnight for Kitty's return. Even with the memory of the reward still fresh in my mind I questioned the wisdom of my actions, now that I was faced with spinning an elaborate web of lies. The second part of the bargain, in her absence, seemed disturbingly remote and abstract.

What the hell had I done?

* * *

Despite a lack of suitable application, within two years I'd completed my O-Levels, achieving acceptable grades. I knew the time had come to run – not walk – away from my childhood, including that deeply regretful day. I needed to reinvent myself, escape the shackles of everything people knew about me, and everything I thought I knew about myself. In keeping with the route taken by Genevieve in 1981, London seemed the obvious destination. I had some vague notion of running into her, but even in my naivety I knew the frightening scale of the capital, and therefore how unlikely such an encounter could prove. Dave, a friend from school, had recently moved with his family to Watford, and his parents allowed me to rent the unused granny flat at the end of their garden. I had a bank account in my name, into which Kitty had regularly deposited a relatively tidy sum of money. I also aimed to find part-time work as I set about joining my friend at his sixth-form college. Not due to leave until September – a further six weeks away – I simply couldn't wait. With Kitty out for the day I seized my opportunity. I couldn't face saying goodbye, and so wrote a short note to leave by the front door, thanking her for her help and support. I had it in my head that I would never return to the cottage; that it had to be final.

Even though my train was booked for midday I found myself awake and up at seven a.m.. An incredibly warm July morning, storms gathered in black swells. I packed everything I considered essential: a few clothes, my Walkman, some art supplies, and various little bits and pieces, until my rucksack could contain no more. Everything else I carried to the edge of the woodland, where, after a few failed attempts, I finally lit a bonfire. On it, with a kind of cathartic ceremony, went the rest of my clothes, various pictures I had drawn, tape cassettes and posters from my walls. I watched as, one by one, they blackened and curled.

Then I remembered something else from my childhood. It suddenly seemed *vital*, although recovery wouldn't be easy, some ten years after dispensing with it. I'd never previously needed it on my person because I never strayed too far from its resting place. I often circled around it, but now I couldn't leave it behind.

I stripped down to my pants and made my way to the lakeside. Reeds tickled my legs as I strode through them, brushing the green leaves and brown heads aside as I waded into the water. The memory of the St Christopher landing somewhere towards the middle remained vividly imprinted on my mind. Not huge by most standards, the lake still presented a challenge: shallow enough at its centre to just about stand in, but in order to scour its bed I had to fully immerse myself. With algae blanketing the surface and silt clouding the waters, I felt and fumbled in the murk; my mind drifting back to the day when, as a child, I felt so helpless in what, back then, seemed a much bigger body of water.

I swept my fingers back and forth over the sediment, then dug them under the top layer, for bursts of twenty or thirty seconds, before surfacing for an intake of air. I repeated this over and over, each time repositioning myself slightly. I recovered a golf ball, two old coins and a strip of rusty metal that looked like a door hinge. I threw them towards the far edge of the lake.

I persevered; not allowing myself to be beaten, even though, short of dredging the lake with professional equipment, I couldn't guarantee success. With each visit for air the sky darkened. Then, as I dove back down, the most incredible thunderstorm burst into full fury. The surface of the water popped and fizzed with hard darts of rain, and for a split second everything flashed bright. I bobbed along the bottom, able to achieve, for no more than a heartbeat, a hint of visibility. The storm hovered directly overhead, the thunder clapping in time with the strobes of light. On the third flash I saw a tiny glimmer in the mingle of mud and clay. The water now darker than ever, I moved closer, and, as I trailed my fingertips over the area, felt the cold surface of metal, and then the links of a chain.

I'd found it.

I stood up, warm rain teeming down. I shook the St Christopher, dislodging gloop and grime, and placed it over my head as if awarding myself a medal. For a moment I worried that lightning would be drawn to it, frying me in the water; and yet, in a strange way – and I'm not quite sure why – I'd have been okay with that. It would have been fate, right? As it transpired, the next crack zipped down a reasonable distance away. I stepped from the lake, dried off with a towel from the kitchen and got dressed; safe to travel, safe to leave.

TWENTY-SIX

Wet to the bone, we scrunch from shingle to shore. "So – do you want to join me in my hotel?" I ask Black. "Just to sleep, I mean. Nothing funny," I add, as we come to a stop on the delightfully smooth, flat pavement.

For a second or two, as she weighs up the offer, I see the look of someone set to reject: a partial, involuntary grimace. But then her face lightens, and there's a hint of a smile.

"Okay then," she says. "*Sleep* sounds good."

"Fantastic!" I reply, with a little too much gusto.

She takes from her pocket a key, holding it out as proof. "I've got to be back in Haywards Heath by mid-afternoon to let my friend in. She's been away – this is hers. I'm staying there for my final few days."

With this information in mind I now plan to spend the rest of the week on the south coast, in the hope that we can arrange a meeting or two before she leaves for the continent. I have to be close by.

Throughout the previous night, as we sat on rotten wood and coarse bitumen, rows of illuminated hotel rooms beckoned from the shoreline: places of comfort and warmth behind the red terracotta façade of the Metropole. I'd always wanted to stay there, only to find that, having finally rented a room, I would end up spending the night a few hundred yards away, trying to work out which unlit window I'd paid for. Despite the grime and decay, I wouldn't have swapped our unique, isolated location for anywhere in the world. However, back on dry land, the stately building appeals more than ever, with its soft bed and the chance to change out of wet clothes. But it will have to wait a bit longer.

"I think we need to go and see Jacob first," Black says, starting off in the direction of his studio. "See if he's all right."

We dry off a little on the quick stroll to the studio. There's no answer at the door.

"Probably hungover somewhere," I say.

"Probably *still drunk* somewhere," she says, turning to head back towards the seafront.

The bed, with its burgundy covers, presents itself to us with a physical allure; our bones and muscles aching for its sympathetic fibres. We take turns to use the toilet, and change into gowns from the closet. In our downy robes we creep under the covers, and lay on opposite sides of the bed, face to face. I don't want to break my promise, and I'm not about to test either her resolve or her attraction to me, and so turn to face the curtained windows, for fear of doing something that might destroy whatever it is that we have. I am well aware that this might be as good as it ever gets. But in the moment, as her breathing falls shallow and her exhalations pulse softly against the back of my neck, that is more than good enough.

TWENTY-SEVEN

"Oh my God, I'm so – look, get him a wet tea towel, a cold wet tea towel. And some butter. Jesus I'm sorry. Are you – *hurry, dammit* – are you okay? No, of course you're not okay, I just don't know why I—"

It's fair to say that my day is no longer going so swimmingly. A middle-aged waitress, bleached blonde hair and crooked five a.m. lipstick, stands beside me, panic stretched across her face as I rise to my feet, pain etched across mine. Coffee, spilt moments earlier, has become a burning glue, adhering itself to my hand.

"Butter?" the café manager asks.

"Yes, *butter*."

"What the hell for?"

"You put it on burns. Everyone knows that. Jesus."

"Why?"

"I haven't got a frigging clue. Because it helps. Just get me some butter!"

As with any minor event, it could have been so different. Minutes earlier, speaking with Black, I'd let my coffee go cold; too caught up in the moment to even take sips, as I tried to find ways to keep the conversation alive. Once she left, the waitress offered to microwave the untouched drink. My future changed when, upon her return, she slipped slightly, and the tray fell from her grasp as she reached for something to halt her fall. Liquid hotter than the solar core seared my skin in an instant.

"Will margarine do?" asks the manager, shouting from behind the counter.

"No, butter. We're not going to eat him. *Butter.*"

"What's the difference?"

"How the hell do I know? Just get the butter. The guy's hand is a mess."

"Calm down, Sally. He's not going to die. Bring him over here — stick his hand under the cold tap. I'll get you a clean dishcloth to put on it."

Little does this waitress know, as she hurriedly ushers me towards the sink – and please excuse the melodramatics – that she has just ruined my life.

The station café sat quiet when we arrived, just after lunchtime. Black led the way to a table in the corner, and as had become the norm, I quickly followed. Despite a couple of hours' sleep in the hotel, we perhaps felt even more tired than at dawn. Though not as alert as earlier, I still found adrenaline pumping. Simply being in Black's company had that effect, but her mood appeared less buoyant. Conversation grew more stilted, and while I understood her exhaustion, I couldn't help but take it personally.

Although fairly certain that we'd see each other again in the next day or two, I didn't want the moment to end. I'd managed to prolong the encounter on a couple of occasions, but I'd run out of options. The clock had beaten me: a muffled tannoy announcement caught Black's attention.

"That's my train," she said.

"I'll come and see you off," I offered, moving to a stand.

"Please don't. It's not necessary. Stay and have your drink. I need to hurry. I'll be quicker on my own."

She leant in to kiss my cheek, and so I offered it. But then – and I'm not totally sure how much of this is imagined – I think she actually moved her lips towards mine, and I instead turned out of what could have been the perfect end to the perfect day.

Even so, I could have no complaints. And I had the phone number of where she would be staying for the next few days written on my hand. Minutes earlier she had taken the waitress's biro, and with it scrawled her contact details. I was so thrilled with the act of her tenderly taking my palm and turning it over, followed by the tickle of the pen tip as it ran across my skin, that I never bothered to study the number.

"You need to get to a hospital," the waitress informs me, applying a cold wet cloth to the back of my hand. "I'll drive you. It was my fault. I'll drive you. I'm taking him to hospital, Elliot." The café manager offers a token resistance, but soon accepts she is right.

We take the short drive to the Royal Sussex County Hospital, about a mile away, in her beat-up orange Fiesta, arriving at an antiquated building whose entrance mirrors that of the train station, with a similar ornate glazed veranda. She rushes me inside after some highly unorthodox parking in an area adjacent to the morgue, and we take our seats in the waiting room. In sharp plastic chairs apparently designed for torture rather than treatment, we sit in awkward silence. Sally makes a few attempts at conversation, but I'm not in the mood. She soon gives up.

In the triage room the dishcloth is finally removed. The damage to my flesh is reasonably severe, but the damage to the ink is even greater. Black's phone number is gone. Maybe if the peeled skin is taken away, dried out, ironed, and pieced back together by the expert conservers who unravelled the Dead Sea Scrolls, then the numerals will emerge intact and in sequence. Instead, my red-raw, blistering hand is cleaned and dressed, and I leave the hospital with a middle-aged stranger, having lost a link to the woman who fit the profile of the love of my life.

I comfort myself with the thought that there's still Jacob; the chance that he knows how to contact Black at her friend's house.

As we step out into blinding sunshine, and wander down the ramp towards the rear of the building and the hurriedly-parked car, a gurney is wheeled from the back of an ambulance towards the morgue.

"Fucking junkies," groans a uniformed man to the porter who pulls open the broad doors, unaware that we are approaching. The white sheet slips a few inches as the trolley moves, and the face it reveals, though pale and distorted with the disguise of death, is unmistakably that of Jacob Dyer.

TWENTY-EIGHT

Jacob and I shared the detached existence of the only child. We felt the abstract presence of the missing sibling: never there in person, but always the awareness of what could have been: the brother or sister who might have stood beside us; the missing, who *never existed*. Also an orphan, his losses proved less dramatic – he was already a young adult when his parents died. But this was now it: the end of his family line, with no known members of an extended family. Although his sexuality made him unlikely to father a child, generations of Dyers ground to a halt with a needle in a toilet. Millennia of procreation, ceaseless struggles for survival and self-betterment, generation after generation, and it concluded like this.

His untimely death left me all the more eager to locate Black, not least because it made it all the harder. I needed to share in the momentousness of the news, and in the deepness of her grief. I also harboured a macabre sense of excitement, at the power of disclosure. If the messenger is sometimes shot, he is also on hand to provide comfort, and to get caught in the crossfire of stray emotions fizzing and firing like pheromones.

My first instinct, upon being dropped off by Sally at the Metropole, was to take a train to Haywards Heath. Walking towards the station I took a brief detour via Jacob's studio. Police tape cordoned off the building. I didn't hang around. I also hurried past the café upon reaching the station, eager to avoid Sally. But with the interminably slow Sunday timetable I spent thirty minutes waiting on the platform, and then ten more sat in a stationary carriage, trying to plan a strategy for when I got to a place I knew nothing about, to find a person whose specific whereabouts were a complete and utter mystery.

The train, once it finally left the station, seemed to inch along, with several unexplained stops. By contrast, my mind raced with all the ways I could break the news, playing out various – albeit largely similar – scenarios of how she would react. In each she played the grateful recipient who breaks down in sorrow, and who turns to me for support – emotional and physical – before, deep in despair, cancelling her trip to Europe. In that instant our lives are fused together: two splintered shards of bone, bound tight by plaster, to heal in unison.

The reality, however, was of a man wandering around a town like a vagrant, picking a direction as if blown by the wind, and finding nothing and no one he recognises. This man slept uneasily on a park bench, and resumed his search in the morning, walking until late afternoon. Defeated, he returned to his hotel in Brighton, to crash for 18 solid hours; awaking just a couple of days before *her* departure, from an unspecified terminal, to a far greater unknown and unsearchable landscape.

The days following Jacob's death involved a litany of moments that rank far from my finest. I wandered up and down the beach, back and forth on the shoreline paths and roads, hopeful of a reunion with Black. So chaotic: action for action's sake. Through the shopping centre and back again, around the Lanes, to the head of the Palace Pier, and then back once more, only this time via Old Steine and the train station, on the way to Jacob's studio. Perhaps there was one place to which I should have remained fixed, for the best part of a week – somewhere that, at some point, she surely had to pass. But instead I felt compelled to keep moving, because to stand still felt akin to doing nothing; taking the risk that I would always be in the wrong place at the wrong time, moving away as she moved near.

I had so little to go on. All I knew was that, having recently moved out of her student lodgings, she planned to kip on a friend's sofa in the days before her trip. College records were off bounds, despite my best efforts at persuading a clerical assistant to divulge information (which, I sensed, pushed her perilously close to calling security). I could find no record of Suzanne Black. A living ghost; alive, but invisible.

Jacob's funeral presented my last realistic hope, the one logical place I could expect to find her – but only if she'd heard the news. And as I waited and waited at the cemetery, scouring the crowd for that one face, it became evident that she hadn't. I had little doubt that she would have postponed her trip had she known. She must have already left for the continent.

Still, I could make enquiries. Awkwardly, I asked strangers, including Jacob's lover Jez, if they knew her, and while some did, none could tell me anything I didn't already know. And so I spent the funeral of a close friend sidetracked by selfish desires. I'd like to say that this proved to be the end of it all, but, alas, it did not – not for that day, and not from then on.

I attended the wake, but made my exit after just fifteen minutes. An idea struck me: with everyone Jacob knew swapping tales in the dank, smoky function room of a nearby pub, an opportunity arose. I saw no other way around it: I had to break into his studio. Inside, I prayed, would be that elusive link. Soon the property would be cleared and sold, the chance gone. I had no doubt: now or never.

The window to the downstairs toilet – where Jacob's body had been discovered – offered itself as the obvious entry point. Secluded from view, its pane of glass shattered quietly. With the last remaining shards knocked out, the gap was big enough to haul myself through. Once inside I stopped for a moment, at the spot where my friend spent his last living moments, to pay somewhat twisted respects. I wished I could honour him with more dignity, but it's not like he was sentimental. Unlike him, I had a life to be getting on with, and in that sense, he would have approved. "Live, man. Live!" he used to say, as he downed another drink.

The studio stood eerily silent, unnaturally still; my footsteps resonating with ripples of echo, nothing else making a sound. Perhaps I also imagined an additional silence – a deathly silence. After all, the space now held an eternal absence. Heart racing, I searched upstairs and down, rifling through personal artefacts: diaries, contact books, scraps of paper. I rummaged through things that took me to the heart of his existence: the art, that most personal means of expression; the clothing, on wire hangers, gradually unforming from the shape of the man;

the treasured knickknacks, with stories bound up in those transparent things. But all I could locate of Black, in both the working and living quarters, had been created by the artist's own hand. Images, not facts. She existed only as simulacrums in sketches and oils – patches of colour mixed and blended, scraped and stabbed, stippled and dabbed. She surrounded me, but never in more than two dimensions. From the front she lit up the room. Side-on she vanished.

Then I recalled the video camera, which documented both the modelling session and my belated arrival. It was unlikely to provide any evidence to aid in my search, but it was a unique record of such a remarkable encounter; one I knew I simply must possess. I hit eject, and the mechanism whirred before delivering the cassette. With it in hand I made my way back upstairs, for one last look.

Fatigue, swirling like a chloroform cloud, had me slump down on the bed. I'd felt feverish for days, since the night on the pier, with my sleep pattern increasingly erratic. Within a heartbeat I lay unconscious, exhausted to the point where I felt myself sliding through the duvet, beyond the mattress, under the floor, beneath the earth, on and on, to some unnamed darkness.

From this comatose state I awoke neither gently nor in my own time. I heard a sound so loud that I found myself bolt upright before I'd even had a chance to break from a dream. Disoriented, until adrenaline injected me to hyper-alertness, I knew nothing other than something serious had happened downstairs. I felt sick. My presence here would not be easy to explain. Big trouble awaited.

Shit.

However, my fears soon dissipated. Upon descending from the mezzanine I saw a giant gull frantically flapping amid the splintered shards of a large window pane, slipping in smears of its own blood. As I reached the final stair it clearly lost its fight.

Able to at last think clearly, with vitality now coursing through every fibre of my being, I had to get out. But one last thing drew me back to the studio floor: the painting of Black, the last oil applied to canvas by Jacob. On the easel, she awaited my rescue. Still wet, I carefully escorted her out through the front door.

It was time to return home to London.

I spent the next fortnight in the capital, trudging through routine with a vacant air. Even though I could do little in Brighton, I felt I had to get back, to be ready and waiting ahead of the following summer. I saw little to lose by relocating and starting afresh on the south coast, and within weeks I'd managed to do just that. I couldn't help but feel optimistic. I had eleven months to forge a link with the unlived part of my life; eleven months to locate my future.

TWENTY-NINE

Kitty's cancer is proving swift and ravenous, spreading like armies of insects eager to join together at a central hub. Tumours race through her, nesting in organs and slowly shutting them down. To them, nothing is inedible; metastases forming in bone and soft tissue, neoplasms leaving bad cells in their wake as they feast on the good. The only thing that slows their progress is her age, and the relative lack of healthy tissue. But for that, she'd be dead by now. Cancer likes the old, but there's more to devour in the young.

For the most part her mind is still sharp, when it isn't in the shifting grasp of morphine. Now mostly bed-bound, nurses and care assistants visit several times a day. The plan, I am told, is to move her to a hospice within the week. I am fortunate to catch her at a good time, with the intensity of pain lower, and a balanced mix of drugs in her system. With a control pad she raises the back of the bed to a more upright setting, and asks how I've been.

"Shouldn't I be asking *you* that?" I reply.

"My health is entirely predictable. I'm dying, end of story. Are you looking after yourself? Eating properly?"

"I've been living alone long enough now, Kitty. I'm okay. No alarms, no surprises."

She turns her head. "What alarm, deary?"

"Nothing. Never mind."

"Oh, okay."

"I've been going through Mum's stuff," I say, as I sit beside her bed. "It was weird reading those old love letters, from all those years before dad was around."

"She didn't only exist once she met your dad. She was once young, and she knew love. But she had… issues."

"That sounds like a euphemism if ever I heard one."

"I don't like using other words, the ones that sound more like labels. She was hospitalised for treatment in her twenties, you know," she adds, coughing into a tissue, before continuing in a rasp that suggests something is lodged in her throat. "They discharged her after a month or so, and years later gave her the all clear, so to speak. But she shouldn't have had you… *Oh,* not that you shouldn't be here," she quickly adds. "It was just too much. Too much for her, too much for the marriage. They thought they weren't capable of having children, that she was too old. You surprised them."

I choose not to linger on this fact, although in its way it still hurts. "Did you ever go to see her in Croydon?"

"No," she says, staring blankly, as if trying to find something lost within her mind. "I don't believe I did."

"What happened between the two of you?"

She sighs. "Nothing too much – no big bust-up – but in the end I gave up trying to help her. I did my best. Maybe it wasn't good enough? But she took herself away, and didn't keep in touch. She wasn't the same girl I grew up with."

"It's so weird, thinking of her as a young woman," I say, seeing my mother in the eyes of my aunt. "Had she managed to successfully stay with one of those men who wrote to her I'd never have been born. And yet part of me wishes that she'd had that happiness. She deserved better."

"You can't change the past," Kitty says, in between deep breaths. "It's not even worth thinking about in those terms. What's done is done."

"It was nice to get a sense of what she was like when she was excited about life."

"Then in its way it's a kind of gift."

I ask a question about my mother's antidepressants, but Kitty seems distracted. "And your father," she says, out of the blue. "Well, he was a useless bugger. Waste of space, he was."

I can't bring myself to hate my father, but she's not wrong.

"Look, deary, can you do me a favour?" she asks.

"Of course."

"Take me out. I want to see the sea. One last time."

"No problem," I say, eager to oblige.

"But first let's have our tea," she says. "There's always time for tea."

Kitty groans as I shift her from the bed into the wheelchair. There is little left of her – a skeleton in skin. In my grip her spine is a row of bony arcs pressing through cotton, and as I lift her up I feel her feet dangling limply against my shins. This close, in a kind of intimacy we've never before shared, a sour odour seeps from her pores. I feel like a parent, moving a helpless infant. Life has reversed our positions; I'm now the responsible one. And yet neither of us is natural in the role of carer.

A warm June afternoon: ideal conditions in which to take my aunt along the promenade. There is, however, a cool breeze, so I'm careful to wrap a blanket over her legs. In her usual way she insists it's not necessary, tells me to stop fussing.

She is still in good spirits, and relatively free from pain, as we make our way from west to east. A man on a motorised skateboard slaloms past, bulky headphones encasing his ears. Beyond him screams *Tranny And Proud* from a luminous pink t-shirt, its wearer not prepared to go under the radar. How must this all look to a woman of my aunt's age, born into a different world?

We pass the sad-looking West Pier, which, after catastrophes at the hands of three of the four elements, is all but gone. Kitty looks hard at the Metropole and the Grand, as I push her along King's Road, as if memories are stirring within her mind — although she remains silent. Then, out of the blue, she says "Take me home."

I stop the wheelchair and begin to manoeuvre a U-turn.

"No," she snaps. "*My* home. The cottage."

I explain that it is much too far to walk when pushing a

wheelchair, and that she had recently given the property to me. I tell her that we went there, a few weeks ago. "Oh," she says, unconvincingly, as if she remembers none of the recent past. "Oh," she repeats, still sounding unsure.

"I can drive you, if you want? I can take you to see the cottage one more time?"

"No. Take me back to wherever I should be. I need my bed."

I walk around the wheelchair, to face her. Her eyes have darkened, confusion etched in a mid-distance stare.

"Where am I?" she asks, lost in her own life.

When I get home I find the ciné film Kitty gave me waiting on the doormat, along with a five-minute DVD transfer. I waste no time, placing the disc straight into the player.

A distorted face crackles on the screen, a twitching mouth flickering at the bottom corner. Lines dissect the jagged features, out of focus from close contact with the lens, until a circle of white with a flaring yellow-red circumference darts diagonally across. The face – that of my father – is gone, dissolved in a flash-fire of sunlight, until a blurred and smudged hand waves before the eye of the camera holder, a *No-no-no* hand, a *You're doing it all wrong, here, let me have it back* hand. The lens is directed away from the sun – a denim-jeaned knee, the rush of grass, approaching fingers – and the camera changes hands. Subject turns to cinematographer, cinematographer to subject.

I see my mother, and for a fleeting moment she is smiling apologetically back at me. And then that is it; the camera pans across the landscape, never returning to the face I want to see. My mother and father, briefly happy before I was born. Fractured memories, held together by film.

For a few seconds they are alive again, and I am young again. And then they are gone again, and I am middle-aged again.

THIRTY

A short distance beyond where the tide dissipates, David and I sit on wooden deckchairs, like gatecrashers staged centrally at a stranger's wedding: everything occurring naturally and spontaneously around us as we incongruously inhabit the scene; surrounded by dozens of disparate people united by a knowledge of how to enjoy the summer. Bikinis, speedos, sarongs and shorts of all styles and colours ripple and stretch on browned bodies as we, two pale men in long trousers, sit with flasks of warm coffee.

"I hate the sun," David says, as we soak in its cutting midday rays.

"How can you not like the sun?" I ask.

"I just hate how I'm supposed to enjoy it. The pressure. Gets to me. Pisses me off."

"Well, it was your idea to come here."

"True," he notes, with a sigh.

Our attention is drawn to a woman— late teens, early twenties – emerging from the shallow water in a white bikini; but for the lack of a conch shell and a different cut of cloth, it is Ursula Andress, 1962. Her figure is flawless, her face distinctive and regal. We watch as she walks to her spot on the beach.

"That could have been her," David says, eyes fixed on the woman as she dries her hair with a towel.

"Who?" I ask, even though there's only ever one answer.

"Marina. She could have looked like that. Could have been here, one sunny day like this. Not a care in the world."

"You think she looks like Marina?"

"Ah, I don't know. Not entirely. It's just that stage of life, that vitality, that… *optimism*. My heart's too old to be broken again, but it remembers what it's like."

"Not at all nice," I note. "But all part of life, I guess."

"She was so beautiful," he says, shaking his head.

"She was. But why is there always so much more fuss about someone beautiful dying?"

"I don't know. Because of all the potential, I suppose."

"The appearance just strikes me as totally irrelevant," I say, still watching the woman in the bikini, as she lotions smooth legs. "*Someone* has been killed. If anything, the beautiful have it easier. What about the poor unfortunate-looking soul who gets bullied, gets overlooked – has a really shitty life – and then gets murdered? Shouldn't *they* be given greater sympathy? Or are ugly people more expendable? Is that the message?"

"I'm sure you know it's not that simple."

"I think it is. The beautiful get all the attention in life, and all the sympathy in death. The ugly are treated much the same as prostitutes in the wake of a serial killing – as if somehow they had it coming. Somehow they won't be missed. It's true, isn't it?"

David ignores me, his eyes locked on the woman as she slowly wipes a squirt of white liquid across her belly. Then again, perhaps he does indeed reply, and it's my mind that's wandered elsewhere.

"I've been meaning to tell you," David says, refilling the plastic Thermos mug over the sounds of kids splashing in the shallows. "The girl you told me about – Black. I thought I'd help you try to find her."

"Really?" I say, somewhat taken aback. "That's very good of you."

"Suzanne Black, you said her name was?"

"Yes."

"Well I went into HQ and searched the database. Nothing, I'm afraid."

"You had my hopes up there for a second."

"Leave it with me, though," he says. "I'll do some more digging. Gives me something else to think about."

"I really appreciate that."

"One thing you never told me is what happened to your wife," he asks, staring ahead, at the horizon.

"How do you mean? Nothing *happened* to her."

"After you got divorced, I mean. Where did she go?"

Due to a slight deficiency in his social skills, where he sometimes fails to modulate the tone of his voice, David's questions can sometimes feel like interrogations. "Why?" I ask, defensively; uneasy at what he might be getting at.

"Just curious. You never talk about her. You talk about the other loves of your life, some of them quite fleeting, but never her."

"She went to Hastings, I believe. It was pretty clear we weren't going to stay in touch. At first I missed her."

"And now?"

"Now it's almost as if she never existed."

THIRTY-ONE

It was 1986 when I dropped out of the Glasgow School of Art, at the end of my first year. I'd grown tired of lagging behind everyone else in terms of individuality and originality; feeling fraudulent when placed up against genuinely left-field thinkers, with their *Fuck-you* clothes and *Look-at-me* hairstyles. I got to know the artists who inspired Jacob, from obvious beacons like Lucien Freud and Francis Bacon, through to Sidney Goodman, Jean Rustin and Tibor Csernus. But I never did understand how they made their marks on the canvas.

Attitude was everything. Art as an excuse: Jacob's enduring approach. The creative process permitted any transgression the imagination could concoct, transcended accepted bounds of decency and taste, even the laws of the land. It could be honest or dishonest; it didn't matter.

"You're too repressed, Clement. Loosen up, for God's sake, boy," my tutor used to tell me. "You have no imagination." I hated him for that, but felt incapable of proving him wrong. "You have no imagination, boy. Open your eyes. Look around. Inspiration is all around!"

While no creative wunderkind, I'm not sure that I ever lacked imagination. Indeed, I spent most of my childhood locked inside my head. But something always stopped that inner world from coming out – *that* was the problem. My English teacher made similar accusations; with a pen I fared no better. I could write well enough factually, but struggled to create a good story. A sense of shame abided at what lay within; an unworthiness, an embarrassment about who I was, what

I felt, and how I interacted with others. It may have proved cathartic to expel it all in one giant emetic outpouring, but I just couldn't translate what I saw in my head, and felt in my heart, onto the callous blank page. I made nice, safe images. I wrote nice, safe sentences. Always afraid of making a mess, getting it wrong, sullying the pure whiteness with my muck.

In a dramatic change of direction, and with my mother's career in mind, I transferred to Sussex to study medicine, but again, in time, came to realise my future lay elsewhere. I lasted twenty months. At least I didn't pass out or vomit during the autopsies, and learned a few things along the way. In terms of a career it didn't prove much help at the time, but it provided some useful life experience and many of the medical basics.

And so it fell to Black, during a simple conversation under the firmament, to combine in my mind the two areas, and set me on the road to a successful vocation: yet another way in which she altered my life. The things – good and bad, great and shameful – that I owe her for. How could I *not* think about her every day?

In the months following her inspired suggestion I was concerned only with her whereabouts. The career could wait. With the savings accrued from a couple of years' pen-pushing in London I finally took the plunge and moved to simple rented accommodation in Brighton, albeit as far away from the cottage as I could get; now officially a full-time daydreamer. I had eleven months – which could be endured with funds topped up by bar work – to learn of the exact location of Black's return.

I conducted my own investigation into her past, but it never went far. I approached the current undergraduates on the course she had completed, but beyond finding a couple of her photographs left in a studio drawer, they offered no insight.

Unable to locate her peers, or any friends or family, I gleaned no further knowledge during the entire time, and Black, as far as I know, never returned to Brighton – either before or after the year ended.

By the autumn of 1994, with hopes of a reunion fading, I finally acted upon her suggestion to combine my areas of expertise. Like someone wishing to please their deceased parents, I approached it with her abstract approval in mind.

I found a workshop run by Richard Harrington, an ageing forensic artist in East Grinstead, whose increasingly poor eyesight and unsteady hand gradually pared away at his craft. He confirmed Black's suspicions: this was indeed my true calling. I studied under him twice a week, working on the real skulls of those who donated their bodies to science. By the time our sessions drew to a close he could barely keep his left hand still. My development pleased him, and through his contacts I soon found work ranging from South London down to Sussex.

It was Richard who first introduced me to David, who, of course, led me to Marina, and this whole new obsession. Unlike Genevieve and Black, this girl cannot get away.

The winter of that year saw fading hopes dissolve into total pessimism, dark replacing light. In between lessons with Richard I maintained my seafront routine, retracing those same footsteps, often unaware of hard rain lashing and waves violently breaking; frequently walking in complete isolation along the promenade, in a different Brighton to the one of eighteen months earlier. I'd gaze at the facades of hotels and shops, with the orange-red rust of ironwork bleeding down walls painted at the start of the summer. I walked in the mornings, once light, and on late afternoons, as streetlights burned up to brightness, in between shifts of bar work.

These walks required no great effort on my part. At least, not when compared with the rather desperate act of a year earlier.

THIRTY-TWO

Seated at the rear of an Airbus descending through thin night fog, I stared out at mini vortexes whorling from the wingtips, spinning in a mist lit red by landing lights. Sweat gathered on the St Christopher clasped so tightly it rendered my knuckles sharp ivory peaks. Sinuses throbbing, eardrums imploding, and with throat and mouth dried out by the air conditioning, I checked my watch, grateful to see that a delay in departure had been redressed by a tailwind.

I loathe flying. My stomach never quite recovers from the moment the engines burst into full fury to send a rattling fuselage bolting down the runway – too fast for those silly little wheels, but never apparently fast enough to project such an unbelievable mass into the air, until, somehow, *it does;* and then, as the buildings shrink away, the point where the power seems to wane, and a banking manoeuvre brings the ground on one side closer, so that it feels like the flight is doomed before even reaching cloud. But most of all I hate landing – those few seconds before touchdown when the descent seems too sharp, the approach too fast, and the plane slightly off-kilter, with one wing higher than the other. All that weight, all that speed, and a hard, flat surface a short distance below.

I breathed hard, every muscle in my body tensed. Constellations of lights pierced the fog – the dot-to-dot of a city at night – and I closed my eyes; holding my breath as the final seconds ticked down.

The things this woman made me do.

Tyres and tarmac collided. A bounce, a jolt, a skid – the back end of the plane swaying left and then right – and the vigorous reverse thrust that sucked the last air from my lungs.

And, finally, *relief…*

Prague, in winter, is unforgiving. This much I discovered on an afternoon spent wandering through snow drifts, with wind-chills that sliced skin from exposed cheeks. Not the ideal time of year to be walking the streets looking for one *specific* face: banks of women passing in the twilight, coat collars turned up, scarves coiled around necks and hooked high over noses, thick woollen hats left to slip down below eyebrows. Still, I had to take the chance. Even with her features shrouded within a balaclava I'd recognise Black's eyes.

"Christmas in Prague", she said on a warm night that now seemed a million years ago, a billion miles away. Knowing that her plan was to visit this city at this time of year, where else could I be?

I did not plan the trip straight away. With winter still in the distance I tried to remain aloof, feeling that such behaviour would constitute desperation. But as mid-December approached I could no longer keep the reality of my desires at bay. Foolish or not, I had to go. What did I have to lose? Some money, but not a fortune. Some pride, but my grip on that had always been tenuous.

I booked a tiny hotel room in Žižkov, a slightly grotty suburb on the edge of the city, its skyline dominated by an immense, ugly TV tower. I dumped my bag on the bed, wasting no time in hitting the streets. The first few hours mixed incredible excitement with an overwhelming sense of the impossible: like finding that one specific snowflake in the white squall. Later that evening I returned to the hotel dejected, but not defeated.

I had no plan, other than to search and sleep. A shower, change of clothes, followed by some food: a cheese and ham toastie whose escaping heat seared the roof of my mouth; and outside again, heading towards the Vltava.

I breezed along a pavement that ran parallel to tram tracks, electric wires overhead awaiting their buzz and vibration at dawn. I passed countless pubs and a handful of neon-lit strip clubs, before heading under a crudely constructed concrete flyover, beyond which modern buildings gradually gave way to those constructed in previous centuries; walking back through time. The city's beauty shone beyond the flakes swarming around me, its architecture illuminated by the flashes of headlights that darted across the facades.

The lights from Vyšehrad, the castle on the distant hill, flickered into view as I turned and made my way up towards Charles Bridge. Once there I could feel the coarse cobbles beneath the blanket of snow as I traversed its camber. Flanking me, a battalion of statues set in two regimented lines: a litany of saints and kings, augmented by the Madonna, and Christ suffering crucifixion. All these and, for just a few minutes, no one else but me, frozen amid their number. I eventually bade them temporary farewell, making my way back to the hotel.

Returning in daylight I discovered what I thought to be a link to Black. By this time – almost noon – mimes, portrait painters and camera-eyed tourists formed dense crowds. One artist, sheltered from the thinning snow beneath plastic sheeting, had on display a sketch of a face that *could* be hers.

Hope rose within me, a warmth bubbling up from my chest. However, my ardour evaporated during a brief conversation with the artist: he'd drawn it a couple of years earlier, from the pages of a magazine. It wasn't her. No matter how far and wide I looked, it was never her.

Settling snow formed to the thickness of a deep-pile carpet on the pavement as I stared out through a café window, watching the first bursts of pale blue light pierce the black between late-medieval buildings. I checked my watch, tapping its glass for no real reason other than nervous habit – sometimes sensing, despite its Swiss precision, that the second hand took a fraction too long to make each move.

Christmas was over, New Year come and gone. So too, no doubt, had Black. I left the remainder of my loose koruna as a tip, stepping out into the gathering blizzard. Weather permitting, my flight to England departed in four hours. I filled my final moments with one last look around the city's nexus, at all times aware that, at best, the attraction I came to see lay somewhere within its vast boundaries, and at worst, in an entirely different country.

On the way to locate the correct tram-stop for the airport I reached the Jewish Cemetery, walled-off and closed to the public out of hours. I circled its perimeter, looking for a view within. A small grate in a gateway gave sight of thousands upon thousands of gravestones jostling for position, cramped within the encasing walls, piled high, one on top of another; a Victorian football terrace of drunken and swaying bodies, frozen to sudden stillness by a wind of pure ice.

From over my shoulder I heard the roar of a large motor and the clangour of wheels against steel, and turned to see a tram pull up outside the adjacent art gallery. I jumped onto the crowded carriage, not certain it would take me to the airport, but prepared to take my chances. I sat between two people reading books with dust jackets removed, and watched central Prague – and possibly, just possibly, Black – speed past in a blur.

* * *

Returning from Prague to a wintry Brighton that, although beautiful in its own way, subdued me with the greyness and familiarity of home, I had yet to fully understand despair and utter futility. That came precisely twelve months later, when the waste of a year-and-a-half spent chasing a pipe-dream hit home.

New Year's Day, 1995, proved the nadir. I'd made friends over the years, but none with whom I wished to celebrate the final hours of 1994. I also avoided returning to the cottage to see Kitty; still unable to face my distant past. The next day, as the rest of the town slept off the excesses of the night before, or sat in the warmth eating and watching television, I wandered the cold, wet streets, heading down to the shoreline at dusk, a recently-emptied whisky bottle in my pocket. Christmas lights – depressing, so long after the event – illuminated the horizon below the leaden skies, until, with the last corner turned, nothing but the dark Channel lay ahead.

I stood at the water's edge for what seemed like aeons, at first lost in my thoughts, then almost lulled to a blank, meditative state by the rhythm of the waves breaking around my feet. I didn't even notice the last vestiges of daylight slip away. My toes, already so cold and wet, did not register the sea sweeping over them. I didn't feel the chill as spume lapped around my ankles, and then my shins, as I took several steps forward. Even my deep-set fear of water didn't keep me at bay; if anything, with perversity, it spurred me on. I don't recall walking further, but I must have, to so quickly find myself in above the knees. The icy water suddenly cut sharply at my inner thigh, like a frozen blade. I waded on, the shock now only registering incrementally, in inches, as each new part of my body slipped below the surface; until a wave blew up over my entire upper body, almost sending me onto my back. On I pressed, pushing against the water's resistance. The next big wave took me under; only then did I realise the depth was now dangerous.

And this is where I expected my will to live to kick in. In testing myself I always thought I'd choose life. The first mouthful of water reminded me of that childhood mishap, and what almost drowning tastes like. As I involuntarily coughed and spluttered, snot and foam frothed from my nose. Everyone fights drowning; the key is to give yourself no way to back out, for when the survival instinct takes hold. In my case, I could already sense how tiredness, and limbs frozen to stiffness, would undermine any attempts to head back to shore. Undecided – I didn't want death, and yet I didn't want life – I sought to buy time by treading water, but of course, at this temperature, I just edged closer to an end. I had neither the strength nor the technique to fight brutal waves. With head spinning and eyes stinging, I caught sight of the blurred lights on the Palace Pier in between increasing bouts of blackness.

Then, out of nowhere, I sensed a presence alongside me.

Jacob!

I reached out to him, but without speaking he took my head in his hands and held it beneath the water. I fought free, amid a flurry of bubbles, but found Black at my side, pushing down on my shoulders. My mother, my father, Genevieve, Kitty: all arrived in the darkness, icicle fingers pressing into my flesh as they sought to push me under. And then someone I didn't recognise – a woman – placed an arm around my chest and a hand under my chin. I resisted, but she held me up, above the waves, and dragged me to shore.

I awoke in hospital, one single heartbeat later. Sat beside my bed, leaning forward: the woman from the water. She introduced herself as Laura, and, after a broad smile that conveyed relief, tenderly readjusted my pillow.

THIRTY-THREE

Fame did not arise in the immediate aftermath of Jacob's death. It didn't happen overnight, the inevitable escalation in the value of his work and the mentions in influential magazines. But there is always something about the finality of a collection: the artist can no longer add to his oeuvre – either to expand it with equally good or higher quality pieces (which make the pre-existing ones less rare), or with substandard work that will tarnish his reputation – and that draws his work into sharp focus.

But there would always be one piece missing from the Jacob Dyer collection: his last painting, unknown, as far as I'm aware, to anyone other than those in the room that summer day.

Though slow to get momentum, his posthumous rise to some kind of prominence came as no surprise. That said, I never once cared about this unknown painting increasing in value, or that it could perhaps become a minor art-world talking point

– I wanted a connection with the subject matter. My interest in the art world would have remained consistent and modest, but it became a passion upon Black's influence; she lived within that milieu. Reconnection would surely come via this world; after all, she had no plans to re-enter mine.

For years I bought books and magazines, and regularly attended galleries and all manner of exhibitions, in London and Brighton – and further afield, if I happened to be in another city. I even turned up at college degree shows. It helped to feel that I was doing something constructive, to keep on her wavelength. Of course, it proved entirely fruitless.

Once someone is out of your life it feels as if they cannot die. You no longer see them in living form, but equally, there is no sense of a conclusive end. Of the people you once knew only to lose contact with, chances are that a few have passed away without your knowledge. Classmates, casual acquaintances, colleagues, exes: some will have fallen by the wayside, with no-one to tell you the news.

As well as keeping an eye on the arts, I scoured newspapers for the name Suzanne Black. It never appeared in stories of tragedy, or columns of obituaries. As much as I wanted her in my life, I might have taken the resounding conclusion of her death, if offered. Because hope can be greatly overrated.

Hope can be little more than hanging on in desperation, as you tell yourself lie upon lie.

* * *

What do we do with the deceased? Well, mostly we bury them. And so, in order to have Black be dead to me, I needed to put her in the ground. After 18 months it seemed the only way to break the cycle of self-destruction, and to actually get on with my life, whatever that now was. Some kind of symbolic burial felt essential.

However, I chose not to include the painting. Too precious to just let rot, I could hide that out of sight in other ways; although, with hindsight, it may have been wiser to inter that too. Still, I had so many other reminders to dispose of: the journal, written in the aftermath, that detailed my inner turmoil; a beautiful fan-shaped seashell found on the shore as we disembarked; sketches, in which I had attempted to capture her likeness before it faded from mind; and finally, the broken video cassette, its tape chewed, twisted and torn to shreds by a faulty VHS machine on only its second play-through. I took all of these items and placed them in an old biscuit tin.

Despite craving ceremony, I still needed the option of retrieving the hoard at a later date – just in case. Burial at sea – casting it high into the waves, hoping it disappeared with the outgoing tide – might have been the most apposite solution, but it wouldn't offer the chance to reclaim her, should the need arise. It had to be a more traditional burial, with exhumation a possibility, and I had just the spot in mind.

It had been well over a decade since I'd last walked a particular country lane, a mile from the cottage that led down to a medieval church and its unkempt surroundings. Little had changed; no new developments or alterations, although winter had robbed the hedgerow of the verdure that made such an impression during my teens.

I made my way to the far end of the cemetery, to the furthest grave, which belonged to a young girl who died almost a century earlier. I hopped over the ancient stone wall, into the adjacent woodland. From here I shuffled up to the foot of an enormously broad yew, whose branches arched back over the graveyard. The gap between tree and wall provided enough space to dig, once I'd located a spot either side of the roots. It was to be Black's final resting place.

Constant, gentle precipitation helped soften the earth. The tip of my trowel sank satisfyingly into the ground, and the topsoil eased from its bed without resistance. I dug down about a foot, scraped earth from against the wall. I wedged the tin into a gap where a coarse stone from the foundation had been dislodged; and, having checked to see that no one was looking, quickly covered it over.

That was it. She was gone.

Or so I thought.

I still catch sight of women I believe to be Black, only to tap the shoulder of someone who, despite some similarities, is revealed in a swift turn to be an impostor. Sometimes the resemblance is not even close.

Perhaps there is an element of the collector about me, in that I am hunting down the rarest of artefacts: that where only a single copy exists. Despite frustration stretching over many years, I cannot deny that I have enjoyed aspects of the search. It has given me a purpose: the lure of a stunning conclusion lurking somewhere undefined in the future. While others grow old and tired, losing faith in their lives, I simply move towards my destiny. Or so, in my brighter moods, I let myself believe.

* * *

She comes at night, this Thumbelina, easing up my eyelids to slip beneath their cover, on those blessed occasions when I finally attain sleep. Without the visitations of Black in these dreams, inserting herself onto my retina like a shadow on a screen, this story may not exist. She could have long-since passed into memory; an interesting tale, but a brief anecdote about one incredible night, rather than a story that abides and grows.

Or perhaps I'm wrong. After all, death cemented her place in my life, with our brief time together inextricably linked with the demise of a mutual friend. As we can all recall, even the most mundane moments remain associated, in memory, with the monumental events they precede. If you are slicing a lemon when you hear tragic news, then that lemon stays with you.

And, of course, there's the painting – which traps the moment in time; evidence to examine, over and over, for hidden clues. But these are from the past: memories and artefacts. Instead, her reappearance in my dreams – often nightly – keeps her *current*, and progresses our narrative in unexpected ways. Even when it's not strictly her, it always *feels* like it is. Sometimes the images are so vivid I'd force myself to blink, if I could. I cannot deny enjoying these visitations, but they are bittersweet: the joy of connection, followed by the disorientation of rejection – occasionally in the dreams themselves, if she gets away again, but *always* upon waking to the real world.

We usually have a future together, as I sleep. But the past is also altered, retrospectively, with that night played out over and over again, only in slightly different ways that, once awake, can be hard to distinguish from reality. It keeps the memory fresh and piquant, but it also embellishes. At times I can't tell if I'm recalling what actually took place, or a later dreamed version, with its distorted truth. Clearly there's no major departure between fact and fiction – the crux remains constant – but certain visions or snippets of dialogue may have been doctored, in sleep, over the years.

Some nights I can smell her perfume: for the life of me I

have no idea what it's called – believe me, I've searched – but it's stored deep in some olfactory memory bank that I cannot evoke when awake. I can feel her stroke the hairs on my arm with the tips of those long nails. I can taste the menthol from her cigarette as I imagine a kiss. And it has a physical effect on me; I feel my heart race, my stomach churn, my skin tingle. It continues in the minutes after I have woken, confused and alone.

The great moment of regret will always be this: *not offering her my number.* If only I had offered her my number instead of vice versa, leaving it in her capable hands, from which point she would have called and…

The moment my life forked in one direction, my dreams the other.

THIRTY-FOUR

It's easy to say now, with the penetrating light of hindsight, but I should have known that Genevieve would not stick to her word. She had become that kind of girl. Once she had what she wanted from you, that was it. I waited and waited for the call to meet her in London, but it never came. For more than a year I hoped against hope that she would turn up unannounced on the cottage doorstep, but of course she never did. She knew I would get into too much trouble if I betrayed our secret, and that I lacked the courage to risk doing so.

The repercussions, however, visited me daily, for months

on end. The worst thing? The concern of Kitty, as well as the countless interviews and statements I gave to the authorities. The police, I believe, never suspected a thing, showing sympathy to the plight of a boy who seemed a genuine victim. (After all, what kind of lunatic would consent to being tied up and beaten?) They wanted to find the two men in balaclavas I hastily invented. Quite by fortune, two unknown men had been seen in the vague area at the time, and their descriptions became those of the pair sought. The innocent duo were never traced, and the case went unsolved. But my guilt did not abate. Even now, I carry it around. Why did I agree to Genevieve's suggestions? What made me so gullible? She set in motion a pattern I would be condemned to follow: falling for the girl already halfway out the door, my heart dragged behind.

At the same time it became apparent to both Kitty and Alice that Genevieve, missing in Derbyshire, had once again run away from home. Luckily for me she'd not been spotted anywhere near Brighton, so no one was aware of her visit. Reports suggested sightings at London Victoria, but the authorities assumed it to be her final destination, rather than the station that linked to the Sussex coast. As far as everyone was concerned, she had simply absconded to the capital, with the indomitable free spirit no mother could curtail, to be lost amid the millions. All still true, I imagine; it just happened to occur after a brief detour to the cottage, and a faked burglary.

I also felt a burden of guilt over Alice's distress, relayed to me via Kitty. I couldn't put either of their minds at rest, beyond noting that Genevieve was a tough cookie who knew how to look after herself. I'm sure they knew she was locked into unbreakable patterns. Forever and ever a runaway.

That was the last any of us heard of Genevieve. Her fate remains unknown. She may well be enjoying a happy existence, in London or beyond. A heartbroken Alice died ten years after her disappearance, without knowing either way.

It provided my first experience of what the missing do to those left behind, and it marked me for life.

* * *

Hard as I tried in my teenage years, I just couldn't let go of Genevieve. Only with the advent of Black could I move on – to a new shadow in my life. In many ways Black reminded me of who Genevieve might have become. What I knew about the precursor – who was more 'real' to me in terms of time spent together – informed my fantasies about her successor, whose power was somehow greater still. However, what I'd learn about Genevieve in her room one summer's day would forever taint my views on the image she projected. Although I knew it wrong to delve beyond its cover, once I'd discovered her diary, lodged behind a chest of drawers, I could no more easily have stopped my heart from beating than put it down. Here resided the interior of her mind, condensed into a bound A5 book; the inside track on her thoughts, open and honest, laid bare on feint blue lines.

But it wasn't what I was expecting. The juvenile nature of the writing, and the girlish tone to her entries, shocked me. It seemed so childish compared with the poised exterior she presented. Perhaps more damning – it was *mundane*. Darren, who, it became clear, lived as a petty criminal when not working as a mechanic or practising the drums, featured quite heavily, but it seemed little more than a schoolgirl crush scrawled in large handwriting. He lacked depth, although that may have been less a fault of her writing and more an issue with his true personality. She mentioned her dream of heading to London with her lover, to be in a band with him and his friends. She went into great detail about their first kiss, and how giddy it made her feel, even though it seems he just thrust his tongue down her throat. However, this was far from *her* first kiss, or sexual partner; previous lovers had been boys her own age, lacking the experience and masculinity of this latest beau. Indeed, she wrote scathingly about boys below the age of 17 – and yet jotted down such musings in a style that signalled her own immaturity (which I now recognise more clearly).

The art and poetry I anticipated was absent. Rather than discuss the lyrics to *Chelsea Hotel #2*, or her passion for figurative expressionism, she gushed about the coolness of Phil Oakey's fashion sense, with love hearts doodled in the margins with the initials of Simon Le Bon. She mentioned some boots seen in a Dolcis window, and even a little sketch of them drawn in pencil. The dates of her menstrual cycle, doctors' appointments, and stylings she had requested at the hairdressers completed the entries.

You didn't need to read between the lines to deduce that she loathed her mother, although much of that may have been pure teenage rebellion. As someone who didn't understand that particular emotion, I felt her lucky to have one. There followed mentions of binge eating followed by days of near-starvation, suggesting that her svelte figure wasn't purely a case of appetite-suppressing cigarettes and the natural shedding of puppy fat.

Of course, I looked for mentions of myself, but found none. The strange and sudden closeness I felt from discovering her to still be a girl at heart – perhaps she wasn't so aloof after all? – was quickly replaced by the distance of *just not mattering*. I didn't even register. I hadn't been expecting declarations of love, but I thought I'd at least warrant the occasional passing reference.

I didn't even exist.

THIRTY-FIVE

David is running late. He asked to meet adjacent to the remains of the West Pier, and I've never been very good at waiting. My mind needs to find ways to fill itself. Absent-mindedly rolling pebbles under my shoe, I can't decide if the colour prevalent on the seafront – on lampposts and railings, bus shelters and balustrades – is turquoise or jade, or some unnamed shade in between. But its glint in sunlight has come to represent Brighton in the summer. It's a colour I will miss – along with the full gamut of greens and blues of the sea itself – if I ever have to go away.

Finally David arrives, and suggests we go for a walk. He's having a better day, he says, and wants to make the most of it – although he still needs the use of his stick. I'm not accustomed to walking at such a slow pace. "You're making me feel old," I say.

"I've felt like a pensioner for years," he replies, wearily. "And I'm still not even sixty. God knows how old I'll feel by then."

"They might discover better treatments. You never know."

"Maybe. Might help if I gave up these things," he says, patting the cigarette box in his pocket.

"So what's this all about?" I ask, as we step from shingle

to pavement; a sensation that always takes me back to that morning in 1993. "We don't usually go for walks."

"All the stories you told me. They interest me."

"How so?"

"They don't all make sense," he replies, bluntly.

"What do you mean they don't make sense?"

"I just don't see how the girl – Black – can vanish like that."

"She went overseas. Maybe she never came back?"

"But where are the traces of her *beforehand*. They should still be there, shouldn't they? You should have found something."

"I tried, believe me," I say, continuing to withhold the story of how I also broke into the studio and rummaged through a dead friend's belongings, to no avail. "You looked her up, too."

"All that did was show she had no criminal record, and that she hadn't been the victim of any crime. Although I did phone the university yesterday, and they couldn't find a record of her either."

"Obviously they wouldn't tell me when I asked all those years ago. Perhaps the files got lost?"

"Maybe. It's still all a bit strange though, don't you think?"

"Well, I never said it wasn't. It's nice that you're taking such an interest," I say, unsure of his motivations.

"I'm like you, Patrick – I like to find missing people. And I hate unanswered questions."

David stops, pauses for breath; wincing as he takes in air. "Just give me a moment," he says, leaning against a shop window.

"We can stop in a café if you want?"

"No, I don't want to seize up," he says, getting ready to move once more. "I need to push on now, rest later, preferably when I'm dead."

I follow his lead, as he takes us up the incline of West Street, towards the train station in the distance. We reach the Victorian clock tower, where West Street becomes Queen's Road. "This way," he says, motioning with his cane to the top of the hill. On we crawl. He comes to a halt as we reach the station's entrance, breathes hard. "So this is where you had that infamous coffee?" he says, as, under the cover of the veranda, we look at what is now a small convenience store.

"It is. This is where it all changed."

"She got a train to Haywards Heath, you said?"

"Indeed she did, David."

"Didn't you ever find out precisely where she stayed that week?"

"No. Again, no trace."

"Come on," he says, leading me back into sunlight.

"Where now?" I ask.

"I want you to show me Jacob's studio."

"It's gone."

David stops. "Gone?"

"Converted into flats."

"But the actual building is still there?"

"In some form. To be honest, I've never been back to look. Not even walked past it. It's been remodelled I think. So I heard."

"Can we walk by?"

"Sure."

I now take the lead, heading down side streets on the way to where the studio once stood. We make a couple of turns, and come to a stop below some flats.

"Here?" David asks.

"Yes."

"It all looks rather old – the conversion, I mean. Doesn't look at all recent."

"It's been two decades."

He doesn't seem to hear me. "I think I'll try and find somebody who knew Jacob, see if they also knew Black. I might have more luck than you. What do you reckon?"

"It'd be amazing if you could," I say. "I asked a few people at the funeral, and they didn't know her, but it wasn't really the time or the place, so I thought I'd leave it until another time. And then later I struggled to get hold of anyone else who was there."

"What about his family?"

"He had none. An orphaned only child, like me."

"He must have sold his work to galleries? People in the art world must have known him?"

"I'm sure they did. I just couldn't find anyone directly connected to him. By that stage we had no mutual friends."

We walk on, back down to the seafront, only now in silence. I wonder what David is getting at. Why does he keep questioning my story? Why is he so interested in finding Black? I can't help but see it as more than the act of a concerned friend.

We reach the shore. His face shows signs of pain. "I need to get home," he says, his limbs beset by tremors. "Can you help me back?" he asks in a weakening voice.

"Of course," I say, aware that I've never been to his house before. It's also the first time I've ever heard him ask for help. I link my arm through his, as with his other hand he nudges his cane across the pavement, and we shuffle along in tandem like the slowest pair in a three-legged race. He doesn't live far, but it takes a good fifteen minutes. Once at his front door he manages to remove the key from his pocket, but his hand is shaking too violently to slide it into the lock. After watching his frustration grow I place my hand over his, ease the key in. An unhealthy odour greets us as the door swings open; a sour mix of damp, dust and cat urine. I help him up the step, then shuffle his awkward body a few feet down a dimly lit corridor. He opens a door to a neat, unremarkable front room, its surfaces still covered with his wife's trinkets and knickknacks, her picture pride of place on the mantelpiece. I assist him into his armchair, and once he's comfortably set, ask to use the bathroom.

On the way to the downstairs toilet at the rear of the house I can't help but glance into the back room, into which harsh sunlight diffuses through a grubby uncurtained window. In sharp contrast with the front room, it is an utter mess. His wife Jean must have passed away a decade ago, and it looks as if it hasn't been cleaned in all that time. There is no visible floor space, just layers of faded furniture, papers, books, chintz and tat. In a cardboard box in the corner sit two curls of animal faeces, and I hear one cat, and see another, crawling above and below the hills of debris. Further down the corridor the kitchen is unclean and almost certainly unsanitary, and the toilet, surrounded by discarded wrappers and tubes, is in dire need of a serious bleaching.

"Tomorrow I'll try and trace some people who knew Jacob," he says, when I return to living room. "If I'm up to it. Think I've overdone it today."

"Whatever you can manage, David."

"How's your aunt?" he asks, changing the conversation, but intoning the question without much apparent concern.

"Not so great, I'm afraid. I saw her the other day, but she was unconscious. She had no idea I was even there. Won't be long now."

"Shame," he notes, with what sounds like sincerity, but adds no more.

On the walk home it strikes me: my days are now split between the ill and the dead. Mine is a life spent in between, stuck with the barely alive and the already deceased.

THIRTY-SIX

Although initially slow to get online, the internet opened up for me a whole new world of search options. Googling Black is now routine; and yet time and again the same unrelated results pop up. Variations on the criteria — such as adding 'photographer' or 'Brighton' — fail to locate the specific hit I am after. At first I visited social network sites like *Friends Reunited*, then *MySpace* and more recently, *Facebook*. Still nothing. Not a Tweet. I visited records offices: Births, Deaths and Marriages. Still no sign.

Then there's Genevieve. I admit to occasionally googling her too, but as a runaway she had disappeared from a far greater radar screen, not just mine. Once I'd met Black I found it surprisingly easy to move Genevieve into the background. I outgrew her. Though still an infatuation of sorts, and briefer in duration, Black was a case of adult emotions rather than adolescent desires. I will always remain curious to know what became of Genevieve, but I am under no illusions.

A sum total of sixteen hours and twenty minutes. Sixteen hours and twenty minutes: a period of time forever imprinted on my mind. How can you fall in love with someone in less than twenty-four hours, and still be in love (or *obsessed*) with that person more than two decades later, despite never having seen them again in all that time? It's the maths I am forever tripping over, trying to justify my feelings. As an equation it simply doesn't work. I've heard it said that if X is the amount of time spent with someone, then X should be the length of time necessary to get over them. By that reckoning I should have been over Black by the Monday morning.

But now, with more than a year having passed for every hour spent in her company, what percentage of my feelings are based in reality? However rational I try to be, there is always a nagging suspicion that she will suddenly reappear. Do these beliefs qualify as in any way legitimate, or are they nothing better than fanciful notions? Is Black now, as an actual part of my life, nothing more than pure fantasy?

You can't invent your own feelings, but you *can* trick yourself about their causes.

And say that I *do* find Black? What if she has aged in the most awful way – less Loren, more Bardot? It's an inevitable process, losing tone, shedding your looks. Once through the hell of puberty you think you are now set in stone; that's it, growing done, change at an end. But then the gradual reversal starts. You know you will age, just *not yet*; and then it creeps up on you. If you are particularly unfortunate, it hoods, binds and kicks the living shit out of you.

In my mind she is still inescapably twenty-one, perfectly formed but on the cusp of that fine line of deterioration, when the first tell-tale signs of the body's slackening appear. I need only look at myself to see the damage of time: hairline slightly receded, a touch of slack skin pointlessly sagging from my chin, eyebrows on the wane, thin wrinkles across my brow. Then again, it could be a lot worse. Truth be told, time hasn't totally trashed me.

It's said that the best way to find something is to stop looking. This is usually applied to the search for love. Of course, it's bullshit. Little in life is going to make its way to you. Why should it? The vast majority – 99.99% – of the world's people, objects and locations exist outside of your own personal sphere. Even if you travelled across each and every country on the face of Earth you'd still barely scratch the surface of its land mass, or bump into more than the tiniest fraction of its inhabitants.

The other thing to do when you've lost something is to try and remember where you last saw it. And that's why Brighton remained the logical place to be. But with regard to finding Black, it's time to give up. I've stopped looking. All this time, and beyond vivid dreams, she didn't come.

THIRTY-SEVEN

The broken oak slouches half-collapsed at the far edge of the grounds, just beyond the barbed wire fence separating the cottage from dense woodland. Beneath its fractured bough sits a patch of soft earth that, late in the damp June of 1981, I spent an entire evening digging with my bare hands. The hole grew and grew, deeper and wider. As darkness set in I backfilled it with rocks and placed a small boulder over the top. I had no idea what purpose it would serve, but it was *mine*.

The next day I created a treehouse: no actual structure as

such, but a den could be determined at the point where the tree split in two. I climbed the broken limb like walking up a slide, and with a saw from the garden shed cut away the thin branches and leaves that dangled overhead, then sliced off a gnarly knot to make the surface flat to sit upon. It provided somewhere to escape to, a secret hideout, even if I had nothing specific to hide from. That summer, after dark, I'd make my way to the tree, to sit in the pitch blackness and listen to the night.

Then Genevieve arrived, to turn my world on its head.

By August I'd begun to spend more time in Genevieve's room. Having already taken some underwear, and not been caught, I started stealing little items: knickknacks and small trinkets, stuff I thought she wouldn't immediately miss. She had a box of cheap jewellery, from which I lifted a ring beset with a fake ruby stone. Loose on a table sat stubs of concert tickets and nightclub flyers; the one I took, adorned with a picture of Siouxsie Sioux, advertised a disco a few weeks earlier. Although she mostly listened to vinyl, she also had a Sony Walkman, for which she had created a number of cassette tapes. From the dozen or so scattered in a draw I grabbed one marked 'Leonard Cohen, The Cure, Japan, various chart music', and slipped it into my pocket. Finally, I helped myself to one of her five hairbrushes.

I had no idea what I would do with any of the items. I didn't have a cassette player. I combed rather than brushed my hair. I had no plans to wear the ring, even if it fit (it didn't). But together, as a collection that included the delectable black bra and panties I'd already stolen, it formed part of her essence; a link to some kind of intimacy. At first I stowed them under my bed, but feared the reprisals if discovered. After all, how could I explain away their presence? Then I remembered the hole. Taking a biscuit tin from the larder, and eating the last of its chocolate Bourbons, I removed the flimsy plastic tray and placed the cache neatly inside, then made my way to the tree. I shifted the large stone capping the cavity, and the rocks I'd placed inside. The tin nestled snugly. I replaced those stones that still fit, and blocked the hole with the small boulder, to form a type of cairn. Still feeling insecure, I dragged, with all my might, the collapsed tree limb, managing to move it, bit by bit, a few inches until it came to rest over the hole.

* * *

More than three decades later, the long-forgotten memories of that burial flash back into my mind.

I rush to grab my shoes.

The sun is setting, but there is still enough residual light to see what I am doing. I circle the lake, traipse through long grass, and carefully climb the barbed wire fence, which, though lacking its tension of old, still possesses a rusty bite. Even though I am more muscular than in my mid-teens, I find the tree harder to shift. The effort leaves me breathless, but eventually I manage to edge it off the capping stone. In the focus of effort I haven't really thought about the emotional impact of what I am doing, but then it strikes me. It almost feels like exhuming a corpse. I clear the rocks from the tin, then carefully lift it out. Red-black with rust, its paintwork has worn away. Despite being fused to the main body of the container, I manage to loosen the lid with my door key. Tentatively I open it up. And there it all is: the ring, the cassette, the underwear and the hairbrush. The flyer has gone – turned to mush. And the cheap ring has oxidised. But the underwear, although damp, has survived, and the cassette, in its protective case, and the hairbrush, are almost like new. Would she forgive me, wherever she now is, if she knew about all this? Strangely, I feel more guilt than I did at the time, when, fevered with hormones, I felt driven to act that way.

* * *

One blurry photo, taken early in the summer of 1981: the only hard evidence of Genevieve Frazer's appearance that I retain. She is sixteen, forever sixteen. Except that now, if she is still alive all these years later, she will be almost fifty. I say it out loud, aghast at the thought.

Fifty.

In my line of work I am occasionally required to age the faces of people who, in decades past, went missing, never to be found. Looking at the photo once more – she is sat on a blanket in front of the lake, neither smiling nor frowning, the big broken oak in the background – it strikes me that I could attempt to draw her as she might now look. Despite the lack of clarity, there is sufficient information present to work with, in terms of her facial geometry. I can measure the distances between her features, and extrapolate the figures to create a life-sized sketch on A3 paper. If it ultimately serves no other purpose, it will at least give me an idea of who she went on to become.

We all age, albeit in different ways and at different rates. But overall, the same things tend to happen to our faces, within roughly the same period of our lives, give or take a handful of years. Unless we resort to surgery, lines will appear. Lines become grooves, grooves become furrows. Already a smoker, if she persisted with the habit it will have taken an additional toll. Time spent in the sun can also impact appearance, although she wasn't one for the great outdoors. Will she have remained slim, or returned to the overweight nature of her early teen years? For the purposes of this drawing I decide on a compromise, with just a little of that fat returned to her features.

With reasonable certainty I conclude that the following age-related changes will have occurred. Her face will present evidence of lateral orbital lines, or crow's feet, curving down from the corners of eyes that are now plumped with bags. There will be a loosening and sagging of the eyelids, with her eyebrows hanging slightly lower. Transverse frontal lines – wrinkles on her forehead – will be fairly prominent, and circumoral striae – vertical lines above the lips – will have developed early, due to smoking. Those lips will have begun to thin, with oromental grooves arcing down from the corners of her mouth. Time will have softened her jawline. And of course, there's a reasonable chance that her hair may have turned grey – although she may still dye it. Older women tend to cut their hair shorter, and yet for some reason I don't see her doing that, whatever its condition. She may now wear glasses, but that's far from certain. Despite the science, it still requires some guesswork.

First I draw the core of her face, as it was then. After all, the position of the key features does not alter. Skin may droop around them, but the eyes, nose and mouth themselves do not move. On top of this I sketch the imprint of time, with muscle and skin weakening, lines rising and falling, grooves and furrows burrowing callously into flesh. With my pencil tilted I shade the cheeks, the temples, and add further shadows to contrast with the light.

After twenty minutes I put down the pencil and step back from the desk to survey my work. The eyes remain clearly identifiable, but I'm not sure I recognise the rest of Genevieve. Perhaps the accuracy of my sketch – or rather, the *lack of* – is the problem, but I just cannot *feel* her as an adult, as a middle-aged woman. In my head she is locked in time, never able to age.

In my head she is sixteen, forever sixteen.

PART TWO

THIRTY-EIGHT

Sleeplessness is now an almost constant state, my life inverted, day for night. I grab micro-sleeps – or rather, they grab me; only to let go, almost immediately, as the most vivid images startle me awake. I get so tired I want to cry. I often beat the mattress in rage, before finally getting up and going downstairs, pottering about in the hope that it will break the vicious cycle. Sleeping pills afford me an hour or two, but leave me foggy and dazed, with a mouth of metal. At times it feels as if there's nothing I wouldn't do for a good night's sleep.

Four or five in the morning, for the umpteenth day running, the sun already rising. I head down to the kitchen, grab a glass of milk. There, sat on the table, is little Monty: fraying at the seams, his tightly-stitched smile still in place, forever winking from the loss of a black buttoned eye. The threads of his armpits have grown loose and ragged, the fabric of his belly tatty and worn. Like me, he has aged. His bow tie hangs slack and saggy on his neck.

He looks precisely how I feel.

In a spontaneous frenzy of movement, fuelled by pure instinct, *I rip him limb from limb*, his soft white stuffing hanging in clouds about my face as I tear him apart. I don't even know why I'm doing it; it's not *his* fault, but then again, he's always present when it goes wrong. As I look down at the clumps of material spread still and lifeless around my feet I am hit with a deep sense of regret, but at the same time I could never stand to see his little taunting face again.

If I explain *everything*, then maybe I'll find some peace.

It's fair to admit that my final encounter with Genevieve wasn't quite as previously described. Anyone who tells their story has interests to protect; a need to portray themselves in a certain light. Is anyone ever *truly* honest? I mean, down to every last detail? I very much doubt it. Why should they be? What's in it for them? We all finesse the details. Only, I've gone a bit further.

Perhaps I also failed to offer a clear enough insight of my trespasses into Genevieve's room. Whenever she and Kitty went out for the day, my first instinct was always to intrude. I just had to be *within*. Once inside I felt the desire to go deeper, probe further. The thrill of simply being in her space – so exhilarating at first – soon waned, with each successive foray demanding greater invasion. Not thrills for thrills' sake; merely the addictive consequence of a need to get *closer*.

Climbing naked into her bed, I would smell the sheets,

cuddle her pillow; the warmth of my skin generating an echo of hers. Having slipped the record player needle into the groove of a Leonard Cohen vinyl – I had the choice of half a dozen – I'd lie back and glance around the room as if she lay beside me, sharing a casual post-coital cigarette. I'd invent conversations that I didn't yet have the maturity to fully understand – the kind of pillow talk I'd seen in films.

As much as anything, the decoration of that room, and the objects strewn across the floor and edging out of open wardrobes and draws, shaped me. I became a product of that environment, soaking up Genevieve's sensibilities. Everything about her seeped into my bloodstream. The startling black and white pictures by trendy young photographers, cut from library books and tacked onto the wall. Francis Bacon's *Triptych May-June, 1973*: depicting the artist's overdosed lover, collapsed on a toilet floor, dead. That's not an easy image for a boy to reconcile, especially in a room of erotic fantasy. I imbibed these stimuli like contracting an infectious disease.

I never wanted to be a liar; between the ages of six and fourteen I was obsessively truthful. I felt an unbearable weight of guilt over my mother's suicide – over the kind of child I'd been. (Which, in truth, was the kind of child that more-or-less everyone is, but my minor misdemeanours came crashing down during the weeks and months that followed.) As a result, I felt myself in some way responsible.

Having said all that, I have always been the kind of person who cannot resist pulling the head from a scab. I think it says a lot about me. I pick at its edges, delighting at the crisp cracking sounds. The satisfaction elevates me way beyond the experience: it shouldn't feel *this* good. A dart of pain – and I quite like the pain – confirms that the scab is still fused tight to the skin beneath, like an unripe fruit unwilling to yield from its stalk.

However, a tiny tickle, and it is ready to be gently levered all the way, until it lays precious in my palm.

Maybe it's connected to the fact that, as a child, I forever took things apart. I wanted to see how they worked, what held them together. Sometimes I imagined hidden treasure inside a toy, only to find, with the case irreparably sundered, nothing but plastic and metal, as well as a surprising emptiness; a moulded vacuum. No secret, and, from that point on, a broken toy.

I just can't leave things well alone.

But for the doggedness of David, none of this would be necessary. I can't help but think he knows more than he's letting on, and that, when out of sight, he's digging away and getting closer to the truth. Things occur without our knowledge, and then – only after the event – do we gain insight. Only young children think there is no world beyond their experience, no life outside their walls, only silence and darkness when they sleep.

Rewriting your past, I now realise, is as futile as trying to wash away limescale with water.

It *is* true that Genevieve arrived that morning, her plan devised and a willing accomplice sought. For patsy, read Patrick. Awoken at five in the morning, I found myself entirely vulnerable, and eager to impress. However, even after the predatory approach, her idea, with Kitty to be the victim of a scam, repelled me. Instead, thinking on my feet, I offered an alternate plan – easier on my flesh and bone, and far gentler on my conscience. Everything up to that point – Kitty, the cottage, the death of my parents – is the truth. But Genevieve's unexpected arrival that early morning started in motion a sequence of events that took me with them, gathering me into their momentum. That's what beautiful girls do to me.

My suggestion revolved around a story I was once told.

Jimmy Smith, the older brother of my school-friend Tony, found himself serving three years for supply of Class A narcotics. This made him something of a schoolyard legend, and Tony, a far meeker boy, received some of this kudos by proxy. Despite being radically different to his brother, a little of that underworld cachet rubbed off. One night, tight in the alcove of a seafront bus shelter as we escaped a storm, Tony divulged his brother's secret: Jimmy had been using a small kiosk at the far end of the West Pier as safe storage for his stash of cash and drugs. And so, as Genevieve hounded me, I found myself blurting out this information, without thinking it through. The sums involved far exceeded anything Kitty had lying around in bank notes. Before I knew it I had dressed, and, thoroughly caught up in Genevieve's enthusiasm, found myself leading the way on the long walk.

In the early morning light – it was still only six a.m. – we reached the shoreline. The smell of seaweed and saline, lavished by the cold dawn breeze, blitzed my senses. Combined with the adrenaline, and the thrill of being of use to Genevieve, I felt more awake than ever before.

The beach lay deserted. Six years after the pier had been closed to the public, and a further six years before an infamous storm ripped the walkway from pier to shore, our task in trespassing was simply to scale the metal gates, and ignore the signs that warned of danger. As I stood and hesitated with my hand on its steel, Genevieve climbed over the barricade. Suddenly it didn't seem like such a good idea. What had I talked myself into? She shot me a withering look, and a shake of the head, as I started to show signs of chickening out. I had no option but to follow, to chase her lengthy shadow.

I'd yet to disclose the precise location of the cache; I had to retain some bargaining power. The offer of sexual rewards as I lay half-awake beneath bedsheets hung as the carrot, and I wasn't about to jeopardise that – although, in truth, I would have been happier with something less carnal but longer lasting: a day spent huddled up beneath the covers, listening to her record collection. I wanted *love*, but guessed it was not an option. The offer? Something quick and clinical.

We passed the first octagonal kiosk – the Brighton Rock Shop – and entered onto the main body of the pier. The walkway narrowed in the approach to the concert hall, then opened out on either side. We took the right-hand path, circling to the west around the low-slung silver building. Once again the walkway narrowed, before expanding to its widest point at the pier head, housing the mighty pavilion. At the south-west corner resided a roofless kiosk, to which I led her.

It stood listing against the backdrop of orange sea. We approached, and located the doorless entrance. A pigeon, disturbed by our presence, flapped wildly upwards, and in turn caused a handful of seagulls to take flight from atop the pavilion. I jumped back in alarm, hyper-alert to any movement, but Genevieve seemed untroubled. "Come on then," she said, impatiently. "Where is it?"

I hadn't bargained for Tony's overactive imagination. Or the possibility that loose lips had led others to the location. Either way, as we moved a mass of mildewed wood from inside the kiosk, scattering it to get at the heart of the structure, I grew uneasy; nothing to be found beyond remnants of an old outbuilding and a flock of dead pigeons. Unsurprisingly, Genevieve got angry.

My only aim was to stop her leaving. You have to believe me on that. I felt a somatic urge to not be deserted; not in that manner. It was a reflex action, somewhere beneath, below or beyond conscious thought.

I meant only to grab her shoulder, in response to the look of disgust she flashed me before turning so sharply on her heels. I didn't mean to push her so violently, but the floor beneath me gave way a little, and I lurched far further forward than expected. I felt the weight of her head for a fraction of a second as my palm forcefully thrust it straight into the corner of the kiosk. There echoed a sickening crack.

She collapsed in a crumpled heap at my feet; her forehead sliced clean open, the wound rising beyond her hairline. Blood streaked through her hair, mixing with a few remaining flecks of red dye. It seemed to gush out. Most damning, her eyes stared up at me, wide and perfectly still: inquisitively asking, *What did I do to deserve such brutality?*

I ran and vomited over the railings, down into the sea. I couldn't face turning back to look at her, and yet I couldn't just run away. My mouth wiped on my sleeve, I moved to stand over her body, shaking uncontrollably, tears streaming down my cheeks. I had no idea what to do. Should I call the police? It may well have been the sensible course of action, but I couldn't afford to take that risk. It *was* an accident, but one borne of rage and confusion. Maybe, just maybe, I meant to be that forceful? Yes, my footing gave way, but I felt explosive anger in that split second. I didn't *think* about killing her, but equally, I couldn't let her get away. I couldn't be abandoned. Not again.

I began to remove her clothes, down to her underwear. I unbuttoned her blouse, and unfastened her jeans, easing both from her pliant limbs. I had this notion about concealing her identity; 'last seen wearing', and all that. Having spent three days with my father's body, I held no fear of a corpse. The repercussions from this particular circumstance, however, terrified me. Incredibly, she remained just as beautiful, and her body – so fresh after death – looked perfect. Her staring dead eyes, however, will forever haunt me.

For a moment I considered dumping her overboard, but concluded that the tide would simply wash her ashore. Cupping her armpits, I dragged her into the kiosk. Frantically I covered her with the scraps of wood, and any other rubbish I could find, building a pyre over her body; not that the damp wood could be lit, even if I had a match. My future depended on never being connected with the scene. Her body must never be discovered. But if it ever was, it must never be *identified*. I gathered her clothes, to later burn in the woods.

And yet leaving her proved the hardest task of all. I anticipated the urge to run, as fast and as far as possible. But the guilt of casting her aside like trash, coupled with the fear of an overlooked piece of damning evidence, trapped me. I crept away, only to stall and pause for thought, turn and look. By delaying I endangered my freedom; leaving too quickly could do the same.

Even then I knew that no matter how thorough my escape, and how great the physical distance, this pier – and Genevieve – would follow me everywhere, forever more.

* * *

My childhood proximity to the dead did indeed lead me circuitously to the world of forensic art. As a mere boy I had committed the ultimate sin. And though I never really knew her, I felt a sense of duty to Alice, and those like her, whose lives are wrecked by never knowing. I hadn't the courage to soothe Alice's particular grief; to point out that her little girl was not in fact missing in London, but instead rotting on a pier. I never could decide which – knowledge or ignorance – would be easier on her soul, but I knew which was essential to my freedom. Guilt crippled me. But it never once made me want to face the lawful consequences of my actions.

Starting my new career, I had only ever anticipated working on modern cases. Historical reconstructions never entered my thinking. I knew artists involved with the recreation of the faces of men found in Napoleonic shipwrecks, and graves from the Civil War. I never imagined offering my services to such a project. But history doesn't have to stretch back that far to be pertinent. It can exist in the more recent past, far closer to home.

As described, David did indeed approach me, keen for a fresh perspective on an old case. I'd worked with him on several reconstructions, and we developed a bond. However, I wasn't quite prepared for the contents of a scruffy manilla file he handed over on the day of the storm, overflowing with pictures of the girl he and his colleagues knew as Marina, but whom I knew as Genevieve. In my mind her body remained as perfect as I left it. That was, until I folded back the beige cover and looked at the crime scene photographs within.

Decades earlier, in May 1982 – almost a year after I ended her life – the *Brighton Argus'* headline informed the town that a body had been discovered. At first I panicked, but it was clear that the police had no idea who the victim was.

Decades on, that remained true.

Back then, as my youthful eyes stared down at the last vestiges of life knocked clean out of her body, Genevieve looked almost normal; I had stopped her heart beating, but, one wound aside, merely turned her into a life-sized doll. Time, and the elements, along with nature's scavengers, ripped her flesh from its bone. I killed her; but they *brutalised* her. That became clear in the photos. Her teeth: I could still recognise the smile her lips would form around them. Heartbreakingly, hollow recesses replaced the eyes, the gaze eaten away.

The crack in her skull showed precisely where forehead met wall. In the months following that conclusive collision her feminine curves pared away to hard asexual lines: the off-white osteoblasts of calcium and collagen. Everything about her had been reduced to something that, at first glance, could be male or female; *AN Other Skeleton*. No matter that on closer inspection an anthropologist, or a reconstructor like myself, could spot the telltale signs of beauty, or identify the gender by the brow ridge or the difference in the sub-pubic angle of the pelvis; her *essence* had dissolved with decomposition. I spared her the harsh reality of ageing, but replaced it with the barbarity of decay.

As in that smoke-filled pub I flicked from one photo to another – a cluster of bones, exposed after the kiosk had been cleared, with the thin under-wire from a bra – I knew that my destiny had come home to roost. David would get there, eventually. It became merely a matter of time.

And so, all those years later, when he asked me to reconstruct the skull, I felt compelled to return to Genevieve her natural beauty – no matter what the consequences of a realistic reconstruction. In that moment, as much as I wanted to decline, I simply had to say yes. I'd been running from it for too long. I had to do my utmost to bring her back to life. I owed her that.

THIRTY-NINE

With great trepidation – I felt my heart gain weight upon hearing the words – I found myself agreeing to David's request. For a decade I'd guessed of the possibility – here was a skull, absent a face – but there existed the sketch artist's original drawing, which I assumed would suffice (even though I could tell it totally failed to capture her likeness; something I obviously kept to myself).

I tried to think of excuses, but none of any substance were forthcoming. There was no point suggesting I had other work to attend to, as he knew I didn't. I couldn't say I didn't have the time, as he knew I did. With all this in mind, what plausible reason could I give?

Decades after that tragic morning, reunion with Genevieve awaited, in the most unusual of circumstances.

I told David to pack the skull in a box, for me to open at my leisure. I couldn't bear to be presented with it, in its full Baptistian glory, and have to disguise my reaction. Just a skull, of course, but I knew the reality that once curved around it. I told him that unwrapping it on my own would be the most respectful thing to do – trotting out some nonsense about needing to be at one with the subject from the start, given the importance of this case – and he accepted my explanation.

The next evening he knocked at my door, cardboard box lodged under his arm. He made some quip about Hamlet, and I forced a smile. Once in the living room he placed the package on the coffee table, and we sat either side, as this *presence* screamed at me from within its thin brown walls. I could barely concentrate on what David had to say, such was the noise – such was the heat and vibration – I sensed from inside that box. I just wanted him gone, so I could have my private moment with a fairly literal ghost from my past. But on he prattled, unaware that this would be so much more than just another job to me: enforced penitence, repentance and atonement rolled into one.

The sun hung just above the trees at the rear of the cottage as I carried the box through to the study, filling the lake with liquid gold. I'd been so eager for David to leave me in peace, and yet as the moment of unpacking loomed I held strong Pandoran fears. How on earth do you confront something like this? I held no meaningful beliefs in evil spirits or voodoo, but I never anticipated such a strange situation; I imagine few people have. In such moments it's impossible not to let your mind wander over myths and legends, to fear the supernatural.

I tried to put such concerns aside. I peeled away the packing tape, lifted the flaps. I lowered my outstretched fingers to clasp cold bone, and with great tenderness lifted Genevieve into the light. My hands shook violently, but I held her fast. And then it blew through me: the need to let out my own demons. All the while I'd envisaged an attack from this sacred object, but instead I suffered an internal crisis. I just about managed to set her gently on the drawing board when the swelling grief and remorse burst up into my chest and funnelled into my throat; exiting via stinging eyes and trembling lips.

I fell to my knees, and wailed. I didn't want any of this. I wanted her, not a life of regret; of persistent hauntings. I looked at her – still *her*, not it – and spluttered "I'm sorry!" over and over; sorrow for my actions, but self-pity, too. I deeply regretted the path she led me down, and my fatal mistake at the end of it.

I began to get cold feet; did I *really* dare capture her likeness? It felt like suicide.

And so I found myself presented with the ultimate test: do my best work, and years of incarceration almost certainly awaited, once someone joined the obvious dots; or betray Genevieve yet again, in the hope of continued freedom, but freedom blighted with constant glances over a guilty shoulder.

Decisions, decisions. I traced my fingers over ridges in her skull; valleys formed where plates fused in infancy. Twenty-two bones in all, joined by delicately woven sutures. Thanks to me, one of these cranial bones had cracked: two fissures radiated diagonally from the impact scar, stopping at the junction with the parietal bone at the top of the head; Genevieve's tectonic plates, disturbed by my earthquake.

As much as I wanted to recreate her living likeness, I remained terrified by the implications. Each path involved its own freedom, its own damnation.

Midnight approached. Midnight passed. I sipped at red wine that looked black beyond the reach of candlelight. *My* time, the early hours; human noise non-existent, even with the windows and doors open. Nature flitted outside, buzzing and twitching and humming. I'd get up and wander to the veranda, look at the moonlight on the lake, listen to the gentle rhythms of the wildlife. And then my mind would wander: insects once nested inside Genevieve's head – that's what I reduced her to.

I had to make a start, perform the basics. The first task: attaching the skull to a stand – a self-made armature – before aligning the head on the Frankfurt plane, which fixes the eye-line straight-on. As if cupping Genevieve's soft-skinned face, I gently adjusted the attitude: lifting her chin, as would a lover when trying to turn a frown into a smile. But there came no involuntary reaction in reply.

Dead. Wholly dead.

Only once the synthetic eyeballs settled into recesses packed with clay did I recall, vividly, how she looked in life. There could be no escaping the decision.

She wouldn't let me fail. I had to do her justice.

FORTY

They should have known, then. They should have guessed. It was not what fifteen-year-old boys did; certainly not ones from supposedly good homes, no matter how detrimental their formative years.

I had held it together fairly well in the aftermath of Genevieve's death, although I feared going to bed at night, aware that in dreams I couldn't escape what I'd done. She wreaked her revenge, via my subconscious. She came at night, this Thumbelina, with an axe to grind.

But on the outside, I don't think it showed – not at first. Already quiet and withdrawn, not a lot changed in that sense. However, I felt it building: stress, in cumulative form. I'd secretly begun to drink cheap spirits, primarily as a means to get to sleep, as the first bouts of insomnia took hold. It couldn't mask the fact that I'd begun to unravel, shedding threads like a fraying fabric in a gale.

Exposed to every one of nature's elements – bones shaking,

muscles shivering, teeth involuntarily punching enamel against enamel – I sat up, vaguely recollecting the notion of going to bed for an early night; an idea that, in retrospect, seemed all the better in contrast to the decision I actually made. Instead: drinking an entire bottle of whisky and sleeping in my clothes on a rain-strewn beach. I awoke, cold and wet, to the sensation of the empty bottle butting up against my side. In the drained vessel I saw a message: *You fucking idiot.*

I wanted to pull myself into the foetal position and slide back to sleep. The sea would come and take me, wash me ashore in Normandy. I'd awake and speak French. Strangers would know my name, and life would resume, plotted along some alternate course. I would be Jacques, in love with Yvette; a normal teenage boy who'd traversed no moral boundaries, an uncomplicated life stretching out ahead of him.

The saltwater in my watch had frozen the hands at 4:17 a.m. The sun was up, and the sounds of a town fully awake could be heard. Moments later I was discovered on the shore, although I have no recollection of my rescue. Rushed to the Royal County Sussex Hospital, my physical recovery seemed relatively swift – days rather than weeks or months – but there followed a series of psychiatric tests, with my mind poked and prodded. In truth, I could easily explain away my reckless behaviour, after such difficult formative years. An abundance of scattered, seemingly random dots meant that no one joined up the relevant ones with the absence of Genevieve.

At least I got a chance at recovery, which is more than I allowed her. But it would be wrong to say that I experienced no punishment. Penitence shadowed me every step of the way. Self-pity, too.

Somehow I survived.

                              * * *

The hardest thing in human existence is to accept that what's
done is done. Death is final. But so too are our actions, each
and every last one of them. We can seek to alter the course of
where the present is heading, and we can apologise, and try to
put right that which we have got horribly wrong. But none of it
can change what actually took place. In modern life, everything
is so easy to edit. Copy, cut, paste, delete. Pause, rewind, fast-
forward. And yet nothing – and I mean nothing – can undo a
moment that we wish with all our hearts could be reversed.

   I didn't want to be this person. And no matter what I do,
and how hard I try, I cannot be anyone else.

FORTY-ONE

Precocious, languidly confident students, with hairstyles,
piercings and beards that leave me feeling old before my time,
lounge and lean on the steps, blocking the entrance to the new
Shoreline Gallery; far too cool to stand beside their work in
search of feedback, or be in the same room as their parents.
They blow smoke into lingering plumes through which I am
forced to pass. Indifference seeps from their oily skin.

   I take from an offered tray a disposable plastic beaker of
cheap champagne: this is the life. The space is stark, clinical,
white-washed. There are alcoves and free-standing walls, but
otherwise it's sparse and spare. Work hangs from slim metal

wires fixed on the ceiling, left to dangle inches from the wall
– on which the obligatory name cards and titles are displayed.
The first I encounter, by a graduate called Tim O'Callaghan,
reads *The Inexorable Plight of the Subconscious Human Mind in
the Face of Irrepressible Social Oppression, No.2*. It is a picture of
a fish. Next to it is a piece called *Cunt*. It is nothing more than
a simple household mirror. I age another year.

And so it is with a heavy heart, and legs that appear similarly
weighted, that, on this searingly hot June evening, I take a look
at the work of the daughter of an acquaintance at a Fine Art
degree show. I have a heavy cold, and I'm already regretting my
decision to attend. I hope for her sake, and mine, that she has
an oeuvre of *Untitleds*.

In some distant way I once belonged to this world. But
now – well, I may as well be just another parent, confused and
awkward, smiling uneasily beneath harsh spotlights as I try to
understand the dark recesses of my child's mind. ("So son, what
is the bloodied sheep's anus supposed to signify?") At least back
then I was included, even if at the periphery. I flick my fingers
through my hair, nervously. My friendship with Jacob validated
me in places like this. The tutors' darling – literally, in one case
– I gained blessings by association. Now I'm left to fend for
myself, and age has further removed any sense of affiliation.
Even some of the parents seem louche and bohemian, as if they
too hail from this left-field world. The sooner I find Amy's work
and get out of here the better.

My mobile phone begins to vibrate. Unsure of the etiquette
in a place like this, I force my way outside, back through the
smoke, to take a call from David.

"Patrick, I need to speak to you."

"What about?"

"Marina."

"Seriously? What is it?"

"I'd rather not say over the phone. Where are you? Can you meet me in fifteen minutes? In town?"

"I'm at this degree show I told you about. I still haven't seen Amy's work yet, or said hello. Can it wait till later?"

"Well, it's waited decades so far, so I guess so."

"Give me about an hour, should be more than enough time to get through this nonsense. I'll see you in The Cricketers, just after seven."

I'm shaking as I walk back inside, bristling with fear. Suddenly the art and its youthful creators no longer bother me. I am involved in something far bigger than any of this. They may look down their coke-twitching noses at me, but I deal with issues far darker than even their most twisted subject matter. They are just playing games. I have *killed*.

I find myself pleasantly surprised with Amy's work, which I locate hanging on the far side of the gallery, a long way from prime position. Relieved, too: I hate doing the fake "it's great" speech, as my tone always betrays me. At first I cannot find her to pass on my regards, so I spend a few moments studying her canvases: bold use of colour, interesting compositions, confident brushwork. It's nothing spectacular, but the figures are vibrantly worked in oil.

She sees me and heads over, and turns out to be a good kid, too. Down to earth, affable, and not at all cocooned in a shell designed to keep others at bay. But I keep things brief. I wish her luck, and mean it.

Now for the real world. What does David know?

I turn, and something on a free-standing wall catches my eye. I'm immediately struck by a strong sense of déjà vu, although it's less a case of re-experiencing a previously lived moment and more like seeing a specific point of my life frozen in a painting. It's hard to explain just how odd it feels. *Obviously* I must be imagining it; I have to be. I move closer. I squint, and then blink. Though heavily stylised, and lacking any great definition, it seems unmistakable.

It is *me*, on the West Pier, as it was *that* night... as *I* was that night.

But it makes no sense: how could a young student have painted a private moment that took place two decades earlier, to which he or she could never have been privy? I look at the name card: Madelaine Vaillancourt. It means nothing.

"You like it?" a young girl asks, sidling up to me. She is of mixed race, possibly a little older than the 21-year-olds who comprise the majority.

"You painted this?" I ask.

"Yup."

"I don't understand."

"It's the old pier." She moves to one side, to look out through the wide windows toward the black frame in the distance.

"Yeah, sure, I recognise *that*. But where did you get this?"

"I painted it – I told you." She takes a step back.

"But who is this?" I am almost prodding my painted face.

"No one. I didn't paint it from life."

The scene depicted is of a naked man on the West Pier, leaning against one of the old rotundas, in a pose that I seem to recall adopting. Behind him the distant blur of colourful lights form a beautiful circle, as the Ferris wheel on the Palace Pier spins. I feel unsteady and seasick, my fever worsening as I stare at the familiar reflection of yellows and reds that fuse into orange on the surface of the water. I feel my vision double, my head grow heavy.

But the longer I study it, the less sense it makes: like a word repeated over and over, its form disintegrates. *Of course* it could be anyone, on a famous public landmark. Reference material in books on Brighton abounds. And the definition on the figure is so vague that I no longer see myself in the smudges of oil.

"Hi honey, how's it going?" asks a woman, and Madelaine turns away, glad to break free from my weird intensity. "Hi Mum," says the girl.

And, for a while, that is the last thing I remember.

The movie cliché, where the victim of a fainting awakes to a circle of faces emerging slowly into focus is eerily accurate to life, I discover. The side of my head feels like it's been struck with a cricket ball – maybe even a cricket *bat*. Grown men aren't supposed to faint, and I'm just about sufficiently aware of what's happened to feel embarrassed. I have indeed fainted, and there's a very good reason for it.

And yet for a second I do not recall that reason, the one that caused me – already feeling unwell and unsteady – to reach the literal tipping point. As I lie partially propped up by the jacket of some unknown person behind me, it still feels dreamlike, looking at too much information to take in at once, particularly with halogen bulbs haloing the row of heads.

But then I clearly see one of the faces looking down at me with concern.

It is Black.

It is Black!

It is *Black*.

After all these years, she clearly has no idea who I am: she calls me 'Mr'.

"Hey Mr, are you okay?"

I recognise her voice, but it now has a slight transatlantic twang. My appearance has changed, and she has yet to engage my fully focused eyes, to see the real me. And she has little to connect me to the event, unlike the link I have to her, with the painting that I now realise is formed from her photographs. Whoever painted it obviously had to know Black, but that didn't mean she expected its subject to randomly appear. Somehow the artist is her daughter, although the ages don't seem to stack up.

I am helped to an upright sitting position, and I instinctively draw in my legs.

"Black? Is that you?"

"*Black?* No one's called me that in years."

I wait for her to remember. But she just stares at me, confused. She smiles, but it is a smile feigning recognition, rather than confirming it. I point at the painting. "It's me," I say, softly.

I can almost sense the penny hanging suspended before its fall. "Oh my God, it's *you*."

In helping me to a stand, with the aid of a suited man I have no interest in acknowledging, Black has touched me for the first time in two decades. It is just a clutch of fingers pressed firmly into my inner elbow, but it is skin against skin. Our faces pass at close proximity on my way to a fully upright position. She still appears surprised, but I'm not quite sure if it's of the pleasant variety. I take a swig from the half-empty bottle of water she offers, acutely aware that our saliva will mingle.

She may no longer go by her surname, but *Black* is still there. Only: a little altered, and a little pulled at, pulled-upon; a little encircled, a little drawn over; a little darkened, a little lightened; a little lessened, a little extended. Time has been at her with its needle and thread, its weights and pulleys, its brushes and swabs. But it has done so with compassion and a gentle hand. Time never totally exempts. But time has loved her. Time has *clearly* loved her.

"Do you have time for a drink?" I ask. "A coffee?"

She hesitates, then confers with her daughter. Madelaine tells her mum she's heading out with her peers after the event, and seeing that she has just met with an old friend, nudges her towards accepting my suggestion. Following a short pause, Black finally says, "Um, okay then."

Absent-mindedly I watch as the spirals of frothy milk blend with the oily coffee, the light swirls merging into the deep brown liquid. Black returns from the toilet and quickly sits, thanking me for her latte. Twenty years ago we shared an instant coffee in a greasy spoon. Now we sit in plush leather armchairs, enjoying exotic South American beans served by immaculately coiffured baristas.

I know this woman so well, and yet not at all. I know her face, but not *this* face. I know her voice, but not this voice. I do, and I don't. Conversation on the short walk flatlined, with, I suspect, too much to say as we strolled; everything kept back until there's adequate time to do our stories justice.

The first thing she notices, with my arm stretched out across the table, is the scar running from my knuckles back towards my wrist. It's hard to miss.

"You didn't have that before," she says.

"What, my hand?"

I am attempting humour, but achieve only facetiousness. She stares blankly back. "Sorry, yeah, I didn't have it before. Although you only missed seeing it by minutes."

She looks perplexed. "How do you mean?"

The things I have thought of saying, upon reaching this

point in the conversation: *That's where I lost you.* That's where you disappeared. You vanished into a mess of peeling, warped flesh. Your number might still be there, the ink unattainably tattooed under the mound of dead, bubbled skin with its ugly pink-red sheen.

Instead: "When you left the café, the waitress spilt boiling coffee over my hand. That's where you wrote your number. I ended up in hospital."

I feel like adding *The surgeons fought for hours, but they couldn't recover what you wrote,* but decide against risking another silent response. My humour, in the presence of such desire, has lead weights, and is heavy. Jokes, I sense, will sink, bomb, crash. I cannot do *funny* in her presence. All those years spent in my mind waiting backstage for a cue to go on and make her laugh has rendered me awkward and over-rehearsed.

"Oh, I see," she says.

"Christ, what a weekend. How much more could have gone wrong?"

"Indeed. So tragic."

"So – when did you find out about Jacob?" I ask, relentlessly stirring my drink.

"A year later. I heard nothing on my travels. I'd phoned a couple of times but got no answer. I sent postcards, but couldn't give a return address as I was always on the move."

"It must have been awful. I mean, obviously it *was* awful. The not knowing, I mean. To realise you went all that time thinking he was…" I trail off, the mixture of milk and coffee complete.

Black dabs her finger at stray sugar granules spilled from a poorly torn sachet. "So, he was already dead – when we spent the night out there."

"I tried to find out where you were staying that week, to let you know. I expected you to turn up at the funeral. Thought you must have heard. I did everything in the days before you left to get in touch. I wanted to see you for myself as much as anything, obviously. But I wanted to find you in case you weren't aware. I didn't want you to read about it in a newspaper. So – in the end, how did you find out?"

"I was on my way to Montreal. I had met Rémi in France, while making my way back in the direction of England towards the end of my year away, and that was it – found myself heading to the other side of the world on a whim. I had no home in England to come back to, and here was this wonderful French-Canadian artist, on tour in Europe, so I thought, why not? We had a whirlwind romance, and within a few weeks, instead of coming home I was on a plane across the Atlantic. Surreal, totally surreal."

"I'm confused. *That* was when you heard?"

"Yes. A whole year after he died. On the plane. I mentioned Jacob's name and Rémi said he'd heard about him, following his unexpected death. I was like, '*What the –?*' I'd been cut off from the art world for most of my trip. I was in my own little bubble."

I nod, sympathetically. But inside I am seething. I *loathe* this 'Rémi' – a man I've never seen, met, nor even heard speak. I know only his name, and in other circumstances I might even think it to be the exotic kind I'd prefer to have instead of Patrick. But now I feel only contempt.

Black continues, and I have to rein my attention back from a spiteful reverie. "I remember feeling sick—" I nod "—and panicky—" I nod "—and wanting the plane to turn around that instant, as if I could go back and cradle him in hospital, as if it was only just happening."

"I know the feeling," I say, experiencing the very same sense of retrospective regret. That *bastard* snared her en route to England. She didn't – still doesn't – grasp that we were supposed to meet upon her return. Yes, it was never agreed, and yes, she doubtless thought that I'd lost interest and moved on due the lack of a phone call before her departure. But she was wrong. I was waiting.

"So Rémi – what happened there?"

The first thing I'd noticed at the gallery, once able to see and think straight, was the lack of an engagement or wedding ring. Weirdly, on some level, no matter how ludicrous the notion, I always expected her to remain single. Unmarried, no partners, celibate. I dare not ask if she is involved with someone new. Until the subject arises, she is free.

"We divorced last year. But we're still very close. Madelaine is my step-daughter. Her mother died from complications during childbirth – which is so unbelievably unfortunate in this day and age, isn't it? So we became very close over the years. She wanted to study in England, so I suggested Brighton. I've been over to London quite a few times, but this is only the third time coming back down here. Strange, really."

It's a joy to see all the mannerisms still in place: the way she absentmindedly plays with her hair, the way she squints ever so slightly when she listens, or raises one eyebrow when the truth sounds like it's being stretched. All bound-up in an older, wiser exterior.

"So – are you married?" she asks, holding her mug just below her lips; oh to be held there, like that.

"Divorced."

"What happened?"

Ah, the unanswerable question: one of those times when the truth is suicide. I don't want to go down the route of yet more lies, but see no alternative. "We just grew apart," I mumble, and she seems suitably convinced. "We're still friends," I lie.

I stand up, ready to order another drink, needing to feed the caffeine habit. Black rejects my offer of a second cup – an offer that, without thinking, I re-offer, so that she has to repeat her refusal. I feel like telling her that I will pay for everything, forever more. And I would, to have her here to pay for. What price her life? How much would she sell it to me for?

"Look, I can't really stay long… A quick iced mocha, if that's okay?" she says, and the prospect of her disappearing back to wherever she came from momentarily recedes.

"What do you think would have happened," I ask, playing with my teaspoon, looking up, "had I not lost your number?"

She breaks from stirring her icy drink with a straw. "How do you mean?"

"With us."

"Us? Well, there never really was an us, was there? It was just one very bizarre night."

"Sure, but…"

She looks puzzled. "But what?"

"Never mind. Did you at least think of me?"

"Well, it was a strange night. The photos were also an obvious reminder, although they sat in the drawer for years. Madelaine asked to take a load of my unused prints to college, to do something with them, so I said fine."

I blow on my cappuccino before lifting the cup to my lips, rippling a furrow in the steamed milk. "So, obviously you never used them yourself."

"I never really found the excuse. They didn't fit in with the stuff I took on my travels, and that became the main focus of my attention. I only developed the films a year later, and I'd half forgotten what was on them. I put the prints in a drawer, forgot all about them."

"You kept with it, though? The photography, I mean."

"Yeah, and I did okay – still do okay – in Canada. Never really found international acclaim. I do some work for magazines, some of it in America, but mostly at home. Nothing remarkable."

"I kept an eye out for your name."

"Well, I changed it to Vaillancourt, before I even got going commercially. And of course, Rémi's name had some cachet, and while I never intended to trade on it, it seemed silly to purposefully distance myself from it. I was proud to be his wife. He was a great man. Still is."

I would have given her *Clement*. Nothing to trade on, perhaps, but it was all I had. Not that she would have taken it. The facts of her life since 1993 have come crashing into my reality like a tidal wave towering over the piers on its way to a total wipeout. I now know better, from just this short space of time, who she was back then, and also who she became. At least I am still suspended in the ignorance of our future. If our past was doomed, then maybe what lies ahead is what fate had in mind all along?

"So what do you do now?" She asks. "You were in between jobs, I seem to recall."

"Well, I never made it as a male model."

At last she laughs. But even this victory is undermined by thoughts of just how ludicrous she might see such an idea. "I'm a forensic artist," I add.

"You took my advice!"

"I did, yes. You remember suggesting it?"

"Indeed I do. So you draw people for the police?"

"Clay reconstructions, mostly. I do a lot of work on finding identities."

"That sounds fascinating."

I can't yet judge her new accent to perfection, but the slight inflection on *fascinating* leaves me a little uneasy. Maybe it's just that the word that is said so often in irony these days, with any genuine usage sounding odd. She must detect this in my expression.

"No – *really*," she says. "It must be very rewarding."

"When we get a result, then yes, very much so. But it can involve a lot of waiting to get there."

"You must be a very patient person."

"Not really. But sometimes you have no choice, do you?"

Every minute is another victory. But what is it all leading to? A half-hearted 'we'll keep in touch' on her behalf? 'Let's be friends', and the utter purgatory that would equate to?

In the excitement I've totally forgotten to meet up with David. I think of texting him but my phone is dead. Everything can wait, now that Black is back in my life.

Perhaps it's just my imagination, but I sense some restlessness creeping into her body language. She shifts in her seat, glances around. Maybe it's just the caffeine; I'm fidgeting too, picking mindlessly at my scar. "It's such a beautiful evening," I offer, looking out at the bustling promenade; at locals and tourists bathed in sharp orange light. "Do you fancy a walk?" I ask. There's a moment when, with a pause, she looks set to reject, but then she smiles – just a little – and lets out a gentle *Okay*.

A surprising late-evening heat – in the air, and rising from the streets – is swept into our faces as we step outside. The distorted bass pumping from a speeding convertible pounds in my chest as it passes. I don't know whether to turn left or right – I have no plan. I'd suggest walking across to the West Pier, for old time's sake, but all that remains are a few black ribs arced across the shallow water. The years haven't been kind: first the collapse, and then shortly after, the catastrophic fire that finally killed it off.

As had been the case all those years ago, she takes the lead. We make our way down to the shoreline, and I draw up alongside her. I feel ready to hold her hand; that the familiarity we achieved in 1993 is once again appropriate. But does she feel the same? I don't want to force the issue. And so my hands remain scrunched into my pockets, uneasily turning over keys and loose change.

A young boy with a bloom of candyfloss brushes past, depositing a patch of sticky pink goo on my forearm. I look around, for a parent, for a reaction, but the boy's father stares blankly back when our eyes meet. I turn to Black and smile, in the hope that she sees me as this benign figure, unflustered by rudeness, even though I want to scream at the child and poke the stick into the man's eye. Could I keep up this act? How long before she discovers the real me? Already it feels exhausting. But living a lie appeals more than the alternative: a truth-filled emptiness.

This time we find ourselves walking to the Palace Pier – renamed Brighton Pier, something that only became possible after the demise of its rival. In the twilight its attractions seem tackier than ever: louder, bolder, bigger, brasher. The overspill of drinkers along the seafront doesn't help assuage my sense of unease as we wend our way along. There's a tension in the air, in the over-loud drunken banter and foul language, and the smell of beer from plastic pint glasses. Black edges closer to me, to narrow ourselves; but no hand is forthcoming as I let mine dangle, just in case.

The pier is an absolute abuse of the senses, bound up within one tightly packed, overcrowded space. It mirrors the excitement that has boiled up within me, but dampens any tenderness. This is a reminder of what it's like to be really alive; but it's also totally disorienting. I'm losing all sense of control, as if I've woken up in someone else's life. Adrenaline pushes me on.

Eventually we make it to the pier head, and into the pub which hunkers apologetically in the shadow of towering fairground rides. A middle-aged woman parades in front of the karaoke machine in the corner, screeching the life out of *Girls On Film*. Suddenly, it's as if Genevieve is present, together with Black, in this room, on this unreal night. Is this tuneless, graceless shrieker what that ballsy young girl could have become? If given the chance, could her youth have burned away to *this*?

Black asks for a rum and Coke, and I order a beer. She finds an alcove at the far end of the bar, which shields our ears from the worst of the noise. And so here we are again: face to face, over the sea. But now we are stuck for something to say.

It strikes me that we are survivors, held together by shared experience, bound by disaster. Ours is a war-tethered bond: reunited comrades who never really got to know each other, beyond the intense experience of one shell-shocked night in the trenches. Perhaps it has limited our conversation to just that one event, through its subsequent link to Jacob's death. Back then we could have gone anywhere in words, with a lifetime ahead of us; now, we are drawn only to *then*, never before. There comes a point in any relationship when you stop asking questions about your partner's past. But in a sense we are already limited to 1993 onwards, because everything should have been broached first time around; to ask is to acknowledge how little of each other's lives we got to know, and therefore, how insubstantial – how featherlight – our connection actually was. To ask is to admit we are, to all intents and purposes, little more than strangers, who never even scratched the surface when first we met.

I try to steer the conversation back towards art. This is our common ground. I'm now far more aware of the significance of her influences, having spent so long researching them, but of course, I'll never get the chance to improve that first impression. Still, I can express some newfound appreciation. I note that I've finally seen the Diane Arbus photo she mentioned.

"Which photo is that?" she asks, taking me by surprise.

"The one with the boy in Central Park. With the hand grenade. You know, the one you said was your favourite?"

"I know the picture you mean," she says, "but it's never been my favourite."

"Really?"

"Really. I like it, but I don't recall talking about it."

"I must have got it wrong."

"Yes, you must have."

I fall silent, trying to understand why she's denying discussing the photo. I can only conclude that it was a long time ago, and that she's mistaken.

I try to spark the conversation back to life. "It was a shock to see myself like that, in Madelaine's painting."

"Could you really tell it was you?" she says, casually swishing the ice in her glass, in between sips. "It's quite abstract."

"It instantly struck me, as if it were an actual memory. The figure was vague, but I could tell it was me, and that I was naked."

She looks confused. *"Naked?"*

"Yes. It was your idea, remember? You made me take your clothes off."

"*I* made you take your clothes off?" She laughs, fully amused, before nervously trailing off. "When was that?"

"When else could it have been? After we smoked the

joint. You made me pose against the kiosk. You insisted I get undressed."

"You *seriously* think that?"

I nod, disarmed by her reaction. Is she ashamed?

"Look, I took some photos of you, but they were candid. I stopped soon after you realised. I always take photos of people, but I *never* ask anyone to pose. Especially not someone I barely know, and *definitely* not naked."

"Don't you remember? It was as a kind of payback for me seeing you in the studio. You said it was your chance to get even."

"Yes, you saw me in the studio. But I think I'd remember asking a stranger to strip for me. I'm sorry, but it's just not something I would do."

"Why are you denying it?"

"Patrick, I have the photos back at the hotel. I got all my old prints back from Madelaine earlier today. I looked at them this very lunchtime. You have your clothes on. *Definitely.*"

"I don't… I mean… You're *sure?*"

"Positive."

"I could have sworn it happened that way. Why would I think it happened that way?"

"Search me," she says, folding her arms in a gesture that suggests she is most definitely *not* free to be searched.

"The pigeons – we played that game with the pigeons?"

"Pigeons? What game?"

"Hitting them off the pier."

"No, we didn't play that game," she says, speaking more slowly, as if explaining something to a foreigner, or a young child. "You whacked some birds out to sea with a plank of wood, if I remember correctly. I didn't want anything to do with the disgusting things."

"It was just me?"

"It was just you."

How can two people have such contrasting memories of the same night? "What about going back to the Metropole in the morning, to dry off and sleep?

"I came back to the room with you very briefly, but we never slept. We made our way to the train station, after stopping by Jacob's studio. Last night was the first time I've ever slept in the Metropole."

"So where did I get that from?"

"Again, I don't know."

I shake my head. "It's funny how the memory plays tricks."

"A *lot* of tricks, by the sounds of it," she says, sharply.

"It's strange, I could have sworn… Anyway, if only I'd phoned you that week. It could have all been so different. We'd have shared the story of that night over the years, cemented the details. There'd be no confusion. We'd know the story."

"Look, I'm sorry to say this, Patrick, but the truth is I gave you a fake number. I was about to go away. You were a little… *intense*. I wouldn't say that you scared me or anything like that, but I did feel awkward."

I exhale, my lungs sucked free of air. "Really?"

"I'm sorry. I could tell you were keen, but I just didn't feel any attraction. You're a nice guy. I just didn't want to hurt your feelings. My life was heading in another direction. When you asked me to write my number on your hand I couldn't bring myself to say no. It seemed easier to just make up a number than explain the truth."

In that moment the sounds in the bar – including another karaoke song – are muted down to bass distortions, as if I'm submerged in the sea, my ears filling fast with water. I can hear a bubbling deep within my eardrums, with just a hint of audible music and chatter. I honestly don't know what to say. All I can do is stare at Black, trying, and failing, to focus my mind with one coherent thought. My eyesight seems equally blurry.

In this pause she checks the time; at first trying to slyly glance at her watch, but finds it fallen halfway around her wrist. As she straightens it the intention becomes obvious. "Look, I best be going. I… well, y'know, it's getting late."

"I'll walk you back to the Metropole," I say, finally presented with an obvious line.

"No, please don't," she snaps. "I'll be fine. Really."

And with a sharp "Bye" she turns and heads towards the door. I sit shellshocked, staring at my half-finished drink, at the bubbles ascending the amber liquid. Seconds later I find myself heading outside, walking into a swirl of noise and colour, trying frantically to pick out one particular head further along the crowded, chaotic walkway, as Black tries, once again, to walk out of my life.

FORTY-TWO

It's a cough that rattles deep within; vibrating in the lungs and the throat, reverberating through tubes and hollows. David is not looking at all well. He's really aged these past few months: bags beneath his eyes further inflating, islands of liver spots conjoining on his forehead, final flecks of colour in his hair and beard absorbed by grey. He's also lost a lot of weight. As we move outside, towards the lake – so that he may smoke – he looks like a man on his way out.

I've aged too. A lack of sleep does that to you. And David has caught me on a day when I fear I shall never sleep again.

"So where were you last night?" he asks, cigarette clamped between shaking fingers. "I waited down the pub for you."

"Oh yeah, sorry about that," I mumble. "Something came up."

"Why did you switch your phone off?"

"It ran out of battery. Sorry."

"Oh," he says, sounding unconvinced. He gives me a strange look. "How did you get those scratches?" he asks, moving in to study the side of my neck.

"I got lucky last night," I note, with a wink. "Say no more," I add, swiftly shutting down the topic. "So David, what's this news?"

"I wanted to give you the heads up that she would be going into today's nationals. I rushed out to buy them all this morning, a couple have reasonable pieces on it. She'll be on the local news, too."

"Marina?" I ask, momentarily confused.

"Yes, Marina."

"Well, that's great," I say.

"Your work will be famous."

"It will, in its way, I suppose. But *I* won't, will I?"

"But at least you do something meaningful."

He's right. But in truth, he doesn't really understand.

"What would it mean to you, to have this case finally solved?" I ask, as a swift breeze rustles the foliage, on its way to us.

"*Everything*. After all, I've nothing else left."

"But why *her*? Why this one? There must be loads of unsolved cases. Why has this one haunted you?"

"I thought you knew all this? I thought you understood?"

He says, disappointment clear in his voice.

"Yes… and no. I mean, I *thought* I did. But I didn't realise just how serious you were. I guess I thought you'd let up at some point. I guess I thought that at some point you'd call it a day."

"No, Patrick. Never. *Never*. When you're young, you're confused as to the meaning of life," he laughs, ironically, "… as if there actually is one. But I'm not going to be around forever. And the older I get, the greater the sense of incompletion." He reaches for another cigarette, hacking almost to the point of choking as he lights up, then dragging the bile back down with the smoke. "I have regrets, but I can live with those. I just can't stand the thought of this never being resolved. When I'm gone, my regrets won't matter. But *she* will."

"But that still doesn't explain why this one case in particular?"

"She spanned my whole career. And I always saw her as an innocent. Not that we can be certain that she was entirely blameless, or pure and wholesome."

"What if she wasn't?" I ask.

"Wasn't what?"

"Blameless."

"She still wouldn't have deserved *that*," he says, with a stern look.

"But would it still mean as much to you?"

"Who knows? But it's just what I've always felt. This girl – you can put your own story onto her, can't you? The less you know about someone, the more personal you can make their story. Especially if they're unable to disagree, and set you straight."

"Fair enough."

"I have another bit of news," he says, flooded with adrenaline. "I tracked down Black's photography tutor. Spoke to her on the phone late last night."

"You did?"

"*Finally* someone who remembers her, Patrick!"

"That's amazing, David. What did she say?"

"The last she heard she was in Canada – Black, I mean. She sent a postcard after a year or so abroad, saying that she wasn't coming back. So there you have it."

"Have what?"

"The reason why you haven't been able to find her. She's been across the Atlantic all this time."

"Incredible," I say, trying to sound enthusiastic. "What a momentous day this is."

"Her tutor gave me an address. You can finally get in touch. Assuming she hasn't moved in the meantime. But still, even if she has, it'll be a start."

"Has there been any news on Marina yet, since going into the papers?" I ask, eager to change the topic. "Anyone recognise her?"

"I don't know yet. I'm stopping in at HQ on the way home. If I can walk that far, that is."

"I'd offer to help you, but I've got lots to sort today."

"No worries," he says, shifting his walking stick to his other hand, redistributing his weight with a groan.

"I'm getting too old for this," he eventually adds.

"Too old for what?"

"Life," he says, wearily.

FORTY-THREE

Mid-evening: unusually late for David to stop by; and even rarer, a second visit on the same day. I open the door expecting a salesperson, but there he is, stood on the garden path, one side of his face bathed in the light of the low sun. Unusually, he looks me directly in the eye as he asks to come in. Clearly, something is on his mind. This isn't his typical casual visit.

He quickly takes a seat in the living room, leans forward with intent. Never one for small talk, he's now skipping even basic formalities.

"What is it?" I ask.

"Developments."

"Really?"

"She's been identified," he says, standing to remove his thin grey jacket. "Marina," he adds, more forcefully, settling back into the chair.

"You don't sound excited?" I note, even though he is clearly agitated; the tone failing to match his body language.

"Nothing's ever straightforward, is it?"

"What's the problem?" I ask, nervousness rattling my voice.

"There's something that really doesn't make sense to me. Either it's the biggest coincidence in the world, or…".

"Or what?"

"Or something is very wrong."

"Oh, I see," I mumble. "Want a drink?"

"Don't you want to hear what I've got to say?"

"Of course. But can't we discuss it over a drink?"

"Whisky," he says, curtly. "Although I might as well smoke, while we're at it," he adds, picking up his jacket and walking through to the study, then out through the French doors, onto the wooden veranda. He sits in one of the two rocking chairs, lights up. I bring out the drinks, placing them on the low garden table.

Once again he looks me deep in the eye, as I sit opposite. "This is big, Patrick. Huge. And the thing is, you *know*."

"Know?"

"Her. Marina. Or, should I say, Genevieve Frazer," he says, tapping ash onto the floor.

At last, my chance to do the decent thing.

"*Genevieve?* You're kidding me?"

"She lived here, with you, at this cottage. *At this cottage!* How could you not tell me about her?"

"Tell you what? She'd run away! That was what everyone thought. She wasn't even in Brighton at the time. She was in Derbyshire. Who says it's her?"

"This guy came forward, Darren Atkins. Says he recognised her as soon as he saw her in the paper. They were planning to run away together, but she didn't make their rendezvous in London. He assumed she'd got cold feet. He had a picture of them together, decades ago. It's the spitting image of your reconstruction."

"*Him?*" I splutter. "He said that? He can't be trusted. I saw him raping her, out by the lake. I saw it, as a kid! If it is her, then I bet he's responsible. *Seriously.*"

"But why would he get involved now?" he asks. "Why not stay quiet? It just doesn't make sense."

"Don't they do that? To see what you have on them? To get a thrill? You told me you had to be wary of anyone who inserts themselves into an investigation."

"Maybe. But rarely after this long. If they get that far away from a crime, they usually want to stay away. Especially if they're grown up, with a family, and so on."

"Maybe guilt has forced his hand?" I say.

"He seems pretty credible to me. *Raped* her, you say?"

"Yeah. A few months before she went missing. Maybe even just a few weeks. But… I was so young, I may have misread it. She was screaming, she looked in distress. But it was dark."

"So you're not hundred percent sure?"

"Well, no. But it didn't seem right to me. And she had a black eye the next day."

"Here's the thing I don't get. You must have recognised her? When modelling the skull. I mean, it must have crossed your mind?"

"It did. But I thought I was imagining it. I often think I see someone I know in the faces I create. Happens all the time. Maybe I subconsciously reference people from my life when I work. Despite all the scientific accuracy, you still need to draw upon your own experience as to what a face actually looks like, above all that bone."

"I suppose so," he says, his tone non-committal. "How old were you back then?"

"Ten or eleven," I say, telling yet more lies.

He murmurs something I don't quite catch. Then he says, "Tell me about that French girl, Isabelle."

"What has that got to do with anything? I told you all about her some time ago."

"Anything you forgot to mention?" he asks, gently rocking back and forth.

"Such as?"

"Well, it's your story, Patrick."

"But you're the one who wants more of it."

"Okay, let me put it like this. You just bade each other farewell at the end of that summer?"

"What are you getting at?" I can hear my tone sound more aggressive than intended.

"The arrest of a young man – Patrick Clement – in 1985, for the harassment of a young French woman. He was a lucky boy, by the sounds of it, with the charges dropped as she rushed back to France."

"It was a misunderstanding. She stopped returning my calls so I went to see her. She wouldn't let me in, but I had no idea what I'd done wrong, why I was cut off like that. She refused to talk to me, wouldn't even open the door. I didn't want to go away until I got an answer. That was all. So I waited. Next thing I know, the police arrived to cart me off."

"I'm supposed to take your word on that?" he asks, looking me directly in the eye.

"I don't know, David. Why not go ask her as you're so busy digging into my past? I didn't do anything wrong. What is this?"

"Her statement says you were trying to break in."

"I was banging on the door to get her attention. Not trying to break it down."

"It doesn't look good, Patrick."

"I can't help how it *looks*," I say, exasperated. "I'm just telling you how it is. Was the door broken down?"

"It didn't say."

"Well then."

"I merely said it didn't say."

"But if I *had* broken the door down, it *would* have said."

"Okay, point taken." He takes a sip of whisky, runs it around his mouth. "There's something else. I spoke to your ex-wife. She came to see me this afternoon."

"Laura?" I ask, as a reflex, even though I've only been married

once.

"Yes."

"Why on earth did you speak to *her?*"

"I left her a message the other day, when I was still trying to track down Black, and not having any luck. I wanted to know what her take on it was."

"Her take on what?"

"Your… *interest,*" he says, slipping the word out through lips initially shaped to form an 'o' that I imagine to be for 'obsession'. "Was it as unhealthy as I suspected."

"Why did you think it unhealthy?"

"Laura agrees with me, for what it's worth."

"Well, she's probably still angry with me. I hurt her. I never meant to, but I hurt her. In many ways."

David delves into his jacket pocket and produces his battered old dictaphone. My first thought relates to the number of times I've told him that his mobile phone can perform the same task; indeed, I frequently use mine to do that very thing, to help me keep track. I am set to lecture him on the issue when he presses play, and for the first time in years I hear Laura's sweet, reedy voice, albeit sounding a little more tinny through such a small speaker.

"For the final few years I'm not sure I believed a single word that came out of his mouth," she says, although I'm too taken aback with the sound of her voice, and the images it evokes, to clearly take in what she's saying. "Most of the time I couldn't prove he was lying, but things just didn't ring true."

"Patrick said you broke up after a big fight?"

"Our first and last. I've still got the two-inch scar."

"Was he often like that?" David asks, to the recorded click-and-whoosh of his cigarette lighter. There's also a rustling, which I imagine to be the denim of Laura's jeans as she crosses her legs.

"No, to be honest until then I thought he was harmless – at least in a physical sense. But sometimes when he was stressed he'd disappear for a few days, just take off without warning. He was… *erratic*. Never violent – at least not until that night. But troubled – I'd say that 'troubled' was the best word to describe him. *Definitely* troubled."

"Yet you met when saving his life?"

"I should have known then – obviously! – that he had some serious issues, but I like to help people. I'm a sucker in that sense. He was so helpless in the hospital. So in need of care."

"What did you know about Genevieve?"

"Genevieve? Who's she? Another one of his fantasies?"

"You *don't know?*" David audibly coughs. "Did Patrick not talk about his past?"

"Bits and pieces. He told me about what happened to his mum and dad, which was so tragic, but not much more. It seemed painful, so I didn't ask."

"What about his prior relationships?"

"He mentioned one or two. Again, he didn't dwell on them, and I'm not someone who likes to ask too many questions. I figured he'd tell me stuff if he ever felt like it. I don't know, in some ways he was mysterious, a closed book, and that attracted me. I do recall something about this wonderful summer with a French girl he met in London. I remember feeling quite jealous, as if he was a much more exciting, romantic character in his youth."

"I wouldn't be jealous," David says, but for some reason doesn't divulge the details. "The story of losing the baby in Cambridge?"

"Yes, that happened," she says, the pain still clear in her voice. "To be honest, he was brilliant that night, and for a short while after. He was so kind and loving, as he could be at times.

But then he withdrew into himself, and I felt I couldn't trust him again."

"Patrick told me about how your father came around to get your stuff, after your big fight."

There's an audible gasp; nothing too dramatic, but all the same a clear sound picked up by the sensitive microphone. "My dad was *dead*," she says. "He'd died a few years before. So obviously there's no way he could have done that. I can't believe he said that! Although, of course, perhaps I can."

Out of the corner of my eye I sense David's face turning to look at mine, but I remain focused on the small machine. I wonder what Laura looks like now? She has re-entered my life merely as a voice, detached from her physical self.

David continues to question her. "You left without saying goodbye the next morning, I understand?"

"I think you know by now that you didn't get the full story. I was going to leave him. And no one leaves Patrick."

"And he accidentally knocked you into the wall? After you damaged the painting of Black?"

"To be honest I don't know what he did. I was knocked out cold, and I can't remember anything from just before that happened. He could have hit me with a hammer for all I know."

"He said he helped you into bed, took care of you."

"*No!*" she says, her exclamation rattling the speaker. "He locked me in a cupboard overnight. I woke up in the cupboard."

"He did *what?*" David says, before belatedly seeming to hear the words. "In a *cupboard?* Why didn't you report it to the police?"

"I just wanted to get out of there, get away from him. And he was crying, sobbing, saying sorry when he let me out in the morning. I've no doubt that he *was* sorry. I just knew that I had to get as far away as possible, as quickly as possible. Don't get me wrong – I'll never forgive him for it. But I couldn't get the police involved."

My eyes remain fixed on the dictaphone, as I wonder how sounds get trapped on mere strips of tape. How does the recorded voice transfer itself so accurately? Also, I wonder if Laura has remarried? What is her life now?

David reaches over and presses the stop button. "She's lying," I say in an instant, feeling cornered as the click snaps me from my reverie. "All lies," I add, even though I didn't catch every word.

"The thing is," he says, slowly, deliberately, "Do I now believe your story about Genevieve?"

"What does *she* have to do with this?"

"I'm just trying to get a sense about you. About the stories you tell."

"But David, you didn't even believe me about Black. You thought she didn't even exist! You were wrong, not me. I wasn't lying. You know that now. I wasn't lying."

"I just don't like things that don't fit together. Now, I accept that sometimes it's just life laying it out that way, but I still need to check. Coincidences, inaccuracies, inconsistencies — they draw my attention. You know that as well as anybody."

"I was just a child when she ran away. I told you, that man Darren is the one you should be speaking to, if it is indeed even Genevieve."

"You don't think it is?"

"It *could* be. But as I said, maybe I had her in mind – subconsciously – when I sculpted her. Perhaps I was in some way influenced and made it look like her. Or perhaps this Darren is mistaken."

"We're trying to trace some relatives for DNA comparison. I guess we'll know soon enough."

"Good."

"I wouldn't go anywhere, though, Patrick. I'm pretty sure the investigating officers will want to speak to you about it."

"Why haven't they already?" I ask, suddenly surprised by this lack of activity, given David's suspicions.

"I said I'd handle you, and they were okay with that. I wanted to hear your take on things. But I will be reporting back to them. And as I said, they've not properly established that it is actually Genevieve yet, so we cannot really move forward."

"Consider this. If it *was* Genevieve, and I had some role in her death, why would I have made the reconstruction resemble her?"

"I honestly don't know, Patrick, but I'm damn-well sure that we'll find out, whatever the truth is. It's coming together, though. Can't you sense it?"

* * *

And that is it; for now, at least. But I'm left like the tiring front runner in a 10,000-metre race, whose great lead has been worn away, and whose fate, as the spikes beat down on the tracks behind, is inevitable. My lies won't keep David at bay for long; he'll check, he'll make discoveries, spot inaccuracies. Soon I'll be running on quicksand.

My options? A full disclosure, and finally act like a man over what I did as a boy. Or, to make some kind of escape.

But no matter what happens now, I *never* got away with it.

At least I've done *part* of the right thing: seeing that Genevieve's bones will achieve identification, so that she is no longer a Missing Person statistic, but instead a girl to be afforded the kind of grave that she once so compassionately tended.

At least I gave her that.

At least, after all I got wrong, I gave her that.

But then, what of my more recent mistakes?

FORTY-FOUR

Time, I feel, to take a break; but only after one last walk around Brighton, in case it never again feels like home – that place where the best and worst happens.

The train station: where I was greeted by my father, and from where I was led, trembling, into a new life; and where, all those years later, another dream terminated. I glance at the shop where once stood the café. I stop on the concourse, which marked the end of all hope of a normal life to a six-year-old boy. The ticket in my pocket that day, although marked as a return, turned into a single. I must take responsibility for my actions, but I was set on a course when abandoned in that train carriage.

From here, I walk down the bustling Queen's Road, with the architecture on my right-hand side little different from all those decades ago – all changes purely cosmetic; the shops below the façades having altered, but little else. No matter how modern and cosmopolitan Brighton gets, it will always retain the hallmarks of its Regency heyday. I pass some greenery on the left enclosing the United Reformed Church, and up ahead, the sea is framed between the street's final buildings a few hundred yards away. I reach the junction where the clock tower stands unmoved, Queen Victoria's face on one facade, Prince Consort's on another. The road is now West Street, and it arrows down to the shoreline, intersecting King's Road midway between the two piers of my childhood. My only thought is to turn right, to the west. Memories whittle away in time, and the older pier is the perfect metaphor: it's down to just the bare bones now.

My path to the west is blocked, however; the Metropole cordoned off. Kitchen staff, waiters, maids and porters hang around outside, beyond yellow perimeter tape.

I ask a waiter what seems to be the problem.

"Someone discovered a body, apparently," he says, matter-of-factly. "Out back, in one of the big bins."

"Oh," I say, stepping back. "That sounds awful."

I quickly turn and head east, in the direction of Rottingdean, on the way back to the cottage; taking in reverse the route walked three decades earlier when I led a mischievous girl to an unplanned fate. Once past what is now the Brighton Pier I approach the cast-iron colonnade of Madeira Terrace, built into the east cliff. Hundreds of arches – complete with turquoise posts and railings – run from the busy hub of the shoreline along the esplanade for what must be at least a mile, down to the more peaceful end of town. A childhood vision of Kitty leaps to mind: dragging me past some attraction, for which she would never hand over the time or the money. Then I think of her now, down to her final hours.

Eventually the final archway blends into chalk and sandstone, and on my right, the last of the beachfront attractions – a crazy golf course – gives way to a natural expanse of shingle. A few hundred yards later I am at the marina, beyond which the east cliff fades to relative flatness, a high wall separating me from road level. A flight of steps, and I am up on Marine Parade, from where I stare across to the smartly redeveloped quayside apartments and, beyond the roofs, the proliferation of white masts in the dock. All the years spent looking on in envy at the apparent carefree lives of those seafarers. Maybe I need to get a boat? Then again, it's probably not the kind of thing you can purchase at short notice. Still, the sea represents freedom, discovery, new worlds.

New lives.

* * *

Every day, the missing of this world are located. Some will simply walk through the front door, back into their old lives as if they'd never been away. Others, sadly, will wash ashore or edge out of a shallow grave as soil erodes. But it's never an end to the story. We choose neat conclusions, all-powerful final sentences, but in life, it seems, there is always unfinished business, ongoing consequences.

Where to draw a neat line? To be honest, until one is drawn for me, I simply don't know.